DISSONANCE

Volume II: Reckoning

AARON RYAN

Plug your ears. And whatever you do, don't look.
The war for humanity continues.

Published in 2024, Edition 1.

Paperback ISBN # 9798990326613. Hardcover ISBN # 9798990326606. eBook ISBN # 9798990326620. Audiobook ISBN # 9798990326675.

Cover art soldier by Pedro Ferreira. Cover art gorgon by Rodrigo Vivedes.

Edited by Denouement Editing and CM LLC. Published independently.

This is a work of fiction. Any similarities to persons living or dead, or actual events is purely coincidental.

For Sweeps, Bren & AJ:
my true loves.

You've helped me to survive.

I CHAPTERS

I NOTE ON AI

We live in an age of AI. Every day, more and more services spring up promising revolutionary and innovative results using artificial intelligence. The authoring industry is not immune to this.

I want every one of my readers to know that not once did I employ, nor will I *ever* employ, the use of AI to sculpt any part of any of my stories. Those who know me know that I am staunchly and adamantly opposed to such cheats.

I'm very proud to be a verified human. The ability to create is a gift that I was endowed by my Creator, and I will never forfeit that nor set it aside to propagate something synthetic and imitative.

Everything you've read by me in this trilogy, and in my other works, is 100% entirely created by me, the genuine article. I'm a verified human, and always will be.

To my fellow authors, I urge you to preserve the sacred gift of human creation and never stoop to such lows. Always cherish this gift you've been given. If you encounter writer's block, take a break. Don't cop out. Don't take the road more traveled by. Don't cheat. Toe the line for all of us, and keep creation – *true* unadulterated creation – alive.

Long live humanity.

Sincerely,

Aaron Ryan,
Verified Human

I PREFACE

Recap from Volume I:

In June 2026, alien beings floated silently down toward earth, holding a geostationary orbit there for three months.

Three months later, on September 3rd 2026, they activated, hunting down all mankind. To humanity's horror, they discover that the alien beings, which they have dubbed 'gorgons', are able to employ a mysterious psychological, telepathic or telekinetic ability to freeze them where they stand, paralyzing them, at which point they can then consume them at their leisure.

Thus, the number one rule was born as it concerns gorgons: *you just...don't...look.*

The ensuing annihilation of the human race took less than four months. By 2027, eighty percent of mankind had been wiped out, along with nearly all other organic biological lifeforms on land, sea, or air. Over the next few years, calamity, disease and natural disaster took another five percent of mankind.

Earth became overrun with weeds and foliage. Nuclear power reactors melted down and powerful radioactive isotopes spread, killing off more of mankind. Rampant disease ensued. But on the very brink of extinction, mankind was eking out an existence in the shadows, learning about their invaders, and preparing for the largest counterattack mankind had ever seen.

Our story then fast-forwards to December 2042. Sergeant Cameron "Jet" Shipley and his brother, Private Wyatt Rutledge, aka "Rut" Shipley, are part of a military Blockade in Clarksville Tennessee, fortified with gun towers and providing solace, shelter, hydroponics, education and training for military reconnaissance missions to find survivors, food, and ammunition.

They are issued a new mission: head up to Austin Peay University and investigate thermal signals, possibly survivors. On their way, they encounter a mass of gorgons at the Cumberland River, but newcomer, Staff Sergeant Joseph Bassett, employs a manual trigger and detonates something akin to an EMP: what the military is calling a "DTF", or *Dissonant Tidal Flood.* This new technology operates similar to an EMP, but on audio frequencies lethal to the gorgons' sensitive hearing, sending them fleeing, or killing them outright in close proximity. The news of this unannounced technology catches both Shipley brothers by complete surprise.

On this same mission, while taking shelter at Austin Peay University's Harvill Hall, they are given a new assignment: they must lojack a gorgon, installing a tracker to monitor its movements. During this tragic assignment, Private Shipley is violently killed by a berserker gorgon: a variant of the gorgon species that is far more aggressive, and far more lethal. Lieutenant Allison Trudy and Joseph Bassett provide aid to Sergeant Cameron Shipley on this mission, as well as comfort.

For their journey back to the Blockade, they are joined by three recruits from Harvill Hall: Jesse, Liam aka "Foxy", and Vera. The team takes shelter from the gorgons at Madison Street United Methodist Church in Clarksville, only to be preyed upon by not only gorgons, but also a lone octogenarian striving for survival who has resorted to lethal desperation. Vera and Jesse are killed, and Foxy is wounded, but the team battles their way out and is rescued by a tank squadron that employs another DTF and escorts them back to an encampment on the Cumberland River, where they realize to their surprise that military operations have been underway for quite some time now, which they have all been kept in the dark about.

The revelations are bittersweet. Mankind is finally on the precipice of launching a major counteroffensive, but the technology has existed for some time now, causing Sergeant Shipley to question why it wasn't deployed sooner, perhaps sparing the life of his brother.

Shipley, in a conference with someone he trusted as a father, Captain Stone from his Blockade, realizes to his horror that the lojack mission that they were sent out on was only a test, directed by President Graham herself, in cooperation with Stone and others.

Confronted with this news, and realizing that Rutty's death was vain at the hands of operations built on lies, Cameron is overcome by emotion, and attempts to assault the Captain. He is brought down by Stone's guard, and knocked unconscious.

He awakes to find himself in the Blockade brig, and is met by Joe Bassett, who informs him that the President is coming to their very blockade, and his thirst for vengeance begins.

The story continues now in
Dissonance Volume II: Reckoning

| | DETAINED

I had had enough.

It was getting stuffy in here.

I had counted off a few days in this stupid cell. My hash marks on the plywood were not hard to etch with my belt buckle, and now I counted six of them. That would put the date at December 10th. My head still throbbed a bit from the butt of that rifle.

A nurse had come in on my first night here. Thankfully, there was mercy to be had, and they attended to my wounded shoulder and cracked collarbone from when I slammed into that berserker in the church hallway. That shoulder had already been hurting from being pinned by the first gorgon in the bathroom with Vera. Anyway, the nurse was formal and took her time poking and prodding. My shoulder "didn't look too bad," she had said blandly. It was on the mend, but she regarded me for what I was: a prisoner whom she wasn't all that interested in treating. She bandaged me up roughly, and then left. I didn't miss her.

The clock on the wall said 0830. The guard must have pounded on the cell wall, which woke me. Oh well, I'll take 0830. No sense getting up early. I didn't have a job to do right now anyway. I yawned and scratched my butt as I sat up on my bunk, reaching for bottled water.

Not that this cell was ironclad or anything: I could probably have escaped easily by now. But there was a solace in knowing that the President was coming here, and I apparently had an appointment with her. I'd give her a piece of my mind at least, so there was no point in trying to break out. In all likelihood, if I were unsuccessful in disabling that guard, he'd (or she'd) surely gun me down. The guards rotated every eight hours.

This friggin' Blockade. Why did I have to get stuck here? Of all the places we could have wound up, why did Dad bring Rutty and me here so many years ago? Ninety miles northeast of us was Mammoth Cave National Park, where the next closest Blockade was, and that would take only a few days to get there on foot. Last I heard, everyone was holed up in there nice and cozy, with gun towers right at the mouth of the cave ready to annihilate any gorgons that dared venture too close. It was a fortress, and I had never been that far before the invasion or since.

Nothing exciting happened here at all. Well, except for the power outage. That was two days ago now, right around chow time. I swear we'd had an earthquake or something because I was napping, and it woke me up. I walked to my door and saw a few scattered personnel running up and down the corridors with flashlights. But they got the power restored soon enough. The guard wouldn't tell me what had happened.

I missed my bunk. I missed Ally. And all of this isolation and lack of information made me miss Rutty all the more. Isolation does crazy things to a person. I was cynical and suspicious *before* all of this had happened. Now, I was almost ready to foam at the mouth while feverishly trying to escape a straitjacket. Prison makes you a bit stir crazy.

Once or twice, I caught the muted thunder of the gun towers, and the alarms even went off one of those times. I bolted up out of my bunk – if you can even call it that – and asked the guard if we were in trouble. He had a com and reluctantly told me that we were fine, but there was a large host of gorgons heading east in a dense throng. They weren't very far overhead, and the gun towers dispersed them pretty quickly. Where they were headed and why they were packed so tightly together, he either didn't know or wouldn't tell me. Probably the latter.

Ally had visited fairly regularly early on, but she was allowed only a few precious minutes to come in and talk, and it was all under the watchful eye of the guard. I wondered if I knew each guard. Their faces were masked. Tall guy this time. Not sure if he was someone I once patrolled with or just some new fresh meat sent in to keep me honest. He was possibly blindly allegiant to Stone and sneering at my very existence from behind that mask.

And Stone? He had checked in every single day on me, offering to talk. I ignored him each time, pretty much. I was so disgusted with him when he showed up the first time that all I could muster was, "Why don't you come a little closer? I think I missed you." He took my meaning: I missed him when I swung for him the first time and would like a second chance, *thankyouverymuch*.

Another time he showed up, I was standing against the wall already staring deadpan at the door. Our eyes met, and I had the rich opportunity to serve him up some cold, steely disdain. The final time he showed up, I turned around and mooned him. He didn't deserve my face, so I gave him the other side. So much for etiquette and order in the ranks.

But with Ally? Most of the time, the guards seemed to leave her and me in peace and quipped up only when we either embraced or started to whisper to each other. "No whispering; speak up!" they would mutter our way, and we would flash our eyes to them in frustration before resuming normal volume. Then, her visits grew more sparse, and the last time I had seen her was the night before last.

Ally smelled so good. I'm sure she was enjoying the fresh showers each day. I missed the smell of that shampoo she had acquired at Harvill Hall: it smelled of lavender back then. I'll never forget that scent. Now, back at the Blockade, it was some kind of cheap minty fragrance she must have brought with her from Alpharetta, but still, it smelled clean and altogether wholesome…and altogether her. I hadn't been allowed to shower but once, and it was under the irritating watch of the guard, standing there and surveying me through the whole process. "Mind giving me a little privacy, or are you enjoying the show?" I asked him. No response, no movement. I probably would have gotten further had I not asked with so much snark, but whatever.

Then, he surprised me with a womanly, "Knock it off, soldier." *Son of a gun or, well,* daughter *of a gun, I guess; you're a chick*, I thought. I felt better after that. I should have guessed it due to her height: a little shorter than me. She also had a lither build than the last guard, who was in fact a guy.

In our last visit, Ally had told me that the President would be here in the next day or two: she had been delayed by a mass of gorgons that had been pushed northward toward them, undoubtedly by the DTFs from the cavalry down here. I wondered what that meant for the folks up at Mammoth Cave. Maybe that's where her last stop was before she intended to visit. And maybe that mass was part of the same throng that had passed overhead previously and tasted the fury of our guns. I had asked Ally, but she didn't know.

Thinking of the date reminded me of Preston back at Harvill when we had told him what day and year it was. The look of catatonic shock that passed over his face was so telling at the time. He didn't expect it to be 2042; he thought it was '38 or '39. I guess you can really lose time when you're hemmed into a narrow place. Maybe Harvill Hall needed some good plywood and a belt buckle for proper hash marks.

I wondered how Bassett was doing and whether he was sidling up to Stone, being all buddy-buddy with him in order to glean whatever intel he could, or if he was genuinely trying to climb the ranks. Couldn't be sure. There was certainly no Blockade DN436 newsletter, and if there was, well, they certainly didn't deliver one to Cell 2A.

And then I thought of Foxy. Poor Foxy. Liam was his real name. I wondered what his last name was, and if he was now going by that voluntarily, or if he was being required to. How was he faring after all we'd been through? Had he been catalogued in the lick n' prick yet, and was he officially in the system? Was he in training? Was it under Stone? I gritted my teeth and bristled.

Considering everything that had happened, I wouldn't blame him if he had wisely thrown his hands up and decided to just go on back to Harvill. I probably would have encouraged him to do that very thing, to get out of this corrupt system while he still could. But I would miss him. He was starting to feel like a little brother after Rutty, and I just couldn't shake that.

The past ten days of my life – *our* lives, actually, including Rutty's – had been incomprehensible. The mission, Ally, Bassett, the EMP, or DTF, or whatever you wanted to call it, the bridge, that stunning heron, the refugees at Harvill, the infuriating mission, Rutty's death, Nevaeh, Amos, Vera, Jesse, my revenge, the church explosion, the tanks, the warship, the memorial, the betrayal, my imprisonment… the President.

All of it: unthinkable, and some of it unconscionable. And here I was, locked in the brig under armed guard, awaiting some pronunciation of fate by a one-woman tribunal: the President of the United States, Jean Graham, who was on her way here even now.

I had to pinch myself several times during my incarceration. Pinching myself hard so as to leave a mark was a million times better than waking up in the pitch black of the night and finding myself crying out for Rutty. That had happened a few times. One night, one of the guards had thankfully come to my door and asked if I needed anything and if I was okay. A little unexpected sympathy goes a long way in here, but all I really needed was, like Rutty, to sleep in heavenly peace.

In one my nightmares, I was inside the belly of a gorgon, and there was Rut: young and healthy, and still in one piece. He gave me that smile. But when he held my gaze, something happened. I tingled, and then I froze. I couldn't move. Then, his mouth unhinged, and he started to devour me whole. I felt every wretched treacherous bite until I woke up in a cold sweat.

I could really use a shower right now. But I didn't get one. Probably wouldn't again until tomorrow night, so I could be squeaky clean for Madame President.

December was creeping along almost to mid-month when here came Ally once again this morning. Just hearing the guard hail someone approaching in the corridor sent a thrill of life down my spine. Something, *anything*, to purge the monotony.

Ally was quite the delightful purge.

The guard stepped aside and let her in. She ran to me and embraced me.

"Hey! That'll be enough of that," said the guard. "Back off!"

Definitely not the sympathetic guard from the other night, I thought.

We flashed a look of contempt at him, separated, and sat down across from each other, but not before I gave her a quick kiss. We held hands: that was something, at least.

"You okay?" I asked her, nodding.

"Am *I* okay?" she retorted. "You're the one in solitary. How are *you* doing?"

"Oh, you know…it's all about opulence and luxury in here, right?" She snickered. "Little to pass the time with in here except imagining what's going on out there. Have the eggs gotten any better? If they have, I'm breaking outta here right now and heading straight for the mess."

"No, unfortunately, they still taste like crap."

"Remember those eggs at Harvill? Man," I said, licking my lips.

"Yeah, I remember."

She seemed to have something on her mind, but there was a lull. Of course we remembered. How could we forget our first real meal in God knows how long. Everything about that little kitchen and the food Ruby had prepared for us filled my senses and flooded me with memories. Ruby and her sister Vera.

Vera. Gone too soon, and not even by a gorgon. *Damn you, Amos*.

"I'm keeping a watch on Liam. He's doing well."

"Good!" I exclaimed. "Thank you."

"Yeah, he doesn't know about what happened, Cam. I figured ignorance is bliss, so, I didn't tell him about the surface-to-air missile or that berserker. Didn't tell Joe yet either. Anyway, the platoons reached Harvill, and some of the tanks are escorting an APC of refugees back here."

"How's he doing? How's his arm?"

"Fine and fine, by all outward appearances," she replied. "He asks about you after each visit. I think he likes you, Cam," she grinned. "You're probably the closest thing to a big brother for him, ya know?"

I did know. And honestly, that's what I had hoped, naturally, since I lost Rutty. I was glad to hear it. Foxy is a good kid, and he had saved me back there. I was glad to know he was doing well.

"Is Rebecca one of the ones coming here?" I asked.

"Yep," Ally muttered slowly, biting her lip in anticipation of what she knew would be my next question.

"Does she know about Jesse?"

She nodded momentarily. "Yeah, she does," she said, heaving a heavy sigh. "Yeah, it sounded like that's why she decided to come. I don't think anyone has told her exactly how, but, well, they don't know about what's been going on behind the scenes with the military, so I think her natural assumption would be a gorgon anyway.

"Preston, well, he decided to stay there. He's a natural leader for them and has led them this far. Some of them were too scared to leave, and, frankly, the war isn't over yet, so, they needed someone to keep things in order. That was Preston, all right. But I think Joe said Ruby was coming along with Rebecca and a few others. Witherspoon too."

"Wow, Witherspoon, huh? I bet his wife didn't look too kindly upon that."

She shook her head. "Probably not."

Ruby. I wondered if she knew that her sister Vera was dead. I wondered if she knew how she died.

I had to ask Ally: "Have you heard about Nevaeh? Did they pick her up?"

She smiled. "Yeah, they got her, Cam."

I bowed my head in relief. Whether she was in such close proximity to that damned church and the stained memory of horror surrounding it, or whether it was just that she was all alone out there, I was truly comforted to hear this.

"Yeah, I think…yesterday?" Ally guessed. "No, two days ago now, that's right. She's not here yet. They are taking them to the encampment on the other side of the Cumberland or something? Where we boarded that ship. I don't know why."

My eyes narrowed. "Why wouldn't they just bring them all here? It's still not safe out there. That doesn't make sense."

She shrugged her shoulders. "I said I don't know why, and I truly don't. It does seem weird. I mean, they have tremendous firepower over there where they're staging, but I know what you mean: nothing beats being under the gun towers."

I agreed, which is why this was perplexing news. But whatever. She'd be here soon enough, I wagered.

We looked at each other in silence for a moment.

"So, back to my first question: you okay?" I asked her, probing.

She smiled delicately. "Yeah, I guess. I miss you. I hate seeing you in here. It's messed up. Joe and I are wondering why Stone doesn't just let you out. I actually asked him to, but Stone thinks you're" -here she cleared her throat and took on a mocking tone- "better off spending some time in quiet reflection." She rolled her eyes.

Quiet reflection. *Sure. If that's what you want to call being locked up and forced to spend my days ruminating over how and why you sent my brother to his death.*

I heaved a sigh.

Ally wasn't finished.

"Cam, I-" she stopped, and looked at me. I tilted my head and raised my brows in confusion. "I know the President is coming here. And I also know you're still upset. You want answers, and you're entitled to them, definitely. But Stone is one thing. This is the President of the United States. I want you to be careful."

My jaw set firmly.

"I'm telling you, as one angry soldier to another, please be careful. When she gets here, you show her the proper respect, okay? Don't go in all guns blazing. Back off and let her speak. Don't pursue some kind of personal vendetta with her. It won't get you what you want."

Ally stared at me firmly, her eyes locked onto mine.

"Lieutenant Trudy," I joked, "you're not telling me to drop this, are you?"

Her expression didn't change.

"I am. For now, yes, that's exactly what I think you should do, Cam. She's not Stone. She's the President of the United States of America, hon. Say your piece, but show restraint. For your own good."

My expression, however, did change.

"I hear you," was all I could say in response.

All's fair in love and war, I guess. But it was sure getting stuffy in here, and I had had enough.

2 | CONFRONTING

I was looking forward to getting out of this place.

When Ally left after our last visit, we had exchanged a brief kiss and then embraced a little too long, much to the ire of the current guard. She had told me to keep my chin up and that she and Joe were working on getting me out of there. Time would tell.

I slept December 10th away fitfully, knowing that any day now I was going to be meeting the one who gave the pointless, futile order that resulted in my kid brother's death. But now, as much as I wanted to jump down the President's throat, Ally's words reverberated in my psyche: I had to heed them. What if there was still something larger going on? Payback doesn't always come at the end of a bullet; sometimes it comes through diplomatic massaging. It comes through the systematic, calculated dismantling of the foundation of bureaucracy, and that takes time, and patience. What if President Graham was only a small part of that: a pawn herself? I couldn't be certain of anything at this point, except that I was going to speak truth to power, even if it killed me. But I would do it carefully, as Ally cautioned.

I shook my head, sighed frequently, and tried to sleep that day away. Too much to think about.

·   ·   ·   ·   ·

The next day slowly rolled around. At some point, I had fallen asleep, though I don't know when or how. Maybe I couldn't sleep because the 11th would mark one week since Rutty's murder. That's what it was: *murder*. By a gorgon. The problem is that there were so many players in the leadup to that; it was hard to pin the tail on this donkey. All I knew was that I still thirsted for vengeance and wanted my brother back. I wanted to erase the pain of the past seven days.

"Shipley. Sergeant Shipley. Shipley," came the dull, muted voice growing in clarity. Something was poking me. My eyes were crusty, and I blinked stupidly at the light and turned over to look at the guard hovering over me with a rifle aimed at my shoulder. "0830. Shower. Today's the day."

·   ·   ·   ·   ·

I tried to count the wrinkles in that plywood knot, but that was ridiculously maddening. Anything to keep from tensing up. And yes, I was tense.

Showered, shaven, shined and in my shoes, I sat on the edge of my bunk in a newly issued pair of fatigues and tan t-shirt that had been placed, folded, and pressed on my bunk after the shower. My boots had been polished as well, and accompanied by new socks. It wasn't the Waldorf Astoria – so I'd heard – but this was nicer than I'd had it for the past week.

Today I had a date with a Chief Executive. I sat there with my hands on my knees, occasionally sipping the coffee that I had been brought. It was no better than what I'd been served up every other day in here, and certainly no better than what I'd lived with in all my time at this Blockade, but it did the job of rousing my wits and preparing me for the inevitable confrontation that would come.

What would President Graham want with me? I'm just a grunt. What was the point of coming all the way here? Would I even get a word in edgewise?

She better apologize, I thought.

This woman was four terms into her presidency, so I guessed that she wasn't about to be talked down to. I didn't even know what I would say: probably more of the same that I had served up to Stone, and that did me a whole lot of good. Maybe if I kissed up to her, she'd let me out of here. No, no, she was probably too smart for that and would expect it. Maybe she even liked or expected a little flippant pushback. Who knows.

What I did know was two things. One, that I was nervous. And two, she had all the power, and I had none.

While in the shower, the guard told me that in this very Blockade, DN436, President Jean Graham had arrived overnight and was greeting the troops in the pavilion. A pang of irritation welled up as I briefly wondered whether Rutty's projection was still up there, along with the others.

Were they being remembered still, just like how they used to fly a flag at half-mast? Or were they already forgotten, drowned out amidst the noise of yet another pompous, fist-pumping, rabble-rousing speech, this time by an elite upper-crust mucky-muck?

I shook my head.

She's here. Now. In this very Blockade.

I looked up at the clock on the wall. 0938. The waiting seemed like an eternity. But it was about to come to an end.

Suddenly, I could feel my heartbeat thudding in my chest as footsteps approached. Someone was coming down the hallway. The guard greeted her. "Ma'am." I stood quickly.

I couldn't see them. The guard's face abruptly popped into the small square window, and he took off the padlock and swung open the cheap, plywood door.

And there she was.

Pastor Rosie.

Not who I expected at all. I tilted my head in confusion but greeted her warmly. "Pastor Rosie, wow, I didn't know it was you...I'm expecting..."

"Well, congratulations," she beamed at me. "When is the baby due? I must confess I thought I'd seen it all, but if you are expecting Miss Trudy's baby, that'll be a new one for my journal." She smiled teasingly.

I snickered. "No, ha, I mean...I was expecting someone else. And I didn't know you knew about me and Ally. Trudy. I mean, not that we're expecting. We're *not* expecting. If that's what you meant. What I meant was-" I stopped, fumbling, while she looked at me curiously.

"I know what you meant, kiddo," she said, and approached me with a warm hug. The guard didn't protest.

And I didn't protest to being called 'kiddo' either. I guess it beat Bassett calling me 'kid.'

"Let's sit. I have only just a minute."

I obliged. Being in the presence of Rosie must be like being in the presence of the Pope. At least, that's what I imagined from my memory of reading about the last pontiff. Gorgons got him early on in the invasion. He went right out and held up a cross in defiance, shouting Scripture at one of them right there in Vatican Plaza. My family saw it on an MSNBC broadcast after the fact. The station did reruns of it over and over, showing the global impact of the invasion. It was a hurricane whirl of red and white robes as he was sucked up in the air and vanished without a cry. His gold cross fell back to Earth, clattered on the ground where he stood, and lay still.

Rosie, too, had an air of royalty about her from a kingdom not of this earth. An elevated supremacy that enveloped her and went before her, but it was graciously coupled with humility. She had on her thin readers, and I knew it was only a matter of time before she started talking to me gently over them. She was dressed in a thin sweater under coveralls. She looked like she had been doing some vegetable planting in the garden of the pavilion. She liked working in the soil, and good, fresh dirt was usually under her fingernails when she wasn't off ministering privately to someone in need.

"I want to thank you for how you handled the memorial. Never got a chance. I really appreciated what you said about Rutty." I nodded to her.

She smiled gently and looked at me over her glasses. "Two things, kid," she said, placing one hand on my knee and scooting over a bit closer to me. "One, you're forever welcome. I know him, and we've talked on more than one occasion. He is a great kid, and he is missed." I appreciated so much that she talked about him in the present tense. There was a sense of forever in that tense that met my heart.

"And two, let's cut the crap."

My eyebrows went up. I wanted to smile out of surprise, but I stowed it. "Cut the crap?"

"Yeah. Crap. Let's cut it," she insisted again.

"Okay?" Now I was deeply curious.

"You got passion and pride, kid. Both are commendable, and I respect you for it. But what you did in Stone's office last week was off the charts dumb. *Dumb*, kid. Just...*dumb*." She scowled as she put a massive emphasis on the word dumb, and her eyes jumped out at me in wide rings.

"Okay, got it - sounds like it was pretty dumb."

"*Dumb,*" she emphasized.

I get it, Rosie.

"You're on to something. You've been hot on the trail since you went out on your last mission, and things seemed somewhat amiss. You were cut out of the picture, the last to know, kept in the dark, and then thrown to the wolves by those whom you trusted. You went with your gut when you took a swing at Stone. That's the dumb part. Now, it's time to channel all that dumb into smarts. It's time to use your head. Remember what I told you, kid. The real challenge is coming. Be ready to receive it. That little stunt you pulled in there that landed you in here wasn't receiving. It was revenge. And revenge never leads to receiving. Revenge only ever leads to dead-ends. Your path goes out, Sergeant Shipley, and I want you to remember what I've told you. Can you do that?"

I nodded. "Yes, I promise I'll remember what you've told me."

She smiled out of one side of her mouth, and I swear it had the tiniest bit of condescension in it, or maybe it was that natural elevated air of hers again. "I haven't told it to you yet, kid. Don't jump the gun."

I let out a chuckle. "Of course. Sorry. What is it?"

She continued to smile as she squeezed my knee. Had I known any better, I would swear she was tearing up. This was affecting her, too, on some level.

"Justice knows no shortcuts, and the wheels of justice have only ever turned slowly. But always remember this: the only way out is *through,* Cameron. The only way out is through."

I took a deep breath. Was she talking about my own justice, what I was going through now? In truth, I was definitely going through my own justice at the moment. Or did she mean someone else's? Hard to be sure. All I could do was look at her and ponder the meaning, promising to engrave it in my memory.

"I'll remember," I barely mouthed. It came out in a faint whisper. I cleared my throat. "I promise."

She looked at me and squeezed my knee one more time, clenching her lips into the narrowest of smiles as her eyes twinkled at me above her frames. She had a sweet, maternal way about her that I really felt myself connecting with.

"Good luck, kiddo." She got up. "Congrats again on the baby. Allison Trudy is a keeper," she said, looking down upon me with another side-of-the-mouth knowing smile. Then, she carefully fished in her pocket and methodically pulled out a silver chain with something clasped on the end of it. I caught a glint of green shining through her hand as she reached for mine.

"For when the time is right," she said, and she dropped whatever it was into my hand. I felt the touch of cold metal. She sealed my hand back over itself, patted it, and smiled. The guard swung the door open, and Rosie walked out. "Hello Richard," she said to the masked and mysterious guard, knowing full well who he was.

I watched her walk out and then brought my gaze back to my hand and opened it.

There, at the end of a faded silver chain, was a piece of an amulet. An actual amulet piece in my hands again: the symbol of our eventual victory and bane of our alien invaders. The silverish surround had been punched through near the top, and the chain ran through it. I turned it over in my palms and dimly became aware of something that had been inscribed into the back.

DELIVER US FROM EVIL.

I choked back a cry and buried my face in my hands.

•   •   •   •   •

I looked up at the clock. 0958. Pastor Rosie had gone, and I was alone with my thoughts and fingering my necklace, which I had clasped around my neck after a long reflective pause during which my whole life with Rutty seemed to come flooding back. I was grateful for the memories. He was still with me.

I couldn't help but glance repeatedly at the clock. If President Graham was being shepherded around by a military escort, then everything would be kept to a nicety in terms of schedule and orderliness. So, I could reasonably expect an appointment to fall on the hour, and 1000 hours was approaching swiftly.

However, instead of footsteps, I heard the guard outside answer a call on his com. "Command, Brig, over." He paused. "Copy that." Movement outside. Footsteps. Another guard.

"Shipley, time to go. On your feet." The door swung open again and the masked guard, now flanked by two other guards, both a little shorter in height, came in. *Wow, I'm a real threat, huh? Graham needs three guards to protect her from me.*

I rose to my feet as they escorted me out. It wasn't a long corridor, but there were other cells that I passed, all seemingly unoccupied. One guard walked a few paces in front of me, leading the way. The other two took up the rear, their guns on me.

As we strolled out of my cell, a waft of fresh air hit me. I'm guessing that the Blockade gate was open. I mean, with all of these handy DTF emitters pulsating all around us, why not? Why would we need gun towers anymore, after all? For now, that fresh air felt and smelled good.

I was on my third meeting with a woman this morning. Hopefully, it was my turn to confront, and not vice versa. Graham was the only one I wanted to confront anyway.

We passed Stone's office on my left. I didn't turn around to look. I didn't care. I didn't know where we were going, but we were sticking to the southern flank of the building, the passageway I'd always known and used. My hunch was that we were heading back to the pavilion. Coincidentally, that route would take me right past Rutty's bunk. I intentionally kept my gaze to my right as I passed, staring at the wall of earth there. I wondered if someone had collected his stuff and put it into my bunk yet. Standard procedure. I wondered if his bunk had already been reassigned. Mine was coming up. They passed us right by it and kept us moving swiftly.

Yep, sure enough, we were approaching the pavilion. We passed a few other grunts as we went through. Some of them I recognized. Pettijohn and Ferro from Alpha team walked right by me. I don't think they knew it was me until after we had passed by them going the other way. Why would they? I was all spit-shined. I could feel them stop and turn in tardy recognition, watching us as we kept moving in an orderly fashion down the hall. It felt strangely like an execution processional.

Eventually the pavilion yawned up on our right, and the earthen walls gave way to that familiar wide passageway leading to the center of our substructure.

The doors were closed, and five additional guards were there, leaving absolutely no doubt that President Jean Graham was somewhere beyond them.

Rosie's words echoed through my mind: *the only way out is through.*

I took a deep breath as the doors opened.

•   •   •   •   •

The first person I saw was Stone. He was talking to someone in what looked to be an officer's uniform. I was unfamiliar with the fatigues he was wearing. They were a hybrid of digital and organic, something I hadn't seen before. He turned to look at me and then dismissed the officer.

I walked straight in. Stone turned front and center to me as I walked in, stiffening his upper lip and heaving a quick sigh. Looked like he was gathering himself for a fight.

I disregarded him and looked around.

Unceremoniously, people were milling around in here, talking in small groups, but I didn't know any of them except for Stone. Guards were placed practically every ten feet around the perimeter of the pavilion. The chairs had been cleared; the trees had been as well; all traces of the memorial had vanished. Yet, on the dais at the far end, there were traces of a meeting held there that had been either hastily assembled or recently cleared. A few easels had been set up, but I couldn't tell what they had marked on the boards that had been positioned on them.

Stone walked toward me. "Shipley."

I looked at him, offering him nothing more than the same cold stare I'd served up for a week now.

"Well, I can see you're still as warm as ever. That's fine. I suppose I deserve it." He attempted a sorrowful smile. "Someone here to meet you, Sergeant."

Someone.

"Right this way." Stone directed me toward the stage and then wrapped us around the other side of the earthen center of the pavilion, passing a few of the groups of personnel talking. The two guards were still behind me. I assumed their guns were still trained on my back.

Suddenly, there she was. I stopped cold.

As if she detected my presence, President Jean Graham turned around to face me.

She was now an elderly woman, and but for her height, which was her most distinguishing trait – she towered over everyone else at six foot three inches tall – you wouldn't have been able to pick her out in a crowd. She was in fatigues like the rest of us. Or, well, like the officer talking with Stone when I entered: that strange hybrid of digital and organic. She was lithe, with her long, gray hair clasped at the back and tucked neatly up and under her military cap. The same piercing green eyes such as I'd seen on television long ago; the same fierce jawline that had been clenched tightly from the tension of a thousand secret briefings. Her face was more lined with care than I remembered it from sixteen years ago or even more recently in any broadcast. But I think you see people differently up close anyway.

Flanked by two guards, she strode over to me with a confident smile. It's fortunate that she didn't put out a hand for me; I don't know that I would have shaken it. I struggled to remember Rosie's and Ally's words.

"Sergeant Cameron Shipley, I presume," she greeted me, firm and resolute, with a slightly gravelly voice, her hands behind her back. Her form and voice betrayed her age. Maybe she was taking some kind of supplements to keep her youthful and fit. Who knows. She smelled stuffy and earthy. Probably all that moving through the tunnels.

"Madame President," I said, clenching my jaw. *Oh, how I would love to call you something else.*

"I'm sorry that we couldn't meet under more ideal circumstances. I truly am." I wasn't sure I was ready to receive that, but I let her continue. "I've read your dossier, and Captain Stone has briefed me on everything that has transpired over the past ten days with you and your unit. I'm truly sorry about your brother Wyatt."

She said it so matter-of-factly, so…remorselessly.

I nodded and bit my lip. That was all I could do, although I think my eyes narrowed a bit at her.

"Your captain here tells me that you were up for a commendation which has since been rescinded. Allow me to effectively negate that recension. Your promotion was well-earned, Lieutenant. You did what was needed. That'll be all," she said, motioning to the guards around me. They nodded and withdrew.

We stared at each other for a tense moment. I don't know if she was expecting me to laud her with praise and gratitude, but a promotion meant nothing to me, not then when Stone gave it, and not now. I wanted my brother back. I wanted to tackle her and rip her face off. In my heart, however, I knew that would accomplish nothing, and here again I thought back to Rosie's and Ally's words about revenge and dead-ends. Revenge wouldn't bring back, let alone honor, Rutty.

She sighed quickly and forced a smile. "Might we have a word, privately, you and I?"

Without a word and expecting me to follow, she turned and sauntered over to the dais, which was unattended. Her gait was vast as a pelican's, and she moved briskly. Graham pulled up two chairs and sat them opposite each other. I obliged and sat, facing the President of the United States, who was gravely assessing me up and down. At last, she spoke.

"Lieutenant Shipley, words cannot ever do proper justice to honor what your brother did, nor what you've had to go through. I know about Harvill Hall, AP University, the bridge, the church, all of it. You've had one hell of a mission that no one deserves to have. But you did what was ordered of you, and so did your squad. And so did your brother. I won't forget that. You've helped pave the way for Operation Deliver Us Fr-" She paused. "My apologies. I had forgotten that that designator carries a bit of sting."

I looked down and heaved a sigh. "Permission to speak fr-"

"Granted," she interrupted me. I shifted my eyes quickly back up to her. I honestly think she was waiting to see if I'd let her have it. "Out with it," she said, and she lifted her palms up and back down to receive.

"Madame President," I stuttered, with cold disdain. I wasn't even sure what I wanted to say, but just tried to let the words flow naturally. "With all due respect, Ma'am, my brother's death could have been prevented. That berserker we implanted was shot down not a single hour after we implanted it in a mission that cost my brother, Private Wyatt Rutledge Shipley," -here I enunciated to make sure she remembered his name forever- "his life." I blinked. I had never addressed him so impersonally before. I cleared my throat. "It cost Rutty his life, and it was all pointless. Then Stone tells me that you – I mean – the military has known all along why they're out there over our oceans. That the berserkers were engineered. That we've had similar operations like this."

My voice and resolve were quietly growing in confidence as I laid it all out before her. She didn't interrupt me. "That the military has all this time quietly been building up a presence in this region and we've had the manpower to take these things down with technology that has just… been… sitting there… waiting in the wings while we put our asses on the line out there every single day. Yet we were sent out on a suicide mission, unaided, while they withheld valuable intel from us, and now everyone plays it off like some early victory dance. And frankly, Madame President, I just find it all a little revolting and keep throwing up in my mouth every time you or anyone else decides to invoke my brother's name or his prayer."

My blood was coursing through my veins. I felt hot. I wanted to strangle her right there, right then. Staring into the eyes of the woman who so cavalierly sent my brother to his death had my thoughts racing and my adrenaline thundering. I wanted justice. No. I truly did want revenge, regardless of the wisdom imparted to me. Ally told me not to confront her, and I think I did a pretty ironclad job of keeping it civil just now, but *dammit, Rosie,* I thought. *Why can't the way out just…be…out?*

Without missing a beat, the President of the United States apologized to me. "Lieutenant Shipley, forgive me," she said, clasping her hands together. "With the intel we had at the time, I made the decision to execute a series of actions that ultimately provided a cumulative success, but that doesn't excuse the casualties along the way. I owe you an apology, soldier."

Well, I certainly hadn't expected that. She almost seemed as gracious now as Pastor Rosie.

"I ask you to forgive the United States Government, and to forgive *me* for the death of your brother," she said in a voice both proud and contrite.

The proud part of it bugged me, but I was willing to accept the contrition. For now. I wasn't about to hug her or anything like that, but I could at least accept her apology.

But wait – had I missed something? Did she say 'casualties'? Plural?

"Thank you, Madame President. However, I must admit I'm curious. You said 'casualties.' Were there other lives lost that we here don't know about?"

She nodded quickly. "Oh, yes, there definitely were. I won't minimize it, but thankfully it was few," she said, proudly, her eyes glinting at me in defense. "Nonetheless, yes. A few operations went south, and it's something that I will forever rue.

"Zooming out and taking it from a ten-thousand-foot view, overall, we have made exponential progress against the enemy in a matter of weeks. But," she paused and clenched her lips in seeming dismay, "it's when you zoom in and look at everything from down here that you see the damage that was caused.

"There are Blockades all across the country that fared differently to varying effect, and that's something you can't just undo with the snapping of fingers. It's something that we have to take great pains to disallow in the future. Which brings us to the next stage."

I wanted to prompt her as to what that was, but I just sat and watched her spill it out slowly on her terms.

"We need you for the next mission. You and your team were the only team – out of thirty-seven nationwide – to observe what happened to the gorgons after two successive DTF detonations. You were at the Cumberland when that first one rolled over you and saw what it did to them. And you were there outside that church when one of our MSU's closed in and decimated their nest.

"It's the *nesting* that we're interested in. We don't know why they're doing it, and we need to. We now have the firepower and the defenses to potentially knock them back into space – or maybe just shy of it – but we need to find their nests and ascertain what they're up to. Then, we blow them sky-high and send them screaming.

"The end goal, Lieutenant, is to pigeon-hole them, corral them if you will, into a few major areas and then take them out for good. We can deal with the few stragglers that remain once that's done."

I looked at her. "And if they refuse to be corralled?"

She shook her head and put her hands up briefly in surrender. "Then we're out of options, and life just goes on as we know it. We revert to the hard ground fight, and we wage the longer battle that will undoubtedly sustain significantly more losses."

"You're talking about ground incursions."

"Yes, I am, soldier," she bit back with the note of someone who doesn't suffer fools lightly. "That's correct. Wherever we can find them. The problem is, as you are undoubtedly aware, that ground incursions are hunt and peck operations with potentially deadly endgames. Those berserkers – and more – are out there, God forgive us."

I shook my head at that. *God forgive us*? You *made them, lady. And what did she mean by 'and more'?*

"The rest of them are out there, scattered randomly all over the planet. Our new mask technology helps to some extent as you've seen, but it would be much more ideal to take them down in a few giant holes than root them out of thousands of little ant-sized ones. We need to take out the whole anthill at once. A massive sweep is what we have to try for first. I'm well aware that in so doing we may also lose soldiers in that process, and that will rip me up inside," she said, and shook her head. "It'll be terrifyingly bad. It's not what I want. But, unfortunately, it's all for the greater cause, and as my papa used to say, 'you can't make an omelet without breaking some eggs,' as horrible as that sounds. We have to take them all out."

"You mean nukes."

She smiled at me. I caught something in her eyes, but I wasn't sure what it was. Condescension? Pride at my comprehension? Or was it irritation?

"Not exactly." She looked away from me for a moment, acknowledging a ten-minute hand signal from an advisor that our time was almost up. She waved back.

"Construction crews are currently laboring on a few locations – that for now need to remain classified – with a massive set of lures and DTF emitters each. Once we've lured in all the gorgons, we take them out. They're calling it the Shake N Bake," she giggled, and I thought that rather juvenile. But then again, we came up with lick n' prick, so, whatever.

Regaining her composure, she resumed. "We lure the overwhelming majority of them, simultaneously, into each of three major areas, and then we blast the shit out of them with so much audio juice that their insides will be on their outsides in a permanent inversion," she said. "That way, there are minimal ground casualties instead of using nukes," she added, almost as an afterthought.

I don't know why, but I couldn't shake the feeling that President Jean Graham was sitting there lying through her teeth to me. But, in all fairness, I'd been conditioned to that lately. Hers just seemed to be wrapped in molasses sweetness, and I was having trouble wading through it.

"So, all that to say, these fine people," -here she waved her arm at everyone else present all around the pavilion- "are all here figuring out how best to do that. And it seems that the best way to go about it would be to create some irresistible lures: figure out what would draw them to us and create these gigantic nests in predefined areas that we've surrounded with DTFs. Then, once we've got them all hemmed in and cordoned off, that's when we nuke, or, well, DTF the hell out of them. With the audio waves that we'll use." She squinted her eyes at me again.

Something in the way she said that sounded like she had slipped up and corrected herself. Did she mean to say 'blast' but accidentally said 'nuke'? Why was she making it so hard to trust her or even like her? My brow furrowed in confusion, and I think she saw it.

Rosie's words came back to me again. If there was still something nefarious here, I didn't think it was my place or my time, the wheels of justice turning slowly, of course, for me to inject myself into any solution. I had to play it cool and play along. *Fine, Rosie.*

I took a deep breath to reset myself. "Alright," I said stoically. "I'm in. What do you need from me?"

She smiled heartily. "I'm so glad to hear that, Lieutenant." Her eyes twinkled. "Captain Stone recommended you highly, and his recommendation is why we decided to come directly here and meet you. We've got stations being set up all over, one of which you saw just over the Cumberland River to the east: the encampment that sent you back over this side in the chopper, where the LST is moored.

"We're readying some tanks for you, and you'll command them. You'll have DTF emitters to protect you, plus weapons and personnel. The tanks are reinforced with ferromagnetic properties naturally because they're steel, but they'll need to launch any DTFs well into the sky or they'll risk being disabled by the EMP properties of those blasts, unless they shut down. Your team will be briefed on that. And we thought that you might like your existing team to support you, so we've already briefed Sergeant Bassett, Lieutenant Trudy, and Private Mayfield."

Ally and I would be together. Thank God. "Mayfield?" I asked her.

"Oh, my apologies," she added. "He's new." She pulled a note out of her pocket and flipped it open. It then occurred to me who she meant even before she said it, and I smiled. "Goes by 'Fox.' Liam Fox Mayfield."

So that was Foxy's last name. Mayfield. He would be on our team as well. My heart swelled with gratitude. That kid had saved me physically and emotionally on the way back. I owed him. It would be good to be with him and Ally. Not sure where Joe stood, however, after our last encounter at my cell door. I'm sure I would find out soon enough.

"Your objective is to connect with the Blockade at Mammoth Cave, DN312, and lead the teams there. They've heard of you. They've heard of what you were able to accomplish at APU as well as at Madison Street United Methodist, and they're ready to follow your lead. They have a lot of new recruits there who need training, and we must train troops for what's coming. And we'll need you to train platoons on ground extermination to whittle down the overall local populations of gorgs after the big blasts are done.

"For all of this, you've been reinstated, effective immediately, with all prior credentials and security clearances, and you've been promoted to Lieutenant as previously granted by Captain Stone." I looked over at Stone, who was out of earshot, but who was watching us intently from across the room.

The President stood. I stood quickly with her.

"Congratulations, soldier. Thank you for your service." She beamed. "Let's all hope we can get this done by December 25th, and we'll give everyone a merry Christmas, huh? I'd call it the best Christmas in sixteen years." She winked at me.

The best Christmas that my brother didn't live to see.

"And please note that we maintain order now," she said proudly. "Absolutely nothing operational for the military happens without my consent. I'm keeping tabs on it to ensure that we have a streamlined counterstrike, okay? I promise no slip-ups or anything happening without my express approval."

She was certainly trying, I'll give her that, and it was eerily comforting. Also, I was definitely grateful to be reinstated. Still, something about it all just felt off. She reached out her hand to shake mine, and I took it. Her smile: forced and a bit saccharin. Her hand: oddly clammy. Was that a trait of the elderly? Was she nervous? It was just...*off.*

In the back of my mind, I couldn't shake a sense of profound betrayal of Rutty. I was so pissed at this lady just over a week ago, but either she was a magician and a silver tongue, all the while the real threat, or the real threat was still out there, playing her. I had to admit that she more or less had me respecting her, though every fiber of my being railed against me doing so. I still wanted blood. I just wasn't convinced now that it was *hers* that I wanted.

"Thank you, Madame President," I mumbled, not without a slight air of indifference. Unsure of what else to say, I looked away briefly, then returned my gaze to her, and managed a weak bit of a smile. Somehow, I brought myself to saluting her, and she mirrored it back to me.

"Report with your team to Captain Stone at 1400 this afternoon for final briefing, please." She held out her hand to shake mine once more.

"Yes, Madame President," I agreed.

"And Sergeant, I – *damn.* Sorry. *Lieutenant,*" she smiled politely as she practically curtsied and looked at me sidelong with a smile, which then faded into a look of sincere reassurance. "Please know that we won't fail you again. And you can have whatever you need. You have my word." She took my hand in both of her hands and pressed it lightly with her last words.

I looked at President Jean Graham. Maybe I had been wrong about her. I was willing to give her a chance. She had all the coziness of a grandma mixed with all the dignified air of a statesman embedded overlong in their prime.

With a nod and a confidence-infused smile, she turned and walked off the stage to my left. I sighed. *Well, that's over, thankfully.* I watched her walk back to her soothsayers as I turned to my right and noticed a tiny projector on the ground there: one of three that no longer emitted any memorial projection.

Deep inside, I couldn't shake a tiny voice telling me that I was being played somehow. I was just confused. Was I wrong about her? If so, how? I wanted the gorgons gone too, and this plan sounded like it just might work. Why was she so freaking dignified and likeable? Did she really mean her apology? I thought – and I'm sure Rosie would agree while peering over her glasses at me – if this is how the wheels of justice turn, so be it. Maybe, it would be better to just unclench a little, remain in the fight, and start believing in people.

Admittedly, I was a cynic. I needed to keep my friends close and my enemies closer. I'd always been that way, and the invasion and subsequent daily survival had augmented that.

And speaking of friends, the thought of being on mission with Ally, Foxy, and Joe again sent a thrill through me. Back doing what I was good at, taking Foxy under my wing, jousting with Joe, and feeling Ally's embrace, I had to confess I was looking forward to that, more than I could possibly begin to express.

Hell. It sure beat staring at a clock and showering in front of a masked guard every few days, scratching off the days into the plywood and hoping for some kind of distracting respite.

So why then did I feel deep inside like such a pathetic, lowlife sellout?

·   ·   ·   ·   ·

The President had returned to her cabinet people, or whoever it was that were milling around her so diligently, eager for an audience with Her Majesty. I mean, if you're a four-term president, then you're practically royalty, right? All of those people were ready to lick her fingers and do her bidding. I wondered briefly how many of them she might send to their deaths without a second thought.

My thoughts were cut short by a young voice. "Jet!"

I turned toward the door. There was Foxy running toward me. And there was Ally, walking with a huge grin, behind him. Here came two that were exactly whom I wanted to see. I wondered if they'd been summoned to come in at the end of my little pow-wow with the President. "Hey," I said, genuinely smiling and walking off the stage toward them. "Come here, you," I said to Ally, and held my arms out.

"Good to see you in tip-top shape, *Lieutenant*," she squealed. *Man,* it was nice to see her outside of that cell. I picked her up and held her in my arms, her body leaning against mine as I tilted backwards slightly.

I heard a young voice clear his throat beside us, and it drew a static chuckle out of me. "Come here, Foxy. So good to see you, man."

"You too, Jet," he chimed in, sneaking in and practically shoving Ally aside so he could get a hug. Same little guy, same blonde locks poking out from underneath some kind of hat. This time, it was military. "Thought we'd never see you again with you trying to sucker punch everybody and all that," he joked. "I expected better manners from a *lieutenant*."

"Well, someone's grown up a little since I last saw him. Getting a little cocky since you're officially a fuzzy patch, yeah? What, Army doesn't cut hair anymore?" I knocked his hat off and tousled his unkempt hair, which had become flattened down underneath it.

"Hey!" he shouted playfully, retrieving his hat and re-donning it. "I don't look good with a buzz cut. Respect the mane, dude."

I laughed. I hadn't felt this good in a week. "I like it too, bud. Good to see you, Foxy." He beamed.

We all shared a moment just looking each other up and down. I broke in. "Well, if you guys are all done admiring me, mind if we hit the mess hall? I'm *starving*."

Ally smiled. "Us too. Let's go."

I noticed that the two guards who had escorted me to the pavilion were no longer there. Seeing them gone was a freeing feeling, like shaking off those shackles. Ally put her arm around me, and so we walked toward the entrance to the pavilion. Stone happened to have migrated back over that way. My smile faded.

The Captain tilted his head and offered up a fairly lame "Good to have you back, Lieutenant."

I gave him an obligatory nod as we slowed. All I could do was confirm that we'd see him at 1400, the hour appointed by the President for the final briefing. I wondered if she'd be there. And I wondered if that would cancel out having him there. Sure, she ordered the whole crap assignment, but at least I could stomach her. Stone sat there and fired bald-faced lie after lie right to my face.

Guess I was in the market for a new 'Dad.' This one had run its course, and the threads of trust that once were strong as mooring lines were now brittle as fibers.

The three of us passed him and walked out.

I was looking forward to getting out of this place.

3 | REUNITED

This was the nicest time I'd had in a while.

1152 hours. Sitting with the gang was so refreshing. I couldn't take my eyes off of Ally, sitting across from me, and I wouldn't let her hand out of mine. No longer in those silly pigtails, her beautiful, wavy hair was tied in the back into a clumsy ponytail.

Foxy sat next to me, all fatigued up and looking every bit the soldier. He regaled us with a few stories of his training and how they had taken him out at one point back to the Cumberland in a tank to meet some of the officers there. He got to board the LST ship. It was called the USS Ellingson and was built in 2025. I still had to see it in the daylight; I'm sure it was an impressive beast.

I still had a *lot* of things to see now that I was back on the outs.

Neither Foxy nor Ally had seen much of Joe. My suspicions grew that he was cozying up to the upper crust and becoming something of a fixture there instead of remaining the heroic addition that I had regarded him as previously. If he was in fact in Stone's pocket, that could mean that Stone was eyeing him for a higher role and maybe something pivotal, as before, with the first DTF. No way to be sure. I appreciated the warning he gave me in the hallway prior to seeing Stone that night, but I had to admit cold suspicion was creeping back in and filling my thoughts.

"Ya know Stone said we'd all get silver stars, huh?" I asked both of them.

"He did?" Foxy exclaimed.

I nodded and sneered. "Last I heard. I dunno, been over a week now. Huh," I mocked confusion. "You guys get any silver stars? No? No silver stars yet? Me neither. Odd."

They caught my sarcasm.

"Wow, silver stars huh?" Ally asked. "That's impressive," she said with an eyebrow raised in disinterest.

"Yeah," I scoffed. Glad to see everyone felt the same sense of *whatever* as I did. I turned and looked at her though, and my disdain was erased.

Ally looked nothing short of beautiful. Foxy was sharing with us some comical interlude about one of the cadets at the encampment on the other side of the Cumberland where he had been doing drills on the side of the Ellingson, and had fallen into the river. He nearly drowned since he couldn't swim, but a sergeant dove in after him and swam him to shore. I didn't catch most of the story; I had eyes only for Ally. With her wavy, unkempt hair pulled back into that bobbing tail and dancing against her neck, she had a few loose strands suspended teasingly across her brow, and her eyes played peek-a-boo behind them. I reached over and smoothed them back over her ear, and she smiled softly at me, taking my hand in hers as it rested on her cheek.

Foxy gradually realized his story was now playing second fiddle, so he nodded and ended lamely, "Yeah, so...anyway."

I snickered. "Sorry, Foxy. I'm not ignoring you, buddy, I promise. I just," -here I looked back at Ally- "haven't seen our dearest Lieutenant Trudy here in a while, and it's been nothing short of lonesome in that cell."

Foxy didn't need me to spell it out for him. He could take a hint. *Beat it, chump.* He knew enough to know how much I appreciated him and was fully confident we'd be reunited soon enough.

"Well, I, uh, ya know, I should go do Private stuff. Maybe you guys should too." He winked.

"Aye, aye, Private," I jested back to him as he got up from the table and gave us a knowing nod and smile. Little devil. I turned back to Ally.

There she was. Lieutenant Allison Trudy. In gorgeous form, cleaned up, and free from duty until the 1400 briefing. What *ever* would be do between now and then?

She raised her eyebrows at me seductively.

I had a feeling I knew what we could do.

•   •   •   •   •

We made it back to my bunk. We didn't really say much along the way. Standing outside there, I was actually fumbling with the lock, and she giggled. "Hey," I protested, turning to her in feigned irritation, "I haven't been here in over a week, gimme a break." She smiled and giggled.

I got the lock off, and we walked in and closed the door. She reached over and switched the light on and then tapped it twice to dim it. I exhaled deeply and took her into my arms.

We both collapsed onto my bunk. I registered that she had tried to steer me to one of the other bunks in there, but I had my rules about the other bunks, and the only one in here that I would sleep on was mine. Mom's, Dad's, Sissy's: those were still sacred.

I took her into my arms again and kissed her, sending my hot breath down her chin and onto her neck as she clawed at my back and drew me in. Passion and heat consumed us, and my heart pounded with anticipation.

I made love to Lieutenant Allison Trudy there, and she to me, while the world rolled by in tanks with DTFs outside, while the President ambled to and fro, making and receiving counsels of war, while sergeants dove off of ships rescuing erring cadets, while gorgons swirled around, dotting the sky overhead, while people scavenged for food, while Nevaeh clung to her teddy bear in some APC returning to the encampment, while Amos lay decomposing in some body bag, while battleships floated slowly up rivers, threading their way through the continents, and while the denizens of Planet Earth massed and prepared for the ultimate revolt.

I stared deeply into the wells of her green eyes, drinking deep the fountain of life there, as our bodies intertwined, enjoined together in the sweet release of all that we had experienced, and whisked us away for an all-too brief escapade through a vast forest of warmth and passionate respite.

Ally loved me with a fury. She had been out here too long as well. She clawed at my back and scratched my wounds, both from the gorgon scratch on my back as I was fleeing to the Blockade with Rutty, and from the wound in my front right shoulder where the other gorgon had impaled Vera and me in that sickening bathroom. Both wounds were still healing, and I hissed at the scratch. She apologized breathily, but I waved her off. In the throes of passion, I hated those memories being stoked, but they vanished into the warm haze of our love once more.

1400 would be here far too soon.

But right now, ignorance was bliss, and our ignorant bliss was right now.

•　　•　　•　　•　　•

I awoke before Ally and looked groggily over at the clock. 1237 hours. Thankfully, as luck would have it, we were undisturbed and had been allowed a little peace. I turned back to her and studied every crease of her soft face, quiet now and slumbering peacefully.

I turned and stared at the ceiling. I was surprised I was able to focus as much as I did with her; I had so many burning questions ricocheting around in my head.

What and who would we find at Mammoth Cave? How long would the training of the recruits take? How would we get there? Would we run into gorgons along the way? Where was Bassett? Would I be able to protect Ally and Foxy?

Foxy – for a moment I wondered where he was. Then, I thought of where Ally and I were, and of where Rut's bunk was. Right down the hall, on the way to mine. And then my heart sank. We had literally passed right by it on the way back from the pavilion, and it hadn't even dawned on me, I had been so immersed with Ally and thinking about getting back to my bunk with her, it hadn't occurred to me that I was walking past his bunk. My spirit deflated for a minute.

Rutty. I miss you, man. I bit my lip and shook my head just thinking back to that library, which only begged more futile questioning. *Was this new job just another asinine assignment? A giant setup once more? Could the President really be trusted? What was left to say to Stone?*

I sighed, and Ally stirred fitfully beside me.

I turned back over to her and saw her stretching and whimpering as she came to. She was comical and adorable all at once. My mouth creased into a smile, sending my fleeting questions vanishing into the ether as I drank in her beauty once more. Her eyelids separated as slowly as the Launch gates, and soon those ravenously beautiful green orbs were staring into mine once more.

"Hey," she whispered through a grin.

"Hey," I mirrored back.

"Hey." She smiled again.

I chuckled and smoothed the hair that had fallen out of her ponytail back from over her brow. "So," I whispered to her, "fraternizing with another lieutenant." I clicked my tongue and raised my eyebrows. "Lieutenant Trudy," I sighed in a self-reprimanding way, "that'll get me a demotion back to Sergeant for sure. That's got to be some kind of record: two promotions and two demotions in under ten days. Whoa."

She shook her head. "Cam, if you think the Army's *that* strict anymore, you've got another think coming. There's a bunch of Army brats back home. Oh, the things we do in our off time," she trailed off, shaking her head in feigned embarrassment.

"Oh, wow, so you're a mobile fraternizer, then. I see," I delivered in mock icy judgment.

She giggled, but then softened into sincerity. "Only with hot and sexy Lieutenant-Sergeant-Lieutenants," she laughed. But then she softened. "No, only with you. I mean that."

Something in the way she spoke told me she did. And I believed her. A science nerd, a hunter, a Lieutenant, part of the original team that wrangled a gorgon, on the team that shot off the first DTF and emerged unscathed from a major mission raid. All of that added up to one thing: I could trust this woman. I could trust her with my life.

I grinned slowly back at her. "I know. I believe you." I looked over at the clock. 1248. "We better get a move on. Gotta report to Stone at 1400," I moaned. "And I've got to check in with Halcyon and see if they have any intel on Mammoth Cave before we go."

"Yeah, I should shower."

"You haven't showered yet?" I ventured rather bravely. "You smell fine to me."

"You're just sayin' that because you love me."

I was. It was true. I smiled back at her. I could tease back and forth with her all day. Unfortunately, we didn't have that luxury.

"You ready to do this whole nonsense all over again?" I asked her through a giant sigh. "Head back out there, I mean?"

She thought about it for a second. "Well, if it means we get to come back here again. *Right here*, I mean," she said, patting my bunk, "then, yeah. I guess I'm game."

I lost myself in her eyes. I smoothed her hair back again and gave it a playful tousle. She giggled.

Pretty sure I'm falling in love with Lieutenant Allison Trudy, I thought. And, truth be told, I think she was thinking the same about me.

Just then she noticed my amulet necklace given to me by Rosie. She had turned over on her tummy and saw it lying on my pile of clothes. "What's this?" she said, fetching it and passing it quietly through her fingers.

"A gift," I said. "From Pastor Rosie. Look at the back."

Ally turned it over and read it, squinting at the tiny lettering. Then she bit her lip. "Wow," she breathed. "Pastor Rosie gave you this? Cam, this is something utterly precious. What a gift. You can't ever lose this," she cautioned me somewhat sternly.

"I won't," I assured her, but I wasn't sure which gift I was vowing not to lose: the necklace, or Ally herself.

•   •   •   •   •

Ally had left, and I was alone to gather my pack and check in with Halcyon on my way to the briefing room where we had had our previous one a little over a week before. I made sure to grab my mask. I silently hoped that we had a lot more masks this time around.

I just kept staring at Rutty's books on my shelf. I had put his last one up there, and they were all stacked neatly. I lightly ran my fingers over them, and memories came flooding back of all the times I would catch him reading. Rutty sure liked to dive into a good story.

I remember he used to read a series about when the rapture happened – I think that's what it was called – and everyone was left behind. All kinds of calamities happened that were frighteningly similar parallels to our own planet's demise. Take out the humans, and all kinds of colossal underpinnings of travesty emerge.

In reality, uncontrolled forest fires ravaged the Earth with no firefighters to mitigate them. Unabated flooding where levees were demolished and water rushed inland, drowning survivors. Earthquakes and structural damage in buildings that eventually toppled. Wasp nests swelled to monstrous proportions, unthreatened. Anthills cascaded out of control and dominated the woods. The earth was groaning under the stress of no custodians left to tend to it. Vines grew up, choked out buildings, and practically pulled them down.

Earth brought mankind's greatest achievements down to itself in a bear hug that, for all intents and purposes, seemed to suggest barren dejection and loneliness. Everything was just so prone to collapse once you subtracted mankind from the equation. We were those custodians. Earth's janitors. Just…far better than Amos was.

But then, we as custodians weren't faring all that well either. With so much animal annihilation, we weren't getting enough protein, and so we needed to rely on beans, peas, lentils, nuts, seeds, soy products, and so forth. Some of us had chickens. We surely did at this Blockade, but never enough. Meat and poultry were in rare supply everywhere. Thank God for canned protein powder. That helped, at least, and I made sure to get some for breakfast this morning, along with that crappy coffee.

Then, we had that giant tornado storm four years ago. Up and down tornado alley, which had been gradually shifting eastward. Summer of 2038. Just our luck, a lot of the gorgons had vanished to God knows where, because it was pretty hot. So, they didn't get hit as badly as we would have liked. It was getting hotter each year, of course. That year, however, was particularly hot. Warm and moist air at the ground; cooler dry air higher up, and wind. That'll do it. We were barraged, and debris was everywhere when we finally came out. One of the gun towers got taken out, but we eventually repaired it. Good thing too, because the gorgons returned in full force to collect and eat their own dead.

Where Rutty and I grew up in Blue Spring, Kentucky, we didn't really see much civilization up there. It was twenty miles northwest of our Blockade as the crow flies, and we only heard about this one because someone mentioned it on their way through, heading south to it. Never found out who they were because we never saw them again. That's what happens when you travel by jeep, which they were doing. Gorgons can hear jeeps.

We went to Mount Pleasant Baptist Church, right there in town, and I was in the kids' program there. I vaguely recall them talking here and there in Sunday School about the second coming, Armageddon, and all of that end times business and the rapture. I must confess that, at times, I wondered if we were living that out right now, and maybe Rut was on to something. The sad part was that you'd just never know until a gorgon got you, and you got to meet the Big Man Himself. At least, that's how I think it went. I never once attended one of Pastor Rosie's impromptu church services. Maybe I should have. Maybe I could have related to Rutty better, and I would have better understood his passion for the Bible, for reading, for joy, for *life*.

One thing he did share with me that I'll never forget was the story of Ozymandias. Rutty loved that story and would go on and on (and I got more and more sarcastic with him as he did so) about how all of mankind's achievements turned out to be for naught, and our plight was echoing that.

Or something. Percy something or other was the author. The poem talked about seeking satisfaction in the things of this world. The speaker came across two giant stone legs in the desert. Lying next to them were this shattered head of a statue and a pedestal with an inscription on it: *My name is Ozymandias, king of kings: Look on my works, ye Mighty, and despair!* Rutty told me about it, how this king Ozymandias – once great and revered – was reduced to nothing. His statue was reduced to little more than crumbled fragments and dust, and his kingdom, once thriving, became a barren wasteland. Nothing remained of it.

There was definitely a message there. Rut knew it, and he tried to tell me.

In his view, in the hubris of what we'd all accomplished as civilization barreled down the track of years, with all our AI and machine learning, all of our automation and industrialization, thirst for knowledge, destruction of natural habitat, commercialization, claiming eminent domain over all the things that God gave us, pride eventually did us in. It does go before a fall after all. Now, weeds grew up through the cracks and choked our cities, covering all of our greatest feats and accomplishments.

I mean, everything always had its caveats, and there were anomalies to that, sure: mankind now had DTFs that they had created to ward off the gorgons. But those, too, came from an alien resource that we had *also* appropriated as our own. We just do that, I guess. Were we right to do so? Time would tell. However you sliced it, right now, it was all we had to fight them off.

That and *borosilicate glass* 3M helmets. I smiled at the memory of Ally giving her talk back at Harvill, sharing how the masks work. I shuddered, remembering their semi-effectiveness in that damned bathroom with that gorgon just before Amos killed Vera. I remember the creeping nausea and the increasing sensation of unease filling all of my joints and the fatigue and queasiness that came over me as I faced off against that thing.

Then, I remembered watching what happened to my brother *without* that mask. He would have stood a chance – if only Witherspoon hadn't had the mask instead.

Instead, Rutty was left behind. There's a sad irony there, I think. For now, all I could do was reflect, and then shake it off. The best way to avenge his death was to get back out there and take those things out. I'd been given a second chance, and I wasn't going to waste it. I think that's how Rosie would see it too.

I lovingly touched Rut's books there on the shelf with my left hand, and then found myself wanting to do something for the very first time in my life. Something strange and alien. Something I was most unaccustomed to.

Though my brain wanted to raise my right arm, palm up, in token of receiving as we'd been taught, my left hand stayed on the books, and my right began a simple unfamiliar motion. I looked down and watched it, as if from far away, watching some scene play out before me. It went to my chest, to my stomach, and then to my left breast, followed by my right. It was almost as if my right hand had a mind of its own, willingly ushering in a spirit of something I had seen Rutty do a thousand times, yet I had always scoffed at it. Now, however, it played out before me, and I found myself welcoming it.

I had just done the sign of the cross.

No matter how you looked at it, my little brother was still with me. And he always would be. I took one of his books, kissed it tenderly, and held it to my chest before I silently resumed packing. But my mind stayed on that new gesture, and it wouldn't leave me.

•   •   •   •   •

1322 hours. My pack stuffed with water bottles, extra shorts, and other sundries, I locked up and headed down the hall. On my right, there it was. 218. Rutty's bunk. This time I made sure to kiss my fingers and lightly tap his door with them as I walked by, pausing ever so briefly. I breathed "Love ya, bud," and made my way to Halcyon.

"Jet!" came a familiar low voice behind me. I turned, and there came Bassett down the corridor toward me.

"Well, well, Mister Joe," I greeted him. "I was wondering when you'd turn up again. Where've you been?"

His southern drawl preceded him. He ignored the question and laughed. "Good old Jet. How ya doin', man?" He gave me a fierce high handshake, and I could see his bicep bulging and straining against the sleeve of his shirt. Somebody had been working out. "I knew you'd get outta there soon enough. Sounds like you took my advice…and Trudy's…and Rosie's," he finished, looking at me sidelong.

"Yeah, well, there's something to be said for getting by with a little help from your friends." I smiled slyly.

"Speaking of, looks like we're back on assignment. I'll be at the briefing this time, I promise. I also promise I wasn't dodging your question. I've been talking with Stone at length lately." *So it* was *true that he was in close quarters with him. Figures.* "It sounds like we're all heading up to the cave. I want you to know that there'll be no surprises from me this time. I promise you that. I'm falling in line,

Jet. You're the point man, and I take my cues from you. I mean it."

I stood still and listened to him. Was there really any reason not to trust him? I genuinely believed that he had done the right thing in trying to save Rutty. I also believed him to be a great leader and effective at what he did. I felt a kinship built in the fiery crucible of our last mission that I wasn't eager to shake off, and I would probably need his experience here as well. Maybe it was time I stopped suspecting everyone of dealing under the table. I had just seen so much of it. But Bassett? He had earned my trust. That much was clear.

"I appreciate it, man," I said at length, shaking his hand again. "Just don't salute me, I hate that."

"Ha, ok, you got yourself a deal, Lieutenant! You ain't a flag officer yet, so you don't gotta worry about that. I'm glad they didn't pull the rug out from underneath ya after all. I really am, kid."

I tilted my head and narrowed my eyes.

Joe dropped his chin and stared at the floor. "Sorry," he said, looking back up. "Old habits die hard."

Don't call me kid. I had warned him of that a few times on our mission to APU, but it didn't sting anymore. "You're fine, Gramps. At ease, soldier," I reassured him with a wry sneer.

"Well, alright then," he said. "You headed to Halcyon?"

"Yep."

"Great, I'll tag along."

We both turned and headed south down the corridor back toward Halcyon and the data room. We could feel the heat wafting down the hall toward us as we approached. The Beast was still running calculations, though I didn't really understand why anymore. I guess my view of the powers that be had been colored. What good is a massive server doing number-crunching when it seemed everyone knew everything anyway, and we now had a weapon that could defeat the enemy? Seemed the Beast couldn't see the forest for the trees. So much for AI and machine learning.

We punched through a blanket of heat as we rounded the corner into the room, closing our eyes momentarily to push out the gust.

Only a skeleton crew of Halcyon was there, working silently, pressed up against their multiple screens, monitoring all kinds of precious signals from surveillance cameras to Beast reports to weather patterns to thermal scans. One of their monitors looked like a mass of tomato soup had been spilled all over it. It was an aerial view of the encampment east of the Cumberland and adjacent to the moored USS Ellingson. All of those thermals massed together made a giant red and yellow sludge, warping and modulating as troops positioned themselves and labored busily.

I wondered where little Nevaeh was in all that, and if she was even there yet. Same for Rebecca, Jesse's mom, as well as Witherspoon and Ruby.

One of Halcyon cocked his head, and then, aware of our presence, turned in his chair and scooted over to us. I'd seen him before, but I've never talked to him. Jocks and nerds sort of thing. Reeking of hot coffee, and laden with facial stubble and a grim, set face with slim spectacles behind wavy black hair, he bobbed over to us.

"Hey, guys," he greeted us with an embarrassing half-assed salute. "Name's Pete. Pete Beckinsale, with Halcyon. Nice to finally meet both of you."

At ease, soldier. I looked at Joe and he at me: we had to chuckle. Like we didn't know he was with Halcyon. His looks screamed it. And they were the only part of the Blockade that kept saluting us. Didn't matter if we told them a hundred times that we weren't flag officers and that a salute wasn't necessary. They'd never remember.

"Nice to meet you," Joe offered courteously. "Any news on what's going on up at Mammoth Cave?"

"Well, we don't have cameras up there as you know, and the satellite relays have been a bit glitchy lately. I'll bet good money that's due to all these DTFs going on all over the place. The constant barrage of them really puts out this rat-a-tat pulse that doesn't quite reach up to the atmosphere but ultimately isn't good for the whole signal interference sphere, if you know what I mean. All that resonance bouncing around all the time here and there really causes some consternation in the bandwidth," he nerdily offered in practically a single breath.

Joe seemed unphased by him. "Yeah, I bet," he agreed. "What about the encampment on the other side of the Cumberland? And your cameras?"

"Oh, yeah! Well, the cameras go all the way out to the end of the spur and then stop a bit before the river. We really monitor only our own land because you guys have never been on assignment beyond that in order to place any cameras over the river. So, we're a bit blind beyond the teardrop. But I think you already knew that."

I already knew that.

"Anyway. The encampment! Yeah. They're continuing to assemble. They call it *Base One* now. There've been no new attacks, and they're continuing to bring down any survivors they find from Clarksville."

"No new attacks?" I asked curiously. Joe looked over at me and then back to Pete. Pete looked at Joe.

"You haven't told him?"

Now, I was ticked. I do *not* like being kept in the dark, and Joe knew that about me already. "Told me *what* exactly, Joe?" I threw at him. Hadn't he literally *minutes* ago assured me there would be no surprises?

Joe shuffled his feet and sighed. "Cam, they did get hit once while you were locked up. It was brief, but it was right after they brought down the little girl. I thought Stone would have told you."

My heart sank and my eyes went wide. *Nevaeh.* "No," I moaned to him. "Pull her up right now. Let me see the manifest, Pete."

"But I don't have-"

"Do it *now*, Pete. Right now!" I hammered.

"Okay, okay," he relented, putting his hands up. He went back to his desk, sat at his computer, and pulled out his keyboard. He looked back at us and then blocked our view with his back as he typed in his password. "Spelling?"

"N-e-v-a-e-h," I said, trying to keep calm. "She better be there." We followed him to the monitor and then leaned onto his desk on either side of him as we traced his movements on the monitor.

Pete's fingers danced on the keyboard and his mouse moved around. His computer whirred. The Beast clicked behind us, quickly humming in answer.

"Uh, African American juvenile, eleven years old, first name Nevaeh, last name unknown, H8199218163. Processed six days ago, December 5th," he verified.

"What's that H code?" I asked him.

"Oh, that's her identifier. The '*H*' stands for human, believe it or not. I know it's silly, but it is what it is. She's roughly human number H8199218163. That's what Beastie assigned her. She assigns everyone a code, kind of figuring on where we would be if-"

"Spare me, Pete. Just tell me if she's alive," I groaned at him, memorizing the number.

"Looking for updates," he droned.

My heart skipped a beat. *Please let her be alive.*

"Nothing new. Says she's still there. I do have a list of all dead. Eighteen were down before they were able to reboot the systems and get those DTF emitters up and running again. Checking."

Another beat. And another.

Eighteen dead.

"Yeah, she's not on that list. She doesn't have a last name reported here, but if there was an eleven-year-old juvenile on this list, it'd be her. There were two other juveniles on it, but they were both male. One civilian and the rest were military. Not a lot of casualties, all things considered, but still, eighteen is a sore blow. I think it took them-"

I exhaled curtly in relief, but I wasn't done. "It's alright, I get it, Pete. Check for a Rebecca. Also, no last name."

"Uh, okay...age?"

"Sixty-three."

He scanned the dead. It didn't take long. There, in green on his monitor, with a cursor blinking after it, was the entry *Burgess, Rebecca (63, F), H8203612851.* My heart sank, and both Joe and I bowed our heads. *Meemaw.* She followed us down here in a rescue, only to be killed herself. Jesse and Rebecca were now gone, and who knows if they had any other family around here. I hated to think what that raid was like or why it happened.

"Sorry, guys," Pete said. "You knew her?"

I nodded. "Yeah, we knew her. She was up at Harvill Hall at APU with us. Her son came back with us and was one of the two that died at the Madison Street church." I took a deep, remorseful sigh. "Dammit," I muttered, shaking my head. I checked the list over his shoulder, scanning it all the way down. I guess it was some comfort that I didn't see Ruby or Witherspoon's names. Ally had mentioned that they were coming here.

"What happened?"

Joe and I stood back up, and he turned toward me, shaking his head as well. "Well, best we can tell, for whatever reason, one of the big bad boys went off. A DTF, like the EMP the same size we saw at the Cumberland. It launched and disabled all the independent units and everything else. Jeeps were dead, tanks were dead. Basically, all of the DTF units and everything else went down for an hour. Most of the vehicles were all powered off and disconnected from their batteries to protect against that. But there were plenty of gorgs beyond the perimeter up north, and they all eventually jetted over to the encampment once they realized they weren't being held at bay."

Curious, I asked, "Perimeter?"

"Yeah, the edge of the DTF range. It's about two thousand meters. A little over a mile diameter where the signal starts to fade out and lessen," Pete concurred. "When that big one went off, it rolled outward, but this time they steered clear of it and fled from the blast zone, outrunning it. Power went out, like a plug had been pulled. They were sitting ducks over there."

"We were shooting everywhere, Jet," Joe continued. "Two of our guys got cut down by friendly fire...but...I think it was for their own good, because they were being frozen by the gorgs."

"Two of *our* guys?" I asked incredulously. "From this Blockade?" I pressed. "When did this *happen?*"

"No, no," Joe said, "not from this one. Just one of the grunts, I mean, no offense."

My heart sank again. *That could have been Foxy,* I thought, *while he was in training!*

"Anyway," Joe continued, "they got everything stabilized, back up and running, but not before…" he trailed off. "It was December 8th. Three days ago. Sometime around 1800."

Right when the gorgons were starting to come out again in force. Then, I remembered when the lights went out here three days ago and had woken me up. Good grief. Reminded me of when Dupre got electrocuted.

"That's when we lost power here a few days ago, wasn't it?"

"Right," Pete said. "That DTF rolled over us. But we're insulated here, below ground, and the Blockade itself has RF shielding. They all do. Long copper magnetic stuff. But only a few of the newer tanks and vehicles over there do, and they're all much more susceptible when they're running. The X-rays from the explosion cause the surrounding atmosphere and air to become ionized, which essentially allows for a massive surge of electrical current along the lines of magnetism, which emits a gargantuan pulse of electromagnetic-"

"But we still lost power," I interrupted him. "We lost power, right, Pete?"

"Right," answered Pete, "it still hits the power grid, which needs to be reset. The battery backups kick in eventually, but not without clearance because they won't last long, and they themselves need to be recharged from the grid. So that took some time here. But over there, yeah, they were down for a good spell."

"But the tanks and vehicles and computer equipment can be repaired, right?"

"Oh yeah," he insisted. "It just takes time, and in many cases, swapping out motherboards and soldering some circuitry. That's tedious work."

All I could think of now was Nevaeh. That could have been her. Or Foxy. But it *was* Rebecca. How tragic. Would the personal losses never end? I had to get out there and make sure Nevaeh was okay. And I really wanted to find Ruby and make sure she was alright as well.

"We haven't had another attack," Pete added. "Everything's been fine since then. I think, if memory serves, an officer was relieved of his position because it happened on his watch, but that makes sense. Other than that, I don't know what to tell you about the little girl."

"I want her brought here. I'm not going out on mission again until they do. I'm pressing Stone on it."

"Cam-"

"Don't 'Cam' me, Joe. That little girl was out there all by herself. We promised her we'd take care of her if she was with us. She didn't have to leave where she was, but she went with them in trust. We gotta make good on that promise. I'll talk to Stone. It's just about time for the briefing anyway." I turned to Pete. "Thanks, Pete. Let us know if you hear anything else please."

Pete nodded and took a sip of his coffee. "You bet. I'll be here. Eyes and ears until you're out of the zone."

As I turned to leave, something struck me as I looked at that giant server in the middle of the room, computing and thinking endlessly. "One more thing. Has there been anything new from the Beast?" I asked him.

"Oh yeah, that," Pete yawned and sleepily replied. "Beastie's been busy compiling all day yesterday and today.

She does that every month, and it's 'that time of the month' for her, so she's pretty grumpy and uncooperative until she's done. Kinda like defragmenting, if you guys remember that, when the old Pentiums ran a bit slower, and you'd always have to run a defrag on them at intervals in order to get all the data consolidated and free up blank space, optimizing it in the process. She's kinda stuck there right now."

I rolled my eyes. Whatever this guy was drinking, it wasn't just coffee. He spoke in a jittery fashion, way too hyped up on caffeine, but it was like he'd gotten ahold of a secret stash of amphetamines or something.

Pete blew hair out of his face. "The last report had her analyzing the coastlines for gorgon activity, but it was nothing new. Oh, hey, w-wait...," he stammered, turning over to another desk next to his and rifling through some of the report paperwork sitting there. "Winston said he saw what he thought was a glitch the other day, something way off the coast of Jacksonville, halfway between there and Bermuda."

He lifted up the stack of papers and flipped until he found the one he was looking for. "Here it is."

Pete brought the report over to us and pointed at it. It was a satellite map of what was essentially the Bermuda Triangle. "Latitude 29°45'53.8"N, Longitude 72°23'28.6"W," he began. "Winston's not here right now. He's on leave, so me and Cody are manning. But before he left, he saw a span of images that were all heading westward, big pack of images densely clustered together."

"So?" I asked him, eager to interrupt.

"Well, I mean what could it be?" asked Pete, hunching his shoulders. "It's not one of ours, and there were no competing DTFs coming from that area, not that far out to sea. We only have them land-based at the moment. And remember, our satellites scanning the ocean have been disabled for a while. This one just picks up barely off the coast.

"But the biggest thing? Gorgons, well, they don't fly in formation, right? Unless they actually *do* now. That's a pretty big signal. So maybe they're massing somewhere. Or maybe these are ones we didn't know about, heading here from Bermuda. Don't know. Beastie saw it and alerted Winnie – that's what we call him – and he got it printed out for the Captain. He's been briefed. You're welcome to ask him before you guys hit the Launch and head out."

Pete pushed his glasses further up his nose.

Great. More questions and lengthy conversations for Captain Stone.

"I'll ask him," I said blandly, taking the report from Pete. Then, I remembered something Stone had told me before I had swung at him. Now was the time to test whether or not the Captain was telling the truth about that.

"Pete, Captain Stone told me that the President knows why the gorgons keep heading us off from the coastlines. You got any info on that?"

Pete shook his head. Either he hadn't been told, or he was in on it too. "I hadn't heard any of that."

"And the Beast hasn't said anything either?"

"Nothing except for that movement I reported."

I thought to myself momentarily. "You got a com you can keep in touch with us with?"

"Of course," Pete said and lifted the headset from his ear momentarily.

"I want you to let me know tidal patterns…uh…water levels up and down the coastlines. Can the Beast report on whether there's been a decrease in our ocean volume, ya know, in the overall sea level?"

Pete glanced over at the Beast and furrowed his brow. "Yeah, anything's possible. It would take some time to compile all of that info, but if it's got any data, I can definitely get it for you. Sea levels are supposed to have *risen,* if anything, due to global warming and glacier melts, at least, about four inches per decade at least. Why? You thinkin' about goin' fishin' and don't wanna hit a reef?"

He sipped his coffee at me with a silly smirk.

"Something like that," I teased. "Thanks. Lemme know what you find, please. You ready, Joe?"

Joe nodded.

"Alright. Well, let's get Ally and Foxy and suit up. I don't know what time we're supposed to head out, but I don't think we're waiting for the morning now that we have all this protection out there. Is there a tank outside?"

"Yep, two of 'em," Joe confirmed.

"Alright. I'm heading for the briefing." 1353. It would be held in seven minutes. "You know where the briefing room is, Joe?"

"Roger, see you there," he confirmed.

I turned to head out. Right then, Foxy walked in. "Hey, man," he said, smoothing his hair back under his hat. "Thought I'd find you in here. You ready for the briefing?"

"Ready as I'll ever be," I confirmed. The two of us walked past the Beast and back out into the corridor toward the briefing room.

"Oh!" he said, "I brought this for you. I thought you might want this on mission." He held up a book that had been slightly bent and rounded. I looked down and took it from him. "You know, for luck."

I unfolded it. It was Rutty's book: the last one he had been reading by Frank Curtiss. The one I had been holding in my hand during his funeral. The one I had crumpled tightly in my fist as I tried to be present during his memorial outside Harvill before I collapsed on my butt.

The last book he ever read.

I clasped it in my hands and then looked at my new little brother, Foxy. My expression changed, and so did his. "Foxy, I…" I started.

He stumbled over his words. "Hey, I- I just thought that you might want it. Sorry if I-"

"No, no," I assured him. "It's fine. I-" I fumbled, "I appreciate it, man. I really do."

My little brother Foxy. I liked the sound of that. *Thank you Rutty.* I looked at Foxy, and he at me. It seemed to my eyes that in the last week he had grown into manhood: confident, experienced, ready. Everything Rutty had been.

We didn't say anything for a moment. Then, I reached over, grabbed ahold of him, and gave him a big bear hug. I didn't want to let him go. "Let's be safe on this one, yeah?"

I didn't just mean him, but also Ally, Joe, and anyone else we might run into on this one. The gorgons weren't gone yet, and as long as they were here, we were in grave danger, all of us.

I swore an oath to myself then and there that I wouldn't lose anyone else on any of my missions.

"Yeah," he breathed. I could tell I was squeezing the life out of him. I laughed and let him go.

Well, this moment was sure the nicest time I'd had in a while.

4 | ENGAGED

Soon, we would be engaged on our mission.

We were heading for the briefing, and then we'd be off. Bassett, Trudy, and Mayfield. Joe, Ally, and Foxy. And me. Like old times, I guess, if old times meant deception, lies, surprise catastrophic weapons, homicidal custodians, and horrific tragedy. *At least, there were good bacon and eggs,* I thought, remembering Ruby.

I still had a score to settle with Stone. By that, I meant I owed him a sucker punch, but for now, it could wait.

Honestly, the first thing I wanted to do was to swing by that encampment, make sure things were back up and running, and check on Witherspoon and Ruby. For us, that was ground zero, where our mission would all begin from. We couldn't afford any giant DTF-downing equipment on our way, rendering us all naked and exposed, especially with civilians present in there. Absolutely unacceptable. I wanted to talk to someone at the encampment who might have more intel on what happened.

We reported to the briefing room, which was just down the hall from Stone's office. Foxy and I walked in, and there he was. No distant peeping-tom, no watching me from afar. Right here, seven feet away from me. First time we'd shared the same close-proximity air since I swung at him.

This time, there was no ashen look on his face after the sudden loss of Dupre or anyone else. He was seated and looked up at both of us swiftly, his face pulled taut with fatigue. He obviously hadn't slept. Whether that was from prepping for this mission or from fear of being in the same room with me again, I wasn't sure. *I'll just assume it's Door Number Two.*

Stone quickly stood, pulling off his glasses and greeting us. We saluted, though I would have liked to have skipped that part.

"Lieutenant Shipley. Private Mayfield."

We nodded. I saluted quickly, with all the honor fit for a steaming pile of feces.

"At ease. We'll begin when the others arrive." He put his glasses back on.

Good. All business, no emotion. I can handle business with this jack wagon, I thought.

And that was that. We sat down, and so did he. I glanced at the clock. Just shy of the appointed hour: 1357. Excellent. Three wonderful minutes of excruciating silence to make him squirm. Foxy and I sat down adjacent to each other on the bench opposite Stone. I kept my eyes on him. He didn't bother to look up and meet mine but was instead penciling something down. Why he didn't bother to keep up with the Joneses and use a laptop or a terminal was beyond me. He'd always been kind of a dinosaur that way. Either that or, in the sixteen years since we'd been invaded, the Joneses really didn't hold any further sway.

1358 hours.

Finally: footsteps down the hall. Ally strode in. Thank God. I stood up to greet her and was reminded of trying to play it cool in front of Joe back at Harvill Hall. I hated doing it here again, but I had to in front of Stone. I wasn't about to clue him into Ally and me. She came in, took a bench opposite me and nodded. She looked toward Stone, who barely even acknowledged her entrance, and then she turned back to me and winked. Apparently, she was okay with playing it cool this time too.

More footsteps. Joe walked in, flanked by two more military personnel whom I had not met or seen before. Joe nodded at me and then sat on the bench next to Ally on her right. The other two, male and female, sat behind her and Joe.

1359. Stone stopped scribbling, put his pencil down with a sigh, and closed the notebook he'd been writing in, in one fluid motion. "Alright folks, let's begin," he said with a huff.

The Captain stood up, walked around to the front of his table, and perched his buttocks onto the edge of it in front of us.

"I assume you're all aware that top brass arrived this morning, including none other than the President of the United States of America," he enunciated clearly.

Acutely aware.

"She's doing a tour of the locals. They stopped at Wright-Patterson AFB in Dayton, Ohio. We've got new orders from her for all branches, including ours. Sergeant-sorry," he appeared flummoxed, "*Lieutenant* Shipley, excuse me, will be leading you all up to the Blockade at Mammoth Cave to train the new recruits. Word is spreading far and wide about what's been going on with the new technology, our reinforcements, and people are joining up. The cave up there has been armored up and equipped with tanks, APCs, weapons, communications, and rations for increased operations, which includes training those recruits. A lot more have joined up there in the past year.

"Sergeant, *dammit,*" he cursed angrily, "excuse me again for cripes' sake. *Lieutenant,*" -here he over-enunciated this time, clearing his throat for comedic effect- "Shipley, you'll command this platoon on the journey, in two tanks, and head up there in one hour. No sense in waiting for the morning for ops anymore; we've now got the extra protection we need for safety."

I guess everyone was still adjusting to my new title. Took the President a few runs at it as well, so, whatever.

If I didn't know any better – and I knew Stone pretty well – I'd say he was nervous.

"Now, uh, I know the four of you" -here he motioned to myself, Ally, Foxy and Joe- "are well-enough acquainted with each other." Something in the way he said "well-enough acquainted" made me look at Ally. I wondered if he actually knew.

"Behind you are some additional manpower on loan from the higher ups. They came with the President's team, and they'll accompany you up to the cave. This is Captain Miguel Monzon and Lieutenant LaShawna Rawley. Do I have that right?" he asked them with his eyebrows raised.

They nodded and voiced "Yessir" in tandem.

"Alright. Now, to our team, the Captain here," -here he gestured to Monzon- "is someone you'll salute, but he's not infantry, of course. Captain Monzon will be installed and stationed at Mammoth Cave to command there. Lieutenant Shipley and his team will command on the road and then fall in line at the Cave. Clear?"

"Yes, sir," everyone but me confirmed.

"Now, here's the rub. The previous captain there has been missing for some time. Captain Vance Cardona. Went AWOL a few months ago and really shook up the Blockade there where most everyone was reportedly fiercely allegiant to him. That's who Monzon here will be replacing. Cardona is considered armed and dangerous, and your orders are to shoot on sight."

Shoot on sight? That was odd. A captain in dereliction of duty, abandoning his post, and his faithful followers in such a time as this? Where would he go out there amongst gorgons that would be safer than his own post? There would be severe consequences for Captain Cardona if they ever found him, but bumping him off seemed a little extreme – this was no spy movie, for crying out loud. And what an order, in a time like this. Was he kidding?

"Why the order, sir?" Foxy asked.

Stone turned to Foxy. "Apparently he's gone off the rails, going mad with conspiracy theories and all kinds of lunacy. He was deemed unfit to lead. There was apparently some kind of altercation there, and he escaped. He's not been seen since. So, DN312 is currently leaderless, except for a few lieutenants there."

There was silence in the room.

Stone paused and then moved over to a board and easel in the corner, ripping back a sheet he'd himself been briefed on earlier. It contained a bit of a hastily drawn map of our location and the cave, with various plot points along the way in blue. There were additional marks in red interspersed throughout the drawing. I guessed those were potential gorgon sightings, or maybe even nests.

"DN312 is the Blockade. They're here," he said, pointing at the upper right of the map. "That's going to be one of our starting points in the coming counteroffensive, but we have to shore up and make safe the encampment there."

Yeah, just like you made safe the encampment here where you lost eighteen people? I shook my head, but I continued to listen.

"You'll probably encounter some gorgs on the way there. There's no way around it. You're exterminators now. You have free reign to shoot to kill, so, *happy hunting.* They should steer clear of you enough due to the emitters."

I looked over at Ally, who had a smile on her face. At last, she'd be able to shoot again.

"Now, with all due respect to you, Lieutenant Shipley, given what you and your team experienced on the last mission, you know what this operation has been dubbed, but, to avoid any future unpleasantness, at present we're just calling it *Operation Deliverance* for short."

My jaw clenched. *Operation Deliverance.* Formerly *Operation Deliver Us From Evil.* What Rutty had prayed. I nodded grimly and strongly hoped that he remembered me taking a swing at him.

"Anyway, it's one of a number of sub ops under the President's new overarching plan, what the higher-ups are jokingly referring to as Operation Shake N' Bake. For this op, you'll have everything you need: tanks, ammo, and these fine folks. You just let us know if you need anything else before you go, yeah?"

"What about the mass of gorgons off the coast that Halcyon reported?" I asked him right away, pointed and monotone.

"Good question," Stone replied wearily, as if he had spent some time assessing that news. "We don't exactly know. They've not done that before, massed together like that, so we're not sure why they've started now. And we, of course, have limited intel on what they actually do out over the oceans, other than steal our water supply. I'm afraid I can't help much beyond that, Shipley."

Suddenly the words of the President came back to me. She said I would have whatever I needed. She promised.

"Thank you, Captain," I began. "I do have one request, actually," I said, standing. "Sir, I'd like to formally request that Subject H8199218163 is to be immediately transferred to this Blockade for shelter and provisions."

Stone narrowed his eyes and tilted his head in confusion. I was impressed with myself that I actually remembered her ID clearly enough.

"Juvenile female, age eleven, African-American, Clarksville survivor, named Nevaeh. Current position is at Base One that was just attacked. I want her here. I want her safely brought to our Blockade."

"Soldier, I don't have the authority to assimilate civilians into our Blockade," Stone said dryly.

"And she gets Rut's old room," I added briskly.

"Lieutenant. Those quarters are for military personnel only. I don't have the ability to grant that."

I was ready for this reply, and steeled my jaw.

"Then, I don't have the ability to lead this mission. Get someone else. The President assured me that I could have anything I need. I have only one request, and this is it. Again, the President said I could have what I needed." It was really two requests in one, but who's counting?

The room grew quiet.

I could feel the ping-pong of the others' eyes as they darted back and forth between Stone and me. He said nothing, but just stared at me acerbically.

Joe cleared his throat, and I looked over at him. "Captain, if I may, we all met her. She was all by herself close to that church, and she may actually have additional information on personnel who were employed there. That might be valuable information if we're trying to catalogue where everyone went, including her parents. Someday, that's gotta be important to that big computer you guys got in there and elsewhere. Seems like a meager request to me, sir."

Joe sat back down.

I smiled at him and then turned back to the Captain. Stone hadn't changed positions and had only flicked his eyes over to Joe briefly during his silly attempt at supporting me. Maybe it was good enough.

Stone shuffled his feet, took a deep sigh, and cleared his throat. He jutted out his chin, pursed his lips, and squeezed a fist. His body language screamed *irritated.* It was wonderful. My eyes didn't leave him, and you could cut the tension in the room with a knife.

Stone slowly walked over to a walkie-talkie he had on his desk and picked it up.

"Base One, Captain Stone, Blockade DN436, over."

There was a pause and then static. "DN436, Base One, Private Lewis, go ahead."

Stone clenched his jaw and looked sidelong at me. Clearly, he didn't like being upstaged by the President any more than my requests superseding his wishes.

"Prepare for escort of juvenile female, name Nevaeh, ID number…" he paused and slowly extended the radio over to me.

I happily read out each number slowly and articulately. "H-8-1-9-9-2-1-8-1-6-3, over." Stone withdrew the walkie-talkie slowly without taking his eyes off of me.

Static scratch again. "Uh, sorry, Captain – jeep drove by, can you repeat, over?"

Stone rolled his eyes heavily, grunted, and thrust the walkie-talkie back at me with a jerk. He was glaring now.

I happily repeated the ID number to the private, giving it my best sing-song voice.

"Roger that. Prepping for transfer. ETA thirty minutes."

"Roger," Stone said stonily, removing his eyes from me and walking back behind his desk. "Will there be anything else, Lieutenant?" he asked in a cascading pitch upward. He was clearly exasperated. "Perhaps some fries and a Coke?"

"Yes sir, that would be wonderful, sir."

Stone stood still behind his desk and looked at me. Deep behind those grim-set eyes and all that bluster, I could swear his eyes were creasing into a smile, one that remembered old unity long-since vanished. Maybe, he wanted it again. I didn't.

He cleared his mental palette and sighed. "Alright," he said, "that's it. You've got one hour. Beat it. All of you," he said and returned his eyes to me.

We rose, slowly dispersed out into the corridor and headed back either to our bunks to grab any last supplies, to the cafeteria to load up on a bite and some water, or to weapons ordnances.

I stood there and raised my arms palm upwards. "I receive this, Captain," I said. "All of it."

Stone just looked at me without a word.

Dad was no more. He was just the Captain to me, nothing more than a cold title of a man I held no honor for and would never again esteem.

I saluted him lazily and walked out. I felt a strange thrill of excitement course through me as I walked out of there: what hadn't killed me had made me stronger. Fate had dealt me and my team a cruel blow, but nonetheless, I would see it through. I was hardened for battle now.

•   •   •   •   •

We would depart at 1500 hours. It was now 1415. Nevaeh should be here in another fifteen or twenty minutes, and then we'd have a brief time to gather and prep for Launch.

The four of us met the two newcomers on the way back to weapons, talking as we strode. I saluted Captain Monzon and shook hands with Lieutenant Rawley. Monzon was a bit younger than Joe, and LaShawna was a bit older. Monzon was graying early and was a stocky Mexican brute with a lumpy face. Definitely had the accent. Shorter than me, but with a commanding brow and guns the likes of which I'd never seen. The guy was ripped, and those biceps could crack a gorgon in half.

Rawley was the complete opposite. Swaggered like she knew how to handle a weapon, but she had rich dark dreadlocks tied tightly into a clasped ponytail in the back and high, curved eyebrows over exotic, piercing eyes. Tight uniform that strained at the buttons. She could have been a pole dancer in another life. I wasn't really sure of her role, but it sounded like, for now, she'd be staying with Monzon up there anyway.

We took a look at a map and charted our course. It would take us about two and a half hours up Highway 79 through Russellville by tank and then east on 68 to Bowling Green. Then, we'd transfer to Highways 65 and 70 up to the cave itself. If the highways were intact and not blocked by abandoned cars, reaching the cave should be a cinch, but we couldn't expect that. Most people hadn't made it that far, and the ones that were caught in the maelstrom of the invasion either became paralyzed and ran off the highway or crashed into intermittent mountains of pileups. Grisly sights, I'm told, but I'd never seen them. We needed to allow some wiggle room for stops along the way. We'd need fresh air, and there would be five of us per tank, and that was one or two too many.

The plan was to head right back the way we came a week and a half before by tank to the Cumberland, Safari over the ship, command two tanks on the opposite side, and then proceed northeast from there. Beyond that, we'd be signing the cross frequently and hoping our own little DTFs held.

Monzon and Rawley shared some good news with us. The Army and US Intelligence had been working overtime. In fortified factories and previously undisclosed assembly lines, they now had portable DTF emitters on all of those tanks, and one day we'd have the kinds you could actually carry or wear on your back. It would be a little while before the latter were available.

Either way, m-decks were relatively obsolete now. We still had some, and they would be in our tanks, but the emitters had a two-thousand-foot range in all directions and would pulse every three seconds. We would no longer have to play such an insidious game of whack-a-mole or hide-and-seek. They'd keep their distance, but we would still have to be wary.

Who would have thought that infernal noise would be such an effective weapon against the enemy? If we had known that in advance, we could have simply blasted annoying political campaign messages on a punishing loop. They would have left us alone. When the former President was killed during the invasion, the speaker of the house was none other than Jean Graham. That's when she was sworn in, and took over as president *pro-tem* right away during an informal swearing in aboard Air Force One. A more formal one wouldn't happen until three years later, since they basically had to keep moving her around, and Congress had been suspended. They actually had to find, educate, and then vote in new members. There were rumors that some were handpicked. That seemed ages ago. But after hearing her in person, she was far less annoying than the previous president or any DTF.

I didn't envy President Graham for having to weather all-out mayhem in 2026 at the outset of the invasion. To her credit, she'd done a decent job. Now, we'd see how she and the other remaining world leaders would do in the taking back of our planet.

It was time for a reckoning.

•　　•　　•　　•　　•

I checked my watch. 1442 hours. We were all assembled and ready by the Launch now. Ally was in my arms and I was cocooning her in front of me, her back to me.

Her hair smelled intoxicating. I kissed her neck, and Foxy told us to get a room.

Everyone was mounting up when the Launch suddenly opened. In wafted unsullied snowy air: crisp, cool, and refreshing. We all looked toward it and instinctively grabbed our guns. The sentry was there, however, and moved in expectation toward the inner hatch, opening it as well. From outside, we could hear the rumble of deep-throated diesel engines.

There she was. Walking through the hatch and holding hands with an officer wearing all black, was little Nevaeh. Same pig tails, same beads in her hair, same ratty old teddy bear clutched to her chest with one hand.

Human No. H8199218163.

The officer escorting her had earplugs in his ears. I wondered what that was about.

I was so overjoyed to see her, I smiled and nearly split at the ears. "Hey! There you are!" I greeted her, and she turned toward me. She wasn't so startled this time, though this environment was wholly new to her, of course. I caught the faintest recognition in her eyes, which narrowed slightly behind her furry bear's ears. "There you are," I breathed warmly again. "Remember me?"

Nevaeh nodded.

I hadn't noticed Foxy right behind me, but he had also ascended the stairs behind me. "Me too? Remember me?"

She nodded again.

"We're glad to see you're okay, Nevaeh. You been holding up well? You doing alright?"

She hesitated, looking around at all of us and the earthen halls before her, probably assessing the safety of the structure and grading it silently in her mind. Momentarily, she nodded again to us.

I smiled back at her. "I'm so glad to hear that, my friend. We missed you! We wanted to take you with us, but we had to get back. Listen," I said, inching a bit closer to her and sitting down on the step in front of her to get to her level. "I know you've been through a lot. I told you we'd keep you safe, and I meant it. I told you there were other children here, and there are. You're going to be safe here, sweetheart, okay? I'm sorry for what happened at the encampment."

She shivered and tensed up. Her eyes grew a little wider.

"Shhh, I know, sorry, I shouldn't have mentioned it. We don't have to talk about it."

I looked back at Ally. It was hard talking to an eleven-year-old. God knows the horrors that she had seen before we even found her in that building so many days ago, and God knows what horrors she had seen since.

Ally gave me a look of exhortation with rounded eyes. *You can do this.*

I turned back to her.

"Uh, listen, Nevaeh, we've got to head out again, but I arranged for you to come here. We'll be back, I promise. Okay?"

"Yeah, just for a little while," Foxy echoed. "These guys will keep you company and get you all snuggled up with your own room, okay?"

I looked at her deeply as I waited for an answer. *Come on, Nevaeh, say something. Give me a break here.*

An eternity passed. Beneath the hum of the base and the increased motion outside, I could barely hear her breathe, "Okay."

"Okay," I answered slowly, and gently reached up and playfully tugged on one of her beads. "You'll be just fine. I'm *really* glad you're here."

"Me too," said Foxy. "Glad you're okay, little one."

I stood up, and the officer led her, with her backpack and little bear, down the metal grated staircase and into the bowels of the Blockade. She was here. She was safe.

As he passed me, he handed me a baggie. It contained my Beretta. What a surprise. It was good to see my old shooter again. I took it and noticed its weight. Heavy. Still loaded. Those were the only two things she had brought with her to Base One. Her backpack looked a little fuller this time, however, and I was confident it contained plenty of relics from 'home.'

I watched the officer escort her down the corridor. I didn't have much faith that Stone would hold up his end of the bargain and let her have Rutty's room, but at least she was here, and she would be safe.

After some last-minute checks, we were good to go. It was now 1500 on the nose. In all my years here, I've never once ascended those stairs and walked directly onto the Launch and immediately out into the open air. Both hatches were still open, as if the gorgons had never existed.

The six of us stepped onto the gangway before the Launch and passed over the metal grating, onto the threshold where once we had to wait in solemnity and palms-up for the sentry. I looked over at the door slides to my right, the ones that Rutty had sprayed with WD-40. No sound there anymore. Would they ever be sprayed again? Would there eventually come an anthem day where we'd throw caution to the wind and let slip the dogs of war with gloriously grinding metal? Would we all emerge through that tiny portcullis, free from our confinement, and breathe anew the sweet fragrance of springtime grass, nevermore to look to the skies in fear?

For now, a light dusting of snow was on the ground outside, and we had to maintain some semblance of caution.

The war was not over yet, but the tide had definitely turned, that was for sure. Awaiting us on the other side of that threshold were, as promised, two tanks retrofitted with a gunner mount and a DTF emitter each, pointing east and ready to go. They looked like M1 Abrams tanks. Those were heavy mothers.

In the bright afternoon, we all looked up. The sky was cloudless. Oh, we could see them all, sure enough, like moving pinpricks in the teal canvas of the firmament, in search of their next meal, but not daring to venture this way, lest their ears explode and their brains along with them. They now seemed such a distant, inconsequential, and marginal threat, annoying but non-lethal nuisances like flies you might swat at, whereas before, we were required to live muted, stunted, shuttered-off lives. Oh, what hope-drenched change had transpired in only eight days.

A cool winter breeze wafted over us. I looked over and watched Ally's hair flutter in the wind under her hat. Her face was pointed upward, basking in the heat and light of the afternoon sun. I could see every gracious line of her face, its edges highlighted in luminescence. Her green eyes opened briefly, and sunlight streamed through them, lighting up a world of emerald. I remembered our time earlier this morning, lost in those green gems, the heat of our bodies as I dove into them. I loved this woman.

Foxy must have taken his cue from her because he was doing the same. It brought joy to my heart. I turned to my right, smiling toward Joe and wondering if this was new for him too. He was grinning from ear to ear. Monzon and Rawley were beyond him, and they were looking at either their watches or their packs. I'd say they looked impatient. Tragic. They had probably been outside and experienced such a sunset already, and were perhaps desensitized to its beauty all too soon in the caravan of the President. But for the rest of us, we were mesmerized, awash with love for the open air, the sunshine, and our world: untainted, undaunted, and the four of us in it, unafraid.

I wished with all my heart that Rutty could see this. My hands went to my necklace, and I cupped it in my palm.

We slowly filtered off the platform and walked down the berm to the waiting tanks, fueled and ready to go. These tanks had a funny-looking black dome on the back, different from what we had seen on the one that had picked us up by the church a week ago. They had an opacity to them, and you could see something going on inside, but it was obvious these were our new hopes. Inside were the new DTF-emitters, the Warhorse Morses for the modern age, mobile and fiercely dangerous to gorgons. I could hear and feel their throbbing hum even as we stood there in the light and heat of the sun glinting off the snow. The ground was amber in its reflection.

We hadn't decided who would ride with whom, but I knew I wanted Ally and Foxy with me. It just so happened that Joe ambled over to the new folks and gave me a wave of his hand. "See you at the rest stop," he cheered over the engines and gave me a thumbs up. Our convoy would have to stop somewhere, yes, but the location hadn't been determined yet. It was over a two-hour journey to Mammoth Cave.

Why was I not surprised that he chose to go with them? Was this some gracious move on his part to allow me space with Ally and Foxy? Either way, we mounted up and made ready to depart.

As I climbed onto our tank, the last to do so, I glanced up the berm at the Launch, as if to bid it farewell. And there, standing on the platform, was Captain Stone. But he wasn't alone. The President, with a few of her advisors in tow, was standing next to him. I didn't know what to make of that. Her, I sort of liked, I guess. Him, I *had* at one point liked but now nearly despised. In any event, I was glad to take my leave of both of them. *Leave them to their warmongering and stratagems,* I thought. *I'm a grunt, and the battlefield is where I belong.*

Still, they saluted me – us – giving us a sendoff with their blessing as we prepared to chart a whole new course. The President cupped her hands to her lips and shouted something, but I couldn't hear her over the roar of the tank engines and the hum of the Warhorse Morse on the back of the *iron maiden* we'd be riding in. I put my hand to my ear and gestured in confusion. She just smiled and waved. I doubt she was even looking at me.

I sloughed it off and descended into the tank, closing the hatch behind me. My healing right shoulder winced as I did so; bending it that way made it angry. I stretched it out and moved it around.

Now, I was inside the steel beast. Glancing around, I saw cases of equipment and dozens of gorgon-deflecting masks suspended on the walls, such as the two that Ally had brought on our previous mission. These, however, looked a bit more sophisticated. And there were cases of weapons and ammunition and even more masks. They even had a rocket launcher, and Foxy was already checking it out. I wasn't sure what it was with nineteen-year-olds and rocket launchers, but he shared Rutty's passion for them.

The driver greeted me and saluted, and the gunner waved from up above. "I'm Simpson!" said the driver. "Nice to have you, sir!" he saluted me as well.

I waved him off. "You aren't required to salute me. And don't call me sir," I waved him off with some cheek. "Lieutenant will do. Or Shipley. Just Shipley is fine."

"Roger that, Just Shipley," he said and laughed. He then quickly informed me that they actually had IRBs now. I had heard of them but couldn't remember what they were. 'Improved Ribbon Bridges:' pontoon bridges that the Army had brought up. There wouldn't be any further need for *one-at-a-time* Safari helicopter seesaw rides, because now we'd be able to travel over an IRB safely and stay in our tanks the entire time.

Those Army engineers. They can work like bees when the need strikes. I guess they had been doing that all along.

Ally and Foxy had stowed their gear and were getting strapped in. I did the same and sat next to Ally. Foxy was across from us, with an empty seat next to him.

Time to go. Long drive ahead. But I was going to check out that encampment first if it was the last thing I did.

•   •   •   •   •

In twenty minutes, we had reached the bridge and were traveling over to the other side. I had the driver radio ahead for Captain Benson, the one with the gravelly-voiced southern-drawl who had greeted us aboard the Ellingson on our return home. I wanted to talk to him. To my knowledge, neither Command nor any of us had given Mammoth Cave an ETA yet, so we could afford a brief stop.

We pulled into Base One, and I got out. The driver handed me some earplugs as I did so. "You're gonna need these, sir."

Ally and Foxy followed me. The hatch popped open on the other tank, and out popped Monzon, Rawley, and last of all, Joe. He had probably played gentleman and let them out first, holding the door for them.

The place was a hornet's nest of activity. *Everyone* had earplugs. That's the first thing I noticed. I guess you had to with DTFs going off all around you every three seconds. Now, I understood why the officer escorting little Nevaeh had earplugs. He had probably forgotten that he even had them in. But they protected against a massive collection of repetitive DTF pulses from the emitters, sure enough.

The whole place was a veritable miracle.

More tanks than I had seen before were cascading in row upon proud row until they seemed like tiny replicas of actual tanks, stretching far off into the distance. As I surveyed them lined up in gallant procession to the south of the bridge ramp, I hadn't turned my attention north yet. When I did, I was greeted by another sight that made my heart sing *and* stop: a *battleship*. There she was, moored a bit north of the Ellingson with her huge gun turrets pointed east and west for a makeshift shield.

I couldn't believe it. I half-expected to see the sail of a submarine trailing up from the river south of us as well. A merry little fleet it would be. The military had managed to accomplish quite a bit in a single week.

I should be in solitary confinement more often, I thought cartoonishly.

I turned to Ally. "Did you ever imagine?"

"N-No," she breathed slowly, her eyes wide. "Bring on the cavalry! This is insane."

Every single one of those tanks had a trademark black dome: a short, reflective hump on the back of them, same as ours. Their own personal Warhorse Morse.

I shook my head and drank it all in. Here, in the heartland of America, transported by river, the armed forces of the United States were prepping for a massive counterattack. And to do that, they were equipping as many Blockades with as much technology, firepower, communications as well as rescue personnel as they could.

Astonishing.

But amidst all the proud structures, the decorum, the orderliness of it all, there was an undercurrent of tension. It was unmistakable. Something had happened here to quicken the pace, and the urgency to set the feet of the soldiers to flight.

An attack.

Dead ahead was a pile of blackened equipment and supports, the structure under which both Army personnel and rescued folks were taking cover. Even from where I stood, I could make out the tattered flaps of canvas that had been stretched over all. This was only three days ago, and a new structure had been erected to our right, past a line of crates, Pelican cases and Army-grade cannisters, hastily lain in rows.

Standing there, surveying the quickly-covered-up destruction, leaving nearly no trace of it (granted, it had been three days), I couldn't help but wonder where Rebecca was when she was killed.

How exactly was she killed? Was she thinking of Jesse when she went? That poor woman.

Meemaw.

I remember her wordless encouragement to me after Rutty died, and how she took my face in her hands. How she covered her mouth and fled from his funeral and how she had taken the lead and fired on those gorgons in the library. She was a brave woman…a mother…a warrior.

It wasn't clear if she knew exactly how Jesse died, but I knew this woman loved her son and had run out after him to give him a picture of her before he left with us. *That small, wallet-sized picture, burning in the fire of the church.* They shared the same fate in life, and they shared the same fate in death. Ironic. Tragic.

And angering.

Why did the DTF go off? Who or what launched it? Was it even launched, or was it detonated? Where? Could it have been prevented? Was it accident, or was it sabotage? If so, why?

I admit that since the day that Joe and Ally arrived in Clarksville I'd become even more of a cynic, and I became a *hardened* cynic after Rutty's death. Even more so in talking with Stone, for I'd never trust again.

So many questions filled my mind, and the answers kept coming back to human action or willful inaction. But if it was either, why? And if it was accidental, how could we prevent this from happening again?

"Lieutenant Shipley," came a low growl. I turned around. Captain Benson, who had descended from the ship, in full officer dress and hat, was approaching me. He looked stern, bent and careworn. Grizzled and with a slow gait. Not the proud commanding officer I had met just a week or so ago as we crossed the USS Ellingson.

I saluted him. "Captain."

He nodded to Ally and Foxy. "Bet you're glad to get back into boots out on the ground, aren't ya, soldier?"

"Yes, sir, I sure am," I said, dryly. His wry face and knowing smile told me that he had obviously heard that I had been in lockup. Wondered how he felt being a fellow captain, knowing that I had swung hard at his contemporary. I wondered if he knew Stone.

"I understand you heard what happened here seventy-two hours ago."

"Yes, I did," I said, nodding. "If I may ask, what went wrong, sir?"

The captain coughed briskly and crossed his arms in the cold. "Well, we're still looking into it, but frankly – and sadly – it looks like human error. That's about all I can say right now."

"That human error sounds like it was costly, sir. Eighteen lives costly."

The captain's eyes glinted. "Yes, it was. But now is hardly the time to go pointing fingers, and that just ends up rankling people. There's a lot of good folks running around here that got a juiced-up shot of adrenaline coursing through their veins looking to end this war in a heartbeat, and we've all never been this near to a decent shot.

"I promise you that at some point, heads are gonna roll. Until that time, we're just chalkin' it up to a bunch of itchy fingers on overdrive from caffeine and nerves that didn't quite know to connect the blue wire and not the red. We had a lot to do to get this place operational as a staging ground, and we were under pressure to get it all ready in time for the President's arrival, as well.

"Plus, we've got all branches of the military here, and despite our best efforts, we still don't know how to talk to each other sometimes." He let out a grim chuckle and shook his head, looking down at his feet while running his hands through his grizzled beard. "It's kinda like making spaghetti with Oreos, mustard, and kippers. Basic training in the worst possible sense integrating all these different units. Each one has their own friggin' lingos and ranks."

As much as I wanted to point fingers myself, I understood what he was saying. Our own basic training, so I was told, was far from the rigor and discipline of days gone by. I can't imagine what it must have been like for all these grunts and fuzzy patches trying to integrate with each other here. And there were so many of them. We hadn't been airborne yet except for that Safari chopper, but it was clear that all branches of the military were there even a week ago, and that speaks to unity, but probably made for one helluva jigsaw puzzle mess.

"Well, look, Captain, we've taken up too much of your time. We're heading up to DN312-"

He nodded. "Mammoth Cave, I know, I heard. Best of luck to you guys. They're lucky to have you up there."

I thanked him. "Well, I'm glad you're making progress up here. Be safe and God speed, Captain," I wished him solemnly. I saluted him and turned to leave. I wished that we could find out where Ruby and Witherspoon were. Obviously, they were not here.

"Shipley," the Captain barked.

I turned back around to him. He didn't say anything, just slowly walked up to me, put his arm around me, and steered me away from Ally and Foxy.

"This little guy here the son of that woman?"

I squinted my eyes, confused. I looked at Foxy. "Oh, Mayfield? No, sir. Rebecca Burgess, was her name. Her son was Jesse Burgess, but yeah, also from APU. We lost him in a firefight up at the church. He never made it this far."

The Captain nodded. "I see. Well, if it's any consolation, I just want you to know that I regret what happened completely. But I also want to assure you that she wasn't cut down by one of our own. We did lose two men that way the night of, and a third succumbed to his injuries later. But all the others who died, the gorgons got." He put his hand on my shoulder and squeezed gently to reassure me. "I just wanted you to know that a gorgon got her, not us. We did our part to protect her. Good, fine, blameless American warriors here, sure enough." He patted my shoulder and smiled in pride.

I was shocked. No words came out of my mouth; I couldn't think of what I would say. Who in the hell would even *think* to say such a thing? Was that supposed to actually console me? It didn't matter how she didn't die – *she had died.* The pressure of speech mowed over me. Was he just covering his ass? As if being killed by friendly fire was worse than a gorgon. How was I supposed to answer that?

Say something, my mind screamed.

"Uh, yeah," I stammered. "I, uh, I know, sir. I appreciate it. Thank you for telling me," I said. Did he have any idea that this woman took my face in her hands after I lost my brother? That she ran from Rutty's burial mound because she couldn't contain her emotions? That she freaking deserved to be protected, and to be alive at this very minute? Did he have any idea that she had lost enough already?

I turned back to Ally and Foxy, and the Captain gave me the creepiest *See-I'm-a-good-guy* smile I'd ever seen. Gave me chills. I still didn't know what to say. I knew what I was thinking though: if Stone and Benson are what captains are, then I would never allow myself to be promoted beyond First Lieutenant. Something happens to you, apparently, as you climb up that rank ladder, and I wanted nothing to do with it. Hopefully, Monzon was different. Hopefully his heart was actually still human.

We climbed aboard and took off, slowly, as Base One drifted away and was swallowed up in the miles we left behind us, as if absorbed by a dream.

I swear I didn't say anything to anyone else in the tank for a good five minutes.

·   ·   ·   ·   ·

"Hey you, Lieutenant Lip-Tie, talk to me. You sure you're okay?"

I guess I had given Ally far too many "fine's" for her liking, and she wanted a solid, honest answer from me. She reached over and pulled my chin toward her. My eyes passed over to Foxy across from us. He had brought along some AirPods and an old iPod and was listening to some tunes. Rutty was into books so much; maybe Foxy's thing was music.

"Yeah, sorry," I breathed, turned in my seat with a groan and faced her. "Benson just gives me the creeps."

"What did he say? What happened?"

"I don't know, Ally. It was more the way he said it. He said that," I lowered my voice to a whisper so Foxy couldn't hear us. "He told me that a gorg had gotten Meemaw and then tried to basically commend himself by saying she wasn't one of the ones shot down by his own men. It was just this" -here I shook my head- "this wacky self-aggrandizing bravado that just reeked of CYA. Like I was going to file a report or something, and that I should be proud of him. I don't know. Just creeped me out. I still feel so bad for her."

"Wow, he said that? That's bizarre." Ally glanced quickly over at Foxy, perhaps to make sure he wasn't listening, being that he knew Meemaw better than we did. "I'm sorry, Cam. Maybe he and Stone are cut from the same cloth. Or," she thought for a moment, "maybe he heard you were close to the President, and he's itching for a promotion. Ya know? Maybe. It could happen."

"Maybe," I quickly replied, and with a huff, I was ready to move on.

"That must have been terrifying for all those people. I wonder how many of them were from Harvill."

My thoughts went back to Witherspoon and Ruby again. Why weren't they there? Where had they been taken? Ally sounded sure they were coming with Rebecca. I thought of Witherspoon's little girl, the one who was so silent back at Harvill Hall. Had she come too? I wondered if that little girl had finally learned to scream. I shook my head again in disbelief. "I don't know, sweetheart. I don't know."

Lost in thought, Ally looked down at the floor of the tank.

For all its heaviness, it was relatively quiet inside except for a low hum. The suspension in these things was a marvel. There wasn't a lot of conversation in here. It was almost as if the darkness inside the tank lent itself to a feeling of nighttime and quiet whispers, even though we were in the thick of the afternoon. I wondered if the other tank was more of the same.

Checking my watch, it was only 1553. We'd been back on the road for a good fifteen minutes now, and we were on Highway 79 approaching Guthrie. It had been silent, and the driver had been running a radar sweep all around us.

Nothing else moving of significance except for the other tank humming quietly behind us.

"So, what are your plans for when we reach the Cave?" Ally asked me as she removed her hat.

I exhaled loudly. "Man, I don't know, Ally. Sounds like Monzon'll be in charge there, so I'll take my cues from him I guess, and offer what I can."

"And what are your plans after that?"

"After what?"

She hesitated. "After we're done there, and it's time to head on home. I mean, things are moving pretty quickly, Cam, and when I saw all those tanks and that battleship, I didn't know what to think. We could be teetering on the precipice of the end of the war, and a lot might change."

I nodded to her.

"Ya know what I mean?" she asked. "It's a little scary because running and hiding is all that we've known, people like us. So much has happened in just a single week; and it could be a whole new world out there in just another week."

Something in her words stirred me. Not just because of the words themselves, but I could see and hear beyond them. Her tone was optimistic and bright, but nervous, and I wondered if she was thinking something beyond what she was verbalizing. Her heart was racing faster than her words, I could tell.

"It'll be okay, Ally. I think it will finally really be okay."

She paused. "Will it?"

I frowned at her in confusion.

She was fidgeting with her neck, the edge of her fatigues, her hair, and crossing and uncrossing her legs. I hadn't noticed it in her line of questioning up until this point, but now it was clear. I smiled at her, curious at what was nagging her. "I think it's time for me to ask if *you're* okay. Are you?" My eyebrows went up as my chin went down.

She quickly nodded, but she appeared nervous. "I guess," she began, but she never let her green eyes waver from mine. "I guess I've never really had a tomorrow, Cam. They've come unexpectedly, and they always brought *something*, but it was always out of my control. I never really could *know*."

In the dim light of the tank, I could see her eyes starting to glisten. "I guess I'm at the point where I want to *know* that tomorrow's coming. Does that make sense?" She bit her lip as if she had said too much.

Now, I thought I got it. Here we were, the two of us, heading off into a world full of gorgons, making loud noises, flying in the face of all that we had known for sixteen long uncertain years now, and she wanted some assurance that her future wouldn't be equally as full of uncertainty.

Out of the corner of my eye, I could see Foxy take one of his Airpods out and start to pay attention to us.

"Ally," I breathed, and turned to her fully. She let out a soft laugh as tears fell from her eyes, and the dam broke. "What is it?"

"I'm sorry," she said, shaking her head. "I just…I'm not good at this, Cam. I never have been. But my daddy always told me to be honest with people, and that's all we really had, ya know?"

I did know. Rutty was that way.

"So," she said, slicking back a tear running down her cheek and composing herself, "I need to be honest with you and tell you I'm falling in love with you. Okay? That I *am* in love with you, I mean. And that, as we're heading out here yet again into gorgon country, I want you to know, Cameron Shipley, that I really love you. That's all. Is that dumb?"

My heart swelled. Warm and unexpected waves of pride, and reverberations of love swelled through me. My spine tingled as I beamed.

"There. I said it. Are you proud of me, Daddy?" she asked, lifting her eyes upward, with a gentle laugh.

I am proud of you, I thought.

I took her hands in mine and looked deep in her eyes. She smiled and composed herself.

"Ally," I breathed once more. "I love you too. And the truth is that I've loved you since I met you, with those silly pigtails you were sporting in the mess hall not ten days ago, hon."

Foxy tilted his head, confused. "Tell ya later," Ally said to him in an aside. He smiled.

"I have loved you from day one, and I want to be with you too. Forever," I said. I swept her into my arms and hugged her tightly, and then as we slowly pulled apart, our chests never quite separating, we sank deeply into a warm caress. My lips met hers; I stole her breath, and she stole mine. I realized again, as I had before, that I wanted nothing more than to be with Allison Trudy for the rest of my life.

I was dimly aware that Foxy was still watching us, but I didn't care. I don't think Ally did either.

I had a sudden idea.

"Hey," I said, "do you trust me?" She tilted her head at me, smiled, and then nodded. I undid the clasp around my neck and pulled off my necklace.

"Oh, Cam – Jet – Cam," she fumbled, not settling on a name to question, "what are you doing? No, no, no," she protested.

"Now, now, simmer down," I said. "It's all good. One gift becomes another."

I slowly extended the chain toward her with the amulet dangling freely at the midpoint. I motioned her to come closer. She sighed gently and complied, leaning forward and sweeping her golden hair behind her head. I reached around both sides of her neck and clasped the necklace behind her, letting the amulet settle into her fatigues to grace her soft neck. Now, the two people I loved most in this world would be together as one: Rutty and Ally. Now I would have them both, together, forever.

Did it feel a bit juvenile? Sure. Was I a bit sheepish about the whole thing? Sure. But I didn't care, and I didn't think she did either. We didn't require formalities, and this moment wasn't going viral anytime soon.

I got off my seat and knelt before her. Foxy joined both of his hands together at the knuckles in front of his mouth and let out a brief girlish squeal of delight.

"Hope you're not judging for quality," I said.

"No, man, you're all good. Go for it, buddy!" he cheered. I laughed and turned back to Ally. She was beaming.

The gunner was watching us as well and smiling. He threw a slap into Simpson's arm while he drove, and Simpson whirled his head around to take in the scene.

"Lieutenant Allison Trudy, would you be my wife, at your earliest inconvenience?" I asked her with a sheepish grin.

All smiles, she giggled like a schoolgirl and threw her head back. For a second, I could see her back in that Blockade cafeteria in those silly pigtails, giggling at the power struggle between Joe and me. I loved her then, and I loved her now, but I loved her *more* now, and I knew that I would love her always.

Her giggle faded to a smile of warm maturity meeting winsome hopes fulfilled, as she stared lovingly straight into my eyes and whispered through tears, "Absolutely."

Then, it was my turn to laugh and cry.

Simpson and the gunner suddenly erupted into cheers and applause, joining Foxy as he burst into shouts and catcalls. Ally and I knew he had seen us, but we were oblivious to the tank crew. We whirled around and gasped in laughter and waved them all off. "Okay, okay, nothing to see here," I jested.

"No! No," Ally stopped me. "There's *everything* to see here." I swept her into my arms, and she kissed me deeply.

The driver grabbed a CB radio and hailed the other tank with a theatrical, coffee-drinking radio DJ voice, "Mobile Scout 82, repeat, MS82 this is MS131, good news over here, ya read?"

After a brief pause, there was a burst of static, and we could hear it through our own tearful laughter. "131, this is 82. What's the good word, over?"

"We have pre-marital bliss over here, like to announce Lieutenants Shipley and Trudy are engaged, repeat, *en-gaged,* bang a gong, get it on, over."

With that, he honked twice, and we could hear the other tank honk twice back, muffled, but still answering our cheerful news from behind us. In Simpson's side mirrors, they were flashing their brights at us as well.

"Roger that, 131, give the happy couple our love, and Staff Sergeant Bassett says he thinks Shipley stacked the deck, over."

Ally and I laughed. Joe was *still* talking cards. I looked over at her. Her eyes were glistening, full of warmth and radiating with heartfelt joy. She looked back at me and mouthed, "I love you."

I did the same and swept her into my arms again. I would never let her go.

Then, we were engaged, right there on our mission.

5 | DEVIATIONS

The road before us was dark.

Ally and I were now a couple. And not just that! We were now engaged to be married. Everything else had happened so quickly, why not this? We both knew. Besides, every single day we went out here, the world might end. I'd rather go out hopeful, and I knew she felt the same.

Something told both of us, though, we had a lot to hope for, and there'd be no ending today. Either that or we were blinded by love and giddily optimistic.

We had talked and snuggled the time away, and even joked with Foxy that he could be the ringbearer. He happily obliged.

The driver informed us that we were now past Russellville on Highway 68. It was 1649 hours. With any luck, we would be to the cave around 1745 or 1750 hours. About an hour to go.

The other tank radioed that they needed a pit stop. Sounded good to me.

I turned to Ally. *My fiancé.* She looked radiant sitting there with my necklace adorning her graceful, soft neck. It was silly, and perhaps a bit juvenile, how we did it; but then again, we'd all been frozen in time with a fair dose of arrested development since 2026. I don't really think anyone would or could blame us if proposals weren't exactly picture perfect. It was she and I, and it was love, and we were committed to each other, take it or leave it.

"I love you," I whispered to her, wrapping my left arm around her and pulling her tightly against me.

"I love you too," she gleamed, but then her expression changed. "But I really have to pee. Bye."

I chuckled. "After you!"

She stood and grasped the underside of the hatch, wobbling with the vehicle and doing her own little *gotta go gotta go* dance until we came to a stop.

When Ally opened the hatch, I'd never seen her move so fast. She barged out like there was a grenade in here. "Be careful, Ally," I barked. We still needed to use caution. None of us had ever been out this way before, except maybe Joe and Ally on the trip to my Blockade in Clarksville. But then, I remembered that they had come through tunnels as well. In any event, they would have been coming from southeast of us, from Alpharetta. The highway our tanks were rumbling up was undiscovered country for all of us.

I popped my head out and checked the sky, rifle at the ready, just in case. All was clear. I thought I saw some movement in the far recesses of the late afternoon clouds, but nothing close. I glanced over at the other tank and saw

Rawley doing the same dance that Ally had been doing. She scampered off not too far away behind some abandoned cars on the side of the highway. Joe popped out next, followed by Monzon. Both sets of drivers and gunners shut off the tanks, emerged, and made small talk while they ate some snacks and relieved themselves. Simpson and our gunner lit up smokes.

Joe leapt off the back of the tank with a heavy thud to the ground below. Not so spry at fifty-two as he probably was at twenty-five, he dusted himself off, grinned at me and sauntered over. "Cam, *congratulations,* man," he said, giving me a high-five. "I knew about you two lovebirds the morning of our mission at Harvill. Before I found you and Rutty in the restroom, you ticked her off by playing Cool Hand Luke. Remember?"

"Yeah, I figured you caught that."

"Never a good idea."

"Yeah, I know that now. Thanks."

"Anyway, congrats. I mean it. I've known Trudy more than a few years. She's quite a lady. Tough, sincere, smart. Quite the fighter. All essential qualities for Mrs. Lieutenant Allison Shipley." He grinned again.

I smiled at him. "I dig it. I can get used to that," I said, fist-bumping him.

He play-slapped me in the shoulder and then moved past me. "Where you goin'?" I asked.

He turned around and looked at me quizzically. "Hey, us married folks gotta pee too. You'll learn," he said, putting his hands out in helplessness. He smiled and turned back around to pee off the highway. I made a note to myself to ask him later about his wife, Maureen. He hadn't talked much about her.

I snorted and turned back to the sky. Sunset was almost here, and that *usually* meant gorgons. It was so surreal. Being out here amidst so much expanse, so far from home, protected by these two shiny humps on the backs of these tanks. I didn't quite feel impervious yet, but darn near close. No one had ever – *ever* – ventured out of DN436 so far, much less returned. I walked to the back of our tank and kissed my fingers, touching them on the black humming hump resting there in a pseudo-blessing. At the same time, I could feel current running through my digits as I received a miniscule electric shock. Sort of like when Rutty and I would dare each other to touch a live, nine-volt battery to our tongue.

Rutty. I wonder what he'd think if he could see us all now. Especially Ally and me. He told us he had a feeling about us in that bathroom back at Harvill, and then led us out of the bathroom as a doorman. Such a gallant goofball. I missed him, but that memory made me smile.

And as if on cue, here came Foxy. "Hey Jet, I mean, *Lieutenant,*" he said, playfully saluting me.

"Hey you, watch the manners, junior." I grabbed him, put him in a loose head lock and gave him a noogie. His hat came loose, and his blonde locks spilled out. "I said respect the mane!" he cried.

I chuckled. "You hit the bathroom? Ready to go on?"

"Yep. Where's the future Mrs. Shipley?"

I smiled. "She's over that way," I said, gesturing in the direction Ally had scampered off to, "and the rest of them are over there. I better hit the john myself. Hold here for me, will ya?"

Nodding, he took my XM5.

•   •   •   •   •

All were done and heading back to the group. Monzon and Rawley were approaching as well. Ally had returned and was now conversing freely with Foxy and Joe. She was showing them her necklace, and I watched them congratulate her with a warmth that filled my heart. The sight of it made me so glad.

I didn't see the tank drivers or the gunners, but Foxy was loudly ripping open a giant bag of stale Doritos in brash defiance of the ever-present terror. He grabbed a handful and mashed them into his mouth, crunching obnoxiously. The others laughed as he did so.

I checked my watch. 1704 hours already. A few minutes from sunset. We'd get in a little later now, but that was okay. Our driver came, walking up behind Joe with his own driver. "Hey, gang. We've never formally met. I'm Simpson, and this is Ollie. We radioed ahead to DN312, so they got an ETA on us now. Should be there about 1800, if we keep making the same pace. Not too bad."

"Yeah," said Ollie, "a little over an hour to go now. You guys ready to load up?"

"Yeah, let's do it," said Foxy.

He had no sooner said that when we heard a distinct radar ping alert coming from the console of the tank closest to us. All of us turned in curiosity, and then looked back up at the horizon, doing a double-take.

Something vast was drawing near. I heard Ally breathe, "What is that?" We didn't wait for an answer. In response, we all silently bolted for our vehicles.

At that moment, to our northeast and coming straight down the skyline at breakneck speed was a dense horde of black shapes, blocking out all light behind them. We needed no explanation; we knew exactly what they were, and they were coming at us *fast*.

We dropped back inside the tanks and donned our masks. I didn't think the gorgons would come anywhere close to us with our DTFs, but they all appeared to be packed so tightly together, moving in formation: something we'd never seen before.

I heard Simpson giggle a pretend fear-based chuckle as he scurried back to the driver's seat. He was *actually* smiling although he looked a bit nervous, but the bravado he had built up – reinforced by the protection afforded us by DTFs, tanks, guns, and helmets – was apparently enough for him. He clambered up and swiftly threw himself into the front of the tank as we closed our respective hatches. The situation felt strangely like my old birds when I would reach my hand into their cage, and instinctively, they'd disappear inside their ratty straw nests.

In our own tank, the radar was now going crazy. I'm sure theirs was as well. As when we had approached Harvill Hall, the screen had a mass of clustered bright blue signal practically dripping from the top of the display, slowly, like thick maple syrup, converging toward the center. Ally, Foxy, and I peeked up into the cab from the back, staring at it. Every time that radar ping would swing around, it grew in mass and density, and the signal was approaching swiftly.

"Contact, forty-five hundred meters, bearing north zero-six-seven east and closing. Four thousand meters. Man, they're bookin'," Simpson uttered.

We were all jockeying for position trying to get our own glimpses out the tiny window on the front. It was crowded in there. Our gunner had hopped in, and he was also watching the radar intently, blocking our view.

So much for a quiet journey. The Captain said that we would most likely run into gorgons on the way up. Well, here came the party, straight at us.

Just then I remembered back in the data room with the Beast and that mass of gorgons flying through the Bermuda Triangle that Pete had pointed out to us. I wondered if this group was the same one. But why were they all packed so densely together like that?

"Three thousand meters, bearing N062E," Simpson sounded. "Twenty-eight hundred, bearing 0-6-1. Twenty-seven hundred." He began to pick his lip.

In a reflex, I cast a glance behind us at the inner walls of the tank. Rows and rows of guns, grenades, rockets, sidearms, and masks, as much as could be fit into the belly of these beasts, still allowing for five humans which was already over capacity. Many of these masks were meant for DN312, the Blockade at Mammoth Cave.

Instinctively, I went for an M5, latched a few grenades onto my clips, and tightened my mask before turning back to them. "What tank model is this anyway?" I asked Simpson, and I could hear the nervous tension in my own voice. He didn't answer; he was focusing on the screen.

"M1E3 Abrams," the gunner said. *So it is an Abrams,* I thought. They're sturdy and rugged. I didn't know what that would afford us, but it was some comfort that they were the best.

"What's your name, Guns?" I asked our gunner.

"Vetas, sir," he greeted back.

"Well, Vetas, let us know what's coming, ok? Don't be shy either and don't ask for permission to shoot 'em down. You go to town on those bad boys."

"Yes sir!" he shouted back over his shoulder, and then snuggled up against his gunsight. "Whoa, baby," he muttered momentarily. "That's a big ol' crowd o' gorgons, sir. Saddle up, everybody, here comes the party."

I tried to shift past Ally to view the radar screen. Peering over her shoulder, I heard her breath catch. She had her grip on her sidearm and was staring intently at the screen. Foxy was beside her, licking his lips nervously.

"Twenty-one hundred, 0-5-9," chimed Simpson. He himself had raised up an XM5 and held onto it as he watched. "Nineteen hundred. Eighteen-fifty."

And that's when we all heard it. The humming. Except, now, it was amplifying. Ally and I had heard that sound up close in the library near Harvill, and I had heard it even closer in the hallways of that forsaken church. But there on that highway, it was like a throng of angry murder hornets intent on a kill. *Murder hornets*, I thought. I shook my head. 'Hear that?" I asked them.

Ally nodded silently and slowly. Foxy was looking up toward the roof of the tank and said nothing.

The other tank was completely silent: they saw them coming as well and were monitoring them just as intently as we were. There was no understood plan except to defend ourselves as best as we could.

"Thirteen hundred. Twelve. 0-5-8," Simpson relayed. "Command, we have numerous inbound signals!" The humming increased exponentially. Simpson turned to Vetas. "Okay. Time to play. Light 'em up, V!" he suddenly yelled, and then he radioed to the other tank. "82, this is 131, thump and dump, repeat, thump and dump! One thousand meters, bearing N060E!"

Our turret began to turn eastward.

"Roger," came the quick burst over the headset.

"Seven hundred fifty meters and closing, bearing N059E!" thundered Simpson. "Hold tight, everybody!"

"What are you gonna-" I tried to say, but then the turret exploded and shot out a massive projectile dead ahead toward the approaching throng. "Ahhhh!" I screamed, falling back and covering my ears. Foxy and Ally both shrieked in pain. The din reverberated like thunder inside that tank Then, another blast rang out behind us from MS82. Both of our beasts launched a salvo of DTFs at the other beasts, and then quickly powered down.

We all eagerly jockeyed for a look out the window. Out through that tiny slit I could see a dark cloud framed against two tiny specks of light.

All at once, the evening sky was lit up like a blinding storm. In the light, I could sense all of us recoil as we squinted and covered our eyes. It was difficult to make out what exactly was happening, but just then the blast wave hit us, and both tanks shuddered noisily. A dim film of yellowish dust was left behind from the blast, coating the window. We could just make out the fierce and angry wailing and shrieking of the enemy from afar, still closing in.

"82, 131, cycle up, go for cycle up!" Simpson yelled, and started the tank back up. It roared to life.

Now I understood. Those big ones still acted like an EMP, and for that, we had to power down, or they'd fry our electronics in that dangerous electromagnetic pulse. The President had said that. However, once it had passed, it was safe to power back up again. The Warhorse Morses were not of the same magnitude, but still put out their irritating three-second-interval DTFs. That's how they were keeping them at bay.

It's not going to be enough. It's not going to be enough, I thought, but dismissed it as pessimism.

The radar was back up, and Simpson confirmed my fears. "Contact persists!" he called out. "Five hundred meters, closing fast. Four-fifty, bearing 0-5-8. They've split! Two groups, 82, repeat, *two* groups: four hundred meters, bearing 0-5-7 and 0-6-1. Oh *crap!*" he screamed. We looked back and forth between him and the radar, our pulses pounding. The hairs on the back of my neck stood up. He was right.

They *had* separated. While the signal truly had diminished greatly in size due to the larger DTFs taking out a bunch of them, they had now split into two distinct groups, blue masses converging on the center of the screen, and closing fast. The surviving gorgons had flown *through* the DTF burst. *What?* I asked myself. *How!?*

"82, this is 131, switch to guns and light up the sky! Go! Go! Go!" Simpson was clearly in a panic. "Go, V, go, baby," he urged. "82, 131, we'll take the left; you've got the right. Repeat, you're on the left; we're on the right."

Vetas didn't waste a minute, and neither did the other tank. The muted thunder scorched the air around us and lit up the early night sky, blasting at the blob that was screaming toward us.

"Simpson! Vetas! No!" Ally shouted. "You're shooting at the same targets; you messed it up!"

"Repeat, 131, did not copy! Repeat, over!" Ollie screamed from the other tank.

Simpson screamed, "Incoming! Three hundred meters! There they are!"

Ally screamed at Vetas. "V, you take *left!* MS131, *you* take the right; *we've* got the left." Simpson whipped around and faced her, staring at her in incredulity, then down at the radar, and then back up at her. "You both took the same group!" she yelled at him. "Don't worry, they got it now! *Shoot!*"

"Copy, we'll take right, over!" yelled Bassett over the com.

"Evasive, evasive!" Simpson screamed, and the other tank, in tandem, roared into action, rolling in reverse and continuing to light up the night sky overhead before us. Treads spinning backward sent us careening back down 68 toward Russellville. It wasn't helping us out by much; we all knew how fast the gorgons were. *Still, every inch helps to stave off the inevitable,* I thought.

I heard a terrific crash behind us as the other tank slammed into the charred husk of an abandoned car and then flattened it. We ourselves ran over something as well, though I wasn't sure what it was. I didn't want to know.

I looked at the radar screen. The numbers had dwindled. "One hundred fifty meters!" I shouted. "What about the DTF? Is it running?"

Simpson didn't answer.

"Simpson!" I screamed.

Foxy shuffled next to me and was breathing hard. "Jet! He didn't power it up! He only powered up the tank! Look!"

I looked at him in fear, and then threw my focus to the cab, searching wildly for where he was pointing. There, under the main console, was the DTF power switch, clearly in the *off* position. "Dammit!" I screamed, lunging forward and flipping on the switch.

One hundred meters.

We could instantly hear the slow whirring of the emitter build up behind us, growing in strength, like one of those old, outdoor heat pumps warming up, and then it was spinning like a dryer with a full load of clothes, putting out that blessed, three-second powerful blip.

The guns continued thundering, but they kept coming. Were they all trying to bum rush us, despite the danger to themselves? Had they figured that if they just ganged up and took out our DTFs that we'd be defenseless, and then they could pick us off? Were they *that* smart?

Vetas hadn't stopped firing; neither had the other tank. Riddled with bullets, gorgons were peeling off of the main throng and falling to the ground. But the rest were still coming, and now they were clearly pissed off. The humming ballooned into a cacophony.

Fifty meters.

The radar signal blob was almost upon us. I couldn't tell if they were converging on just one or both of us. But there were still *far* too many of them.

"Ahhh!! Get down, everybody!" Vetas screamed.

Twenty-five meters.

"Get down?" I asked wildly toward him. "What are you – wait. No! Vetas, *NO!*" My voice cracked from the pressure of the scream as I watched his hand, in near slow-motion, move in desperation toward his other trigger. Everything seemed to slow to a crawl. I tried to get to him. *He couldn't do this.*

Vetas could, and Vetas did.

In one last desperate attempt, he launched another DTF, a big one, at short range out of his other turret.

Ten meters.

The tiny candle flew into the sky and exploded in a blinding flash. Our tank literally lifted off the ground momentarily due to the proximity of the colossal burst and then thudded back down, dislodging every one of us. Curses echoed throughout the cabin.

Outside the window, I watched a thunderous rolling pin of dust and light go spinning off across the plain in all directions: the aftermath of that blast. I could make out some of the gorgons exploding in agony, wrenching and convulsing midair; most of them slammed into our tank and ricocheted off of us with dull thumps. A few, long, spindly arms slapped up against the window as more than one painful shriek was heard outside. Dark blood smeared from an alien hand onto one side of our windshield, and then a fierce spray covered the whole thing.

One after another, they fell from the sky in piercing agony, wrenching and wailing in their sonic grief.

Our tank rocked left and right from the falling impacts. Others plummeted to earth and skidded down the highway beside us. The other tank fared no better.

The gorgons were dead. The mass of approaching signal was gone from the radar, but so was the radar itself. So was everything else that ran on microchips and circuitry in here.

In one fell stroke, Vetas had destroyed the computer systems that powered our tanks, rendering us completely inoperative.

We were saved, but unfortunately, we were still an hour out from Mammoth Cave, and now, we were sitting ducks as well.

We were all alone, defenseless, and the road before us was so dark.

6 | PATIENCE

This was not going to be easy.

I cracked a chemlight. Ally did the same. All of us looked at Vetas with stirrings of anger and throbbing incredulity. Foxy went off the rails and cussed him out. All Vetas could mutter was "I did what I had to do…I did what I had to do," and shook his head.

We couldn't radio the other tank, we couldn't radio Command, we couldn't radio Mammoth Cave.

We couldn't anything.

Ally breathed out a solemn, remorseful sigh, squeaking out a long hiss like air being let out of tires. She whimpered, and I swear she was about to cry.

For me, I was ticked. I tried to stop him, but I was too slow. Vetas pulled what should have been the last resort when all else failed, and he shouldn't have done it. That throng was thinning, for sure. Who was to say those gorgons would have been content to simply endure the audio barrage whilst pummeling our tanks with their wretched muscly forms, shriek and then move on? No one would know the answer to that now. Vetas hung his head even lower, if that were possible, and exhaled loudly.

I could only imagine the conversations in the other tank. They had to know Vetas fired that DTF, and I wondered if they were looking at our tank and watching us to see if we'd climb out first. We couldn't communicate with them.

My thoughts were cut short, and I didn't need to wonder anymore. There came a rap on the hatch, and we all looked up, startled. I moved to open it, and Foxy exclaimed "No, Jet, don't!"

"It's okay, Foxy. Gorgons don't knock. It's gotta be one of us, and if it is, I'm sure they surveyed the area for more of them before they came over here. Everybody just relax."

I turned away from him and rotated the hatch lock. It popped outward, and there stood Joe. Without a word, he dropped in with us and set his rifle on the ground. Traces of thin, vaporous green mist followed him in, eerily amplified by the sickly venomous green of his own chemlight.

As if we had the extra room. It was crowded in here already with five.

I closed and locked the hatch after him. His face was grim and stern. Joe let go of the hatch grips and looked over at Vetas with an expression that could curdle new milk.

"Get your m-deck in gear. Get 'em in gear, *now.* Turn 'em on. *Right now.*" He was forcible in his instruction. But he was right! The motion detectors! I whipped around, looking for them.

"There!" pointed Foxy. I followed his direction and saw a cluster of them mounted to the wall and instantly moved over to unstrap them and post them up on the top of our tank. The batteries were stored elsewhere, so we grabbed some and inserted them. Would they all still work?

"We'll point ours north and south. You point yours east and west. Let's go. Hurry," Joe urged.

Foxy helped me. We opened the hatch once more, positioned them on top of the hatch well and powered them on. Mercifully, they started right up. They weren't complex machines, and these batteries had survived the blast, as I'd heard most would.

We listened. No pulses...yet. I whispered a quick thank you to the Man Upstairs that we even had them. *Obsolete,* I thought them earlier? *Lo contrare.* Not anymore.

I turned back to Joe.

"Well, folks, we're cooked. Nothin' works in our rig. How 'bout yours?" he asked, his eyes not leaving the back of Vetas' head. Joe didn't need an answer. The question was rhetorical and full of shaming. "You did us good, gunner, real good." And just like that, he exploded. *"Real damn good indeed, soldier! Just what the hell were you thinking???"*

"Joe...just..." I waved him off. "...don't. He knows. Besides, there's nothing we can do now except bail out of the tanks and leg it all the way up there, and no one wants to do that. Let's just keep our cool with the limited air we have in here." I took a quick peak at my watch. 1724. "How are Monzon and Rawley and your guys?"

Joe sighed, alternating his focus between Vetas and me, and then shook his head. "I don't know. *Fine.* I mean, we're all just dandy out here, right?" He huffed noisily, and then slammed a thick, hairy fist into the wall. Ally started. "*Man,* I miss Maureen right now."

His wife. I wondered how long he was supposed to be stationed out here with us before he was cleared to return back to Alpharetta: his own Blockade, his own life, his own wife. I turned to Ally, and she gave me a slight forced smile in recognition of his pain. She understood.

Simpson turned around in his chair and looked red-faced at Vetas with momentary disdain, but he put an encouraging hand on his shoulder as he faced us.

"Well, folks, last I saw, we were still in Auburn, on 68 bearing east," he said with an exhale. "Last sight I caught was of an old building on the south side of 68, but that was some way back. It was just slopes on either side of us. We're gonna have to double-time it up to DN312 at the cave. I mean, we're pretty much at the Rubicon now, and I figure it'd take us at *least* fifteen hours with breaks if we had to walk it. The rest of the highway looks peppered with cars here and there. We *could* hide out in and amongst them, duck and cover, but we're still thirty-two miles out from the caves as the crow flies…longer if we're stickin' to the highway. There'd be uneven terrain between here and there if we go in a straight shot, with who knows what to traverse or what we'll run into."

"You're talkin' about leaving the tanks and *walking?* With those gorgons out there? No way, man," Foxy protested. "Screw that. Just give me a sippy."

I bowed my head. "Don't you ever say that again, Foxy," I breathed. "Don't talk like that," I said, sternly. "We're not done here yet." Cyanide pills were no laughing matter, and were a horrible solution at the end of all hope. But we hadn't lost all hope yet.

Everyone looked at the two of us. Moment of truth.

"I say we stay right here," Simpson continued. "Sooner or later, we get declared overdue, and they'll send a team up after us. Mammoth Cave will say we're MIA, and then base'll send a few more units our way, right?" he insisted, growing more optimistic with his appraisal as he continued. "And they had to have seen those DTFs go off."

It was sweltering in here. Thick, reinforced hulls keep gorgons out, but they keep hot air in, and we couldn't stay in here forever. I realized I was sweating, and so were all of us. A/C was out. We were all crammed in here like sardines. One thing we'd need to do would be to leave the hatch open if we wanted any air at all. I looked behind me, and grabbed some bottled water stowed against the side of the hull and passed them out to everyone.

"He's got a point, Jet," said Joe. "I mean, we can ride it out and wait, sure. We got guns, we got rations, we got masks. I say we ride it out and wait. We've been in tougher fixes than this." He looked at me. He was talking about the church and Amos.

I thought for a moment and then turned to everyone else. "Is that the consensus?" Virtually everyone nodded. Not a single one of us relished the thought of venturing out into uncharted territory with only our masks, our guns, and our wits, for fifteen hours with gorgons everywhere. Such an action would be construed either as suicidal desperation or possibly even abandoning our post if we left our tanks with all these supplies meant for the Blockade up there.

I scanned their faces. Foxy cleared some sweat dripping down his forehead, and removed his hat. His blonde hair fell down in dark, matted clumps, and rivulets of sweat streamed down his cheek as he wiped them away with his sleeve.

"Alright, here's what we do," I said, clearing my throat. "Joe, you head back and tell the other unit we're holding steady. Keep your hatch open. We'll keep ours open too. We won't survive if we don't have air; we'll suffocate in here. Make sure you guys have enough masks, water, guns, all that, yeah?" Joe nodded.

"I want a watch posted in both tanks. Round the clock, with binoculars, thirty minutes each. Divided by five per tank, that gives us each two hours to sleep, with a half hour on watch each." I looked up through the hatch at the clear night sky. The moonlight kept it from being pitch black, and the sky was dotted with stars. "Our m-decks should help us. We've gotta keep quiet. Two per tank: you point yours north and south, and we'll take east and west, like you said."

Joe nodded quickly. "Thank God those were off, though they're somewhat unidirectional with a limited span." He was right. A DTF *might* have killed those too had they been on. "We can try to repair the circuitry in here; anybody got any experience with motherboards and soldering?" he asked.

I remembered what Pete had told us back at the Blockade about repairability. Replacement parts and time.

Vetas raised his hand quietly, not looking up. Everyone around me glanced around the tank, as if searching for someone better.

"Well, you did this," huffed Joe. "If you can *un*-do it, even better. We might just get out of this alive if you do," he growled condescendingly, in no mood to award credit for volunteerism.

Vetas' chest sank a bit further at that remark. Everyone let Joe's guilt trip sink in for a moment as they looked around them doubtfully. Vetas said nothing.

I didn't see the need to beat a dead horse. And maybe this was the chance he needed to redeem himself. After all, we were no longer under attack.

I turned to him.

"Alright, Vetas, you give that a crack, yeah? And as far as the m-decks, it's all we've got for now, so we'll take it. Post that watch, keep those m-decks on, and look for any radios. I don't know where we've got 'em in here, but we'll look too. That'll help us with communications since those should have been off as well. We get separated or have to bail, we'll need those. And look for any backup headsets in your tank. I don't think there are any, and I don't see any in here. Mine's not working."

Simpson shook his head, confirming he didn't think there were any.

I took off my headset, not realizing I still had it on. It was useless now; they all were. Now, it was more of a felt presence amidst the sweat that began to drip profusely down from my short, wavy, and now drenched hair.

"Anyone has to go to the bathroom, you're going to have to go in an empty water bottle or something. Don't drink too much. Strip down, don't overheat. Conserve. Get as comfy as you can. We're in for a long night."

•　　•　　•　　•　　•

Joe slowly stuck his head out of the hatch, looked around, and then exited like a field mouse.

The others followed my orders and removed hats and jackets. Foxy took off his shirt and wrung it out; it was nearly drenched. He pulled a new shirt out of his pack but didn't put it on yet. I didn't blame him. It was stifling in here.

Simpson took first watch. He said he wanted out of the driver's seat, but I suspect that he and Vetas were close friends; however, now he wanted to just get away from him.

Vetas set to work on the repairs.

It was now 1735, and I hunkered down next to my bride-to-be. Ally was trying her best to get comfortable against the inhospitably steel hull of the Abrams. In the dim light I could see her: calm, pensive, but the slightest trace of a tremble.

It was quiet in the tank, except for the periodic staccato pulse of the m-decks, sounding off a blip-blip...blip-blip in near unison, one slightly offset from the other. Right now, those were our radar, and our ears were bending towards them with all attention.

I scooted over to her and put my right arm around her. Stretching my arm out made my shoulder wince, but she leaned her head into my chest, and I relaxed my arm.

"You okay?"

"Mm-hmm," she echoed, slightly nodding her head. "Super cozy in here," she smirked.

The warmth was putting her to sleep. I put a knuckle in my own eye and rubbed to ward it off. A yawn escaped my lips nonetheless. "Yeah."

I combed some loose strands away from her face that were plastered to her forehead with sweat.

"We'll get out of here, Ally. They'll come for us. Simpson's right: they had to have seen both of our DTFs, and our tanks will have relayed coordinates back to the Blockade. I'm sure they shut down their own stuff in time. And the Blockades are supposed to be shockproof anyway. They're pretty reflective, but they will have watched. They won't see any movement, and they'll come for us."

I said it, but in my heart, I wondered. *Would* Stone actually send someone for us? Would someone else? Would anyone? If they received intel about the gorgons and now two heavily armed Abrams tanks were down, they might take their own sweet time figuring out what to do rather than instantly dispatching any kind of rescue mission.

Nonetheless, I needed to be brave for Ally, and for all of them. I put on my best reassuring face. "Someone will volunteer and head out after us, or they'll be assigned. They'll come for us."

"They'll come for us," she repeated, half in a dream, as I kept stroking her hair. Her gorgeous, sea-green eyes drooped heavily. I remembered getting sucked into them back at the Blockade. And that prompted another memory.

"Ya know," I began, "speaking of volunteering, you still owe me a story, hon."

Her eyes opened and she squinted. "Huh?"

"Don't *huh* me, silly. You were going to tell me why you volunteered back there at Harvill, but then we got sidetracked, and then sidetracked some more."

She smiled faintly and answered sleepily, "You're still on that, huh?"

I smiled back at her. "Uh, *yeah* – you owe me a story, darling."

She did still owe me the story, after all. It was only fair. Ally grinned. "Well, we appear to have plenty of time, and nothing else to do."

She sat up slowly. Then she looked around, almost as if she didn't want the others to hear. Foxy was wide awake. Vetas was sitting alone in a corner, focusing on a few motherboards, but I could tell he was listening to us. He still had his hat on. Despite the heat in here, he kept it on, probably to shield his eyes – *and* his countenance. Simpson was standing halfway outside the hatch, his turn to watch. He had twenty-five minutes to go before the next rotation at 1800.

"Remember what I told you about Nick and Badger?"

I nodded. *Her brothers.* I remembered how she had slowly, painfully recounted how they had defended her during the initial invasion, how Badger, the younger of the two, had shielded her body with his, dying in the process.

She nodded back to me. "Yeah." She took a long, slow breath, followed by a noisome exhale. Then, she turned suddenly to me. "Are you sure you wanna hear this?"

I nodded again. "Yeah. I do."

Her eyes slowly shifted away from me and blinked.

"Well, it was September 3rd, 2026, right? At the tail end of summer."

I had forgotten the exact date, which seemed odd. But a memory flinched in me: that was the date the gorgons suddenly 'activated' and began to hunt us down, though they had all set up a geostationary orbit for three months prior, interspersed all around the planet. All I remembered was that it was in the early evening. Everything happened so fast.

"I guess we all remember where we were, right?"

"Yeah, I do."

"I don't," said Foxy. "I really don't. I was just a toddler, actually." I remember thinking he must have been just three when it happened.

"Yeah, well, parents and grandparents – and others – recalled afterward that there were five events they would always remember where they were when it happened. Pearl Harbor, JFK, Challenger, 9/11, and the Invasion.

"I told you about where we were. Liam, I hadn't really met you yet," she said, looking over at Foxy. I admired her preference for calling people by their real names. She did the same with Wyatt, my brother Rutty. "My brothers protected me as we made for the nearest shelter we could find. It was a Subway restaurant. They were doing like a human shield over me. Then, they were just…gone. Badge turned around, and, well, he got frozen. My older brother Nick went back to get him." She paused. "I lost both of them that day." Foxy swallowed hard. "I never rejoined my parents or found out if they were still alive. I still don't know.

"Well, a week or two went by in that restaurant. I was hiding in the manager's office with an older man who was in his sixties. He was very, very sweet," she said, turning and looking up at me with those green wells of melancholy. *Sixties. A little older than Joe Bassett.* I wondered if that's why she was paired up with him. Paternal archetype bonding and all of that.

"He really took care of me. We played card games quietly, we talked quietly, he would tell me riddles and stories quietly. Everything…quietly. We dared to go out and grab food, while it lasted, before it got stale. He'd go out and literally bring me back a Philly Cheesesteak sandwich that he'd whipped up with chips and soda, as if I had purchased it." She snickered to herself. "Dude was like super well-acquainted with sandwiches. I don't know, maybe he was a regular there. His name was Holt DeLapp. I'll never forget his name. And he was really kind, when I had to go potty, he would take me out and make sure that the door was locked with me in there, and he would stand guard outside. Just a really sweet guy overall.

"Anyway, we learned over time that the gorgs more or less disappeared during the day, so I think we got a little too big for our britches. Started venturing outside the shop more and more, further and further, searching for anybody else that might still need help."

She stopped, and her voice trailed off. Ally seemed to remember something sad, but said no more of it. "We never found anyone else because, well, you know."

She shrugged. We did know.

"Holt, as it turns out, was diabetic. He needed his insulin, and there was a pharmacy, a CVS I think, across the street. He was going to go to it after he had grabbed some dinner, so he was in there before us. Well, he never got it, and he was getting sicker. Ketoacidosis. I never forgot that word," she said, laughing sillily. "It was a big ten-dollar word for a little girl like me."

Foxy was listening intently. I too had a feeling I knew where this was going. I glanced over at Vetas, looking briefly over at us eerily underlit in green by a chemlight he was holding as he was trying to conduct his repairs. He was watching her intently. All bets were that Simpson was eavesdropping as well.

"Well, he was getting sicker and sicker, and he had to pee like *all* the time. Dry skin, dry mouth, headaches, stomach pain, nausea, flushed. All of it. So, he took it upon himself to go over there and get it, or he could literally die. I was only eight, but I was stubborn."

"What? You don't say," I chirped, my words followed swiftly by an elbow to my ribs. "Ow! Hey."

Ally let out only the slightest trace of a laugh and nervously picked her lip. She waited a bit, lost in pensive thought.

"We had been in there for twelve days. I actually had my ninth birthday in there with him," she sheepishly admitted. "Saddest birthday ever," she said with a sigh. "Holt had decided to make the journey by himself. I mean, *journey.* Not really a journey for anyone else, but for a diabetic in the throes of ketoacidosis, it would be hard for him. So," she took a huge breath, "I volunteered for him."

Ally smiled proudly in honor of her brave nine-year-old self.

"Wow, Ally, really?" Foxy asked. "What did he say? I bet he tried to stop you."

She nodded briskly. "Oh yeah. He did. He said it was my birthday present." Foxy tilted his head. "See, he felt God put him there to protect me, so him taking care of himself was actually him taking care of *me*, he said. And that would be my gift. I had lost my family, and that's what he felt called to do. Really, *really* sweet guy. I mean, I could have wound up with some weirdo. I thank God for Holt. I don't know what would have happened to me without him."

"What did you do?" I asked.

Ally turned to me and met my eyes ever so briefly there in the dark. "Well, he was too weak to stop me. I told him I was going to get his medicine for him, and that it was my gift right back to him. We got into a funny gifting war argument. He actually passed out from laughter."

Foxy laughed. "Seriously?"

I laughed too. Pretty sure I heard Vetas chuckle.

"He did. So that was my moment," she said, proudly. "Little Allison Trudy was going to be his hero, and he'd wake up to one of those injectors in his face. And a Philly Cheesesteak," she added proudly. "Yeah."

She looked at all of us. I'm sure it felt to her that we were waiting with bated breath, because we were. I couldn't shake the feeling that we were all inevitably being drawn toward a tragic end, and I was already preparing to mourn Holt with her.

She looked around at us, reluctant to continue.

"Well, it was a Friday afternoon when he passed out. It was still pretty hot, which helped. I slunk out of there as quietly as I could, going out the front, and not daring to look over at where my brothers had died. That was really the hardest part that I hadn't thought through fully beforehand.

"I checked the sky, I checked the streets, I checked all around," she said. "Credit that to my dad teaching me stealth while hunting quail with the bros," she said, playfully firing a finger bullet at Foxy and clicking her tongue with a wink. Foxy smiled back.

Then, her smile faded, and she went sullen for a moment. *Here it comes*, I thought. My heart went out to her for what she was about to share. It didn't take a genius for any of us to realize that Holt's chapter was about to come to a tragic close.

"Well," she began slowly, "I was halfway across the street when I heard coughing. It had taken me ten minutes to muster up the courage just to cross the stupid street!" she exclaimed defiantly. "But I heard it, and I turned around, sheltering behind an abandoned car. By this time, there weren't any humans left. The gorgons had picked off all the rest. I remember being astonished that there wasn't a single other survivor. Only Holt and me.

"Well, there he was, leaning out of the building, blinking stupidly in the light, and he was crying out and calling for me, telling me to come back. Like, full-on calling my name, waving me back into the restaurant. I just crouched there and shook my head frantically. I put my finger to my lips for him to shush. He just wouldn't. Crazy man," she said and shook her head.

Ally looked down, and I could feel her body tremble slightly at the memory. Her voice dropped to a whisper as she emitted a labored sigh. "It didn't take them long to come. They flew in from a few directions and just tore him up. I think he was in so much pain that he had his eyes closed anyway, but…" -here she turned to me- "I don't know which is worse, being paralyzed and then eaten…or just being eaten."

I shook my head. I had no idea, and I didn't want to know either.

Ally dropped her head. "Poor Holt. The sweetest guy. I don't know if I would have made it that long without him. Dammit, I felt guilty for weeks after that. I peed myself," she said, hiding her face in my chest. "Isn't that silly?"

"No way," I breathed. "Not silly at all." Foxy agreed by clenching his lips and shaking his head. I wondered if the little Foxy had done the same.

Ally continued. "I stayed under the car for two… whole… days," she breathed, heavily enunciating her last words. "I felt so bad for him. All kinds of self-recriminations went through my head. *I wasn't fast enough, I wasn't brave enough, I wasn't powerful enough.* All of it.

"Anyway, that little nine-year-old girl vowed that the next time she volunteered for anything, no one would die. Imagine that," she said, somberly looking up at me as if to ask for forgiveness.

"Hon, don't even. Seriously. You can't even be thinking Rutty's death was any part of your vow. You did your best. You and Joe."

You guys. Not me. I couldn't help but leave myself out of that story. I had stayed in place, rooted to the ground in horror when Rutty fought that berserker. I swallowed hard. "Don't," I repeated.

No one spoke for a bit. Ally was the first to do so after a somber minute passed. "Yeah, well, that's the story. Except for the vial."

I paused. "What vial?"

She turned and looked up at me again.

"The *vial*. I went in and got it, finally. It's in my backpack. Holt's insulin."

I couldn't believe it.

Neither could Foxy. "*You got Holt's insulin?*" he cried. "No way!"

She nodded, her eyebrows pointed down, as if she didn't understand my surprise. "Yeah, I'll show you."

Ally scoffed as if she were surprised that we were surprised, and there was the pig-tailed spicy newcomer I remember from the Blockade not so long ago, chewing her gum noisily and studying me. She sat up, opened her pack, fished out a vial, and showed it to me. I held my chemlight up to it and read the prescription.

Novo Nordisk human insulin, ReliOn brand. DeLapp, Holt. Use only as directed.

I was floored. The brave young girl before me, all alone back then, had done what she had set out to do. For Holt.

"I keep it in my pack for luck. Always." She looked at it wistfully as if recalling something about Holt, and then she drew her eyes back up to me. I smiled proudly at her, as, together, we studied that vial. I could relate. In my own pack, I also kept Rutty's book for luck.

Staring down into the green gems of this beautiful soul that I had found, the one who made my tummy tingle, I had a newfound appreciation for Lieutenant Allison Trudy right there and then. What a brave young soldier! If there was any doubt whether she was fit to serve, all you had to do was listen to her story of the young, terrified, orphan girl who completed her mission.

I took her in my arms and held her tightly. No one else said a word, but I grabbed that vial and clutched it close.

For luck.

•   •   •   •   •

1800.

Time to rotate the watch. Simpson climbed down through the hatch and got ready to swap with Foxy. He took his mask off and curled up to sleep almost immediately. I found that a little odd given that it was only 6pm.

Foxy had already called dibs on the next watch, as he was still sweating. *He must naturally run a bit hot,* I thought. He donned his mask and made ready.

I looked out briefly before Foxy went up and glanced back toward the other tank. They were swapping out sentries there too. Good. As neat and tidy a guard as could be reasonably expected out here.

A marked difference in temperature was instantly felt once you popped out past the tank hatch. The frigid, snowy air felt brisk, yet immeasurably welcoming and refreshing. It had a coolness that awakened you at once with the bite of winter's chill. I actually looked forward to when it would be my turn to be on watch.

It had been roughly forty minutes since the DTF. By all rights, we technically should have arrived at Mammoth Cave by now.

Vetas, of course, had had other ideas.

Sweating like a pig, he was now busying himself with the control panel and the circuitry in the corner. Good thing it was off, or I'm sure he would have fried himself like bacon.

I watched him as Ally slumbered against my shoulder. Pretty sure she was asleep, or nearing it. She had stirred as Simpson and Foxy had traded places. She was nestled up against my right shoulder, which was protesting being flexed at that angle. I rubbed it briefly with my left hand.

The memory of Amos and that church came back to me. We all would have gotten out of there alive had Amos not done what he did.

We all would arguably be at Mammoth Cave now had Vetas not done what he did. Human error – especially intentional – costs time, money, and sometimes, human lives. I hoped to God that this time, it wouldn't cost any lives. But whereas Amos' error was to kill, Vetas' error was to survive. There was of course a profound difference.

By now, both Blockades would have declared us MIA and would hopefully be prepping a rescue op. I just wasn't sure which one it would come from, nor when. We were all hoping against hope to hear new, fresh tanks rumbling up the highway behind us, bringing much-needed rescue and reinforcements.

But I wasn't sure if Stone would sit back in his cozy chair and armchair quarterback it, allowing the experience of other good souls to carry out the rescue mission, or if

Mammoth Cave would step up and come save their new saviors.

I wasn't sure if we'd get out of here alive. That's just the thing: we were living in a world of complete uncertainty.

No one could be certain of anything anymore, and none of this was going to be easy.

7 | RESURRECTED

The clouds lay thick over the land, and night was falling. The moon barely showed its light through the wisps of strata floating silently overhead. *Silent enough to mask a gorgon's approach*, I thought.

I couldn't sleep and glanced up at Foxy. He was steadily rotating back and forth, no doubt scanning the horizon. The steady pulses of the m-decks continued to sound. "You okay up there, bro?" I asked him.

He whispered back down, "Affirmative."

Affirmative. Man, that kid had been swiftly militarized. I wondered how long he had been sheltered there at Harvill, like a trapped thing yearning to be out there, free, brandishing his weapon, and going to town against the gorgons in a spray of bullets and torpedo fire. My thoughts went back to the church once again, in the fellowship hall when he fired that RPG past me. He had definitely been in his element from the word *go*, and already had the scars to prove it.

Ally stirred against me, moaning something about just needing water. Her head was now in my lap, and I took her jacket and dabbed the sweat away from her brow, and then from mine.

Vetas was still working. At one point, he had come past me and fetched a soldering kit from one of the ceiling compartments. He was now busying himself with soldering wires and circuitry together back in the corner. He had stripped down to his pants, socks and boots as well. The cold outside air was getting inside, just not enough. He had also found a headlamp in here somewhere, so that was a nice break from the chemlight green we had all been accustomed to. And it would help him see the wires more clearly.

"How you doin' over there, V?" I asked him, employing Simpson's nickname.

Vetas took a bit of time to respond, and then grunted in a husky, low tone. "Alright, I guess. It's coming along." I couldn't get any more out of him except for the slow, steady exhalation of smoke from his soldering iron. Thankfully it dissipated fairly quickly in the air by being sucked out through the hatch.

I checked my watch. It was now 1813. I wondered why my watch hadn't been killed by the DTF. It was electronic. Sure, I couldn't get a cellular signal on it anymore for weather or communications with the Blockade, but the readout still worked.

I remembered reading about EMPs in high school – if that's what you could even call the scholastic training we received in the Blockade – and that they affected devices differently. Some completely, some partially, some temporarily, some permanently. Older devices survived better than newer ones because the newer ones had more electrical parts: computers, microchips, and so forth.

This tank was a newer device, unfortunately, one of the last developments from sixteen years ago when we were all frozen in time and nothing was ever manufactured en masse again. I could only hope that Vetas was really able to get us up and running again. If so, then he could potentially jumpstart the other tank as well.

The night was getting on.

•   •   •   •   •

At 1819 I had dozed off somewhat, when I heard a bit of a muffled commotion outside, and our west-pointing m-deck sounding some blips. I grabbed my rifle, but there was no reason for alarm. Foxy was talking to someone. Evidently, one of the guys from the other tank had come over to us. "Awesome, I'll get them to him," he said.

I looked up toward Foxy, and a torrent of sweat went cascading down the back of my head and into my shirt. I grabbed Ally's jacket and blotted the back of my head with it and then turned back toward the hatch again as I gulped a drink of water.

Foxy pulled himself back down through it and handed me two walkie-talkies.

"Jet, look!" he exclaimed with subdued joy. "Look what the other guys found. They want you to try it right away!"

"No way! What a score," I breathed. "Do they both work okay?"

He winked. "That's what we're about to find out. They've got two over there. Channel six, bro. I mean, sir."

He saluted me and smiled.

I took them. "You salute me one more time, and I'm gonna knock you bald-headed. At ease, soldier."

Four walkie-talkies, I thought. *Please let them work.* Setting one down on the pad next to me, I felt the weight of the other. It definitely had a rechargeable battery inside it. A bright light turned on me from the corner of the tank. Vetas was eager to see them work as well, and he lit me up. Ally, in her sleep and illuminated by Vetas' dazzling headlamp, crinkled her eyes and rolled over.

I switched it on. And there, on its display, was a beautiful amber readout. Wasting no time, I tapped 0-6-enter into the keypad. Thank God most batteries are resistant to the effects of an EMP. That more or less explained my watch still working.

Right away, I heard a blessed sound. The static blip of a receiving signal. "82, this is 131, do you read, over?"

Nothing. Tense pause. Then, "Loud and clear, good buddy, this is 82." Right away I knew that thick drawl, and my mouth curved upward in recognition.

"Hey, Joe. Mighty nice development! Where'd you find them? And I take it the batteries were stowed separately, over?"

"Sure enough, Jet. And you gotta know that both Blockades'll be scannin' the bands too. So, we best be makin' a joyful noise and see if they'll hear us. Amen?"

"Roger that. Hallelujah, good Reverend," I said. "Nice find, over."

Static burst.

Well, it wasn't the Blockade on the other end of the radio, but these would help, and maybe, just maybe, they'd find us on these bands. I didn't know what kind of long-range communication equipment Mammoth Cave had access to, or if they would in fact be actively scanning yet, but it was a foregone conclusion that they should be scanning for us given that we were MIA.

We were now an hour past the DTF explosion, and about a half-hour overdue at Mammoth Cave, so one or both of them should technically be watching the radar and scanning the bands for us. Additionally, Halcyon would be scanning the night sky anyway. If a working satellite passed by *and* they could catch us on thermal fast enough, they might just have our precise location. We surely didn't have it ourselves.

My watch read 1825. Almost time for Foxy to swap out. I would let Ally sleep and take her watch. Vetas needed to continue to work on the repairs, and, I think, more out of a profound sense of penitence than any kind of sleep he might actually need, he wouldn't want to leave that post. He owed it to us, but I think more for himself.

I lovingly lifted Ally off of me and laid her gently down. She startled as I did so. "Wait – I just...what?"

I snickered. Sissy used to do the same thing, way back when. "You're fine, hon. Just rotating the watch soon, and I'm up. You sleep." I winked at her. She smiled, closed her eyes, and was out like a lamp.

•   •   •   •   •

Foxy and I swapped at 1830 as planned. He took off his mask, drank some water, put on his jacket, and instantly went to sleep just as Simpson had done. I donned my mask, took the walkie-talkie up with me and kept it at the lowest volume, communicating at regular intervals across multiple channels, while watching the sky.

It would soon be too dark to see unless we put up some floodlights, and we would have to rely wholly on the m-decks. But the eyes have a way of adjusting to the dark and seeing shadows against shadows. I'd been out on enough recons to know that all too well.

When I emerged from that tank, oh my, that was refreshing. The chill December air bit at me, but was so welcome after the close stuffiness inside that steel hull. The temperature was decreasing in there with nothing running. It still felt like a sauna, but one that had been recently switched off. My watch read forty-three degrees out.

At 1841 hours, Joe came on the radio after a brief burst of static. "Jet, this is Joe, over?" I don't know if he saw that I was on watch out of their window, but he was whispering, thank goodness.

"Go ahead, Joe," I whispered, looking around and brandishing my M5 by my ear, pointed upward.

"Calm night."

"Yep. Nothing over here. I can almost hear your blips over there too. Is that you on watch?" His voice sounded a bit echoey. Someone's head protruded from their hatch, masked and watching.

"Nope. Baxter's up. He's our gunner. Ollie, Monzon, and Rawley are all down here with me."

"Why are you still up?" I whispered at him.

"Are you kiddin'? It's 6:41, for Pete's sake. Right now, Maureen would be puttin' out supper."

"I never knew you had a wife before tonight," I laughed quietly as I looked around. All this whispering made me feel like we were both on some 1-900 phone line. "You always struck me as a career vet with no time for love."

"Very funny," he quipped. "Couldn't be further from the truth, and my Maureen, my sweet Maureen. Ahh. I'm just sorry you haven't met her, that's about all I can say. She's amazing. I miss her. Sure could go for some jambalaya right now." Joe chuckled.

"Oh, man, don't do that. We're surviving on ration packs, Joe; you *never* mention home-cooked meals when we're on ration packs. These things were probably packaged before we hit this millennium."

"Yeah, I'm sorry. You're right." He paused. "Miss – er - es." His message cut off.

"What was that?"

"I said I sure miss her eyes. Maureen has these blue-gold eyes, and one of 'em has a bit of a darkened wedge below the retina. It's an amazing imperfection that is just...perfection."

"She sounds nice, buddy," I whispered.

Joe paused.

"Funny thing," he began, "and I know I haven't said hide nor hair of this since Harvill, but when we got that gorgon, I saw its eyes. They're just dead, Jet, ya know?"

I did know. Jarringly, my memory was whisked back to that bathroom in the church where that gorgon had impaled Vera and me. I saw right into its dead, lifeless eyes. My shoulder spasmed briefly as if it read my mind in aching memory. "Yeah, I've seen 'em. More up close than I would have liked to. There's nothing there, except that horrifying power they have behind those eyes."

"Nothing."

"Except death."

Now all I could think about was Rutty. Where was this conversation going? I hoped he would get back to Maureen and avoid this painful stroll down memory lane.

"I miss Maureen's eyes. They stand in stark contrast, man. The Bible says, 'The eye is the lamp of the body. If your eyes are healthy, your whole body will be full of light. But if your eyes are unhealthy, your whole body will be full of darkness.' Those eyes, man. It's like a dog's eyes when they go blind: opaque, milky, nothin' behind them. Dead. I *sure* miss my wife's eyes, Jet."

"You'll see her again," I encouraged him. "Don't you go getting' soft on me, Sergeant Bassett. If there's anybody in our battalion that has faith, I would have guessed it would be you."

There was another pause.

"I know. Maybe it's the heat of this tank." He laughed. "Feels like a sauna in here. You?"

"Nah. Not right now, at least. I'm on watch. But I know what you me-"

Just then my radio burst static and a blip, as if Joe had turned his radio off. "Joe. Come in. You there?" I asked.

"Shipley, Lieutenant Shipley, come in, over?" came a voice I didn't recognize. My heart leapt, and my eyes widened. *Someone had scanned the bands and found us!* "This is Mammoth Cave, DN312, do you read, over?"

"DN312, this is MS131, Lieutenant Cameron Shipley, go ahead, over?" I shifted my legs below and stood up at attention, I was so excited.

Joe had to have heard as well. He was now silent. I bet he was waking everyone up over there. I looked down into the hatch. "Foxy! It's Mammoth Cave!" No answer. He must have fallen asleep now too. "Vetas!" I hissed downward.

"Yeah?" came the quiet whisper in response.

"Got Mammoth Cave on the line; tell the crew!"

Shuffling below me. Halting whispers and stirs of movement. Ally eventually looked up at me through the hatch and then poked her head up to squeeze through with me. I couldn't put my arm around her since I was holding my weapon and the radio.

"We picked up your chatter. What's your position, over?" came the transmission.

"Mammoth Cave, MS131 and MS82 are stranded somewhere along US-68 outside of Auburn, over? Exact location unknown. Both units disabled from large-scale DTF, repeat, frozen in the blind, over?"

No response.

Finally, a burst of static. "Stand by. DN436 patching in now."

Another pause, followed eventually by quick static bursts. "Shipley, this is Captain Stone, do you read?"

One big happy family, all on one party line. No big deal. I knew I'd have to talk to Stone sooner or later.

"Stone, Shipley. Loud and clear. Stranded outside Auburn on Highway 68 with two units downed by DTF," I reported.

"Roger that, Lieutenant, we've been informed...we're on our way to you. Stand by."

Ally shivered and slunk back into the tank.

I loved the waiting in between.

Just then I heard Baxter on lookout in the other tank let out a light cough and clear his throat. My west-pointing m-deck let out a faint blip briefly as he did so.

"Shipley, Stone," he came back on. "Aside from your location, which we got, gimme a sit rep."

They must have gotten our location from one of our watches.

Situation report. I gathered air into my lungs and didn't waste any time quietly muttering out all the details. "All present and accounted for. DTF disabled MS131 and MS82 at 1720 hours. DTF emitters inoperative. Tanks inoperative. We're scanning on four m-decks in all directions and maintaining defensive posture. Vetas, our gunner, is working on repairs. He thinks he's almost there. We have water and radios. No sign of gorgons since the attack."

"Who set off the DTF, Lieutenant?" Stone asked briskly.

That seemed unnecessary. I didn't want to throw Vetas under the bus, but no one else was to blame. "Vetas, sir. He's working on repairs right now."

"Was it intentional?" came the quick question.

My brows furrowed. What was this, an inquest? *Let it go, Stone.* "Affirmative. A reflex. A last-ditch effort to save us, which worked, Captain," I sighed. I thought I could hear Vetas exhale in shame below.

Another pause.

Stone came back on. "Well, you sure sent one helluva flock our way. The skies were lit up with gorgons fleeing from up there, over St. Bethlehem. Got a few rescue patrols up there that saw them screaming west overhead, clearing out. Then your blast hit them. They're down too. Fortunately, Halcyon saw it coming, and Base One *and* our Blockade were able to kill power, but only just in time. A *very* close shave. Please do *not* do that again without advance warning."

It suddenly occurred to me that whoever was left in Harvill must be quaking in their boots and anticipating the end of the world by now, what with all the DTFs they had experienced of late. Hopefully, they were all rescued out of there and in safer housing by now.

I didn't answer Stone.

"Okay, Lieutenant, just hold tight. Three units were dispatched to you, after you went MIA. They're coming up 79 right now, north of Olmstead. Fresh emitters. ETA 25 minutes. Just hold tight and lay low, copy?"

"Copy that," I whispered and checked my watch. 1848 hours. That meant they'd be here around a quarter after seven. 1915. "You read all that, Joe?"

Bassett buzzed back in. "Yep, roger that. Hallelujah once more! Command," -here he turned his attention back to Stone- "thought it might also interest you to know, and perhaps to encourage you guys to step on the gas, we've got ourselves a couple of newly engaged folks over here."

I rolled my eyes and filled my chest with air.

"Lieutenant Shipley and Lieutenant Trudy are now pledged to tie the knot, so whatever you can do to run some red lights, we'd be much obliged," Joe finished.

"Congratulations to the both of them," he said to Joe, and not to me, which didn't surprise me at all. "No promises. Hold your ground. They'll be there as soon as they can. Good luck," Stone urged and clicked off.

Yeah, thanks Stone. I said nothing in reply.

Glancing over at Baxter in the other tank, I held up my radio in a victory pump. He echoed that back. Made me smile.

Ally appeared below me, smearing fresh lip balm onto those beautiful, succulent lips. I could smell the mint from up here.

"You catch all that, hon?" I asked her.

"Yeah, that's good news." She looked up at me, and I could see the twinkle in her eyes. She was delighted at the news that the cavalry was coming.

"How's V coming?"

Ally turned to him and repeated my question. Vetas murmured something back to her, which carried a note of optimism. She turned back to me. "He thinks he's almost there, Cam."

"Good. How's Foxy?"

She looked over at him, then back at me, and chuckled. "Yawning and rubbing his eyes. So is Simpson. You ready to switch?"

"Nah, I'm good. It's 1850. But their ETA is 1915, and I'm not tired. You rest. I'm good. I'll get any update and tell you guys when to prep for evac."

I turned and looked down the highway past the other tank, back toward Russellville. The cavalry wasn't far beyond the city lights, which faintly illuminated a billowing shelf of cloud wall above. As I looked back, I caught a glimpse of some trace movement against the reflection of an abandoned car. It looked like a wisp of low, night fog rolling slowly across the road. That would bring in some extra cold, which might be even more welcome for the next watch.

I cleared my throat and went to say something to Ally, when our m-decks suddenly started to pulse with a frenzy. The slow staccato blips turned into rapid-fire buzzing pulses: *both* of them.

I looked over at Baxter in his tank, and he was doing the same: studying his m-decks and then whipping around frantically and looking in all directions, around and above. Brandishing my M5, I did the same, as my heart raced. "Masks and guns, get 'em now!" I whispered harshly down below. "We've got company!"

And that's when the highway became *alive*. The slight motion I had seen earlier wasn't fog; it was *vapor*. Showing up clearly now in the cold light of the moon for what it truly was, the blueish-green mist swirled angrily as a hundred gorgons slowly increased their speed along Highway 68 toward us. They had been crawling *under* the radar pings of the m-decks. *Crawling!* I thought. *How did they know to stay under the pings and 'under the radar' as it were?*

My thoughts were cut short as a vast dark shape silently whisked up and over the back of the other tank, grabbing and yanking Baxter clean out of the hole and off into the sky. Baxter grunted and wheezed as he was sucked out of his hatch.

My hairs all stood up, and I shook with fear as my eyes went wide watching them fly overhead. All that was left in Baxter's place was a cloud of festering vapor as he sailed past.

Baxter reflexively fired skyward with his XM5, and the gorgon screeched and dropped him just east of our tank. He landed with a thud and a howl fifteen feet beyond us from a solid twenty-foot drop. But he got up quickly, fueled from adrenaline, and limped off toward an abandoned car over in the ditch. The gorgon that snatched him also flailed and landed with a crash and a hiss beyond our tank close to him. It spasmed and then lay dead.

In horror, I suddenly saw the rest of them. In every direction, gorgons had been slowly slithering along the ground, imperceptible as snakes, and now, revealed in the pale moonlight, they were panting and salivating, their deadened eyes leering at us. Their mist rose up about them as a cloak, their shapes and quantity concealed by the swirling, hellish scene drifting toward us. It encircled our tiny battalion, alone in the middle of nowhere.

Foxy quickly emerged through the hatch, rifle first, and put his back to me to cover the other side. His jaw was firmly clenched, and his eyes flashed with intensity.

The commotion was deafening now as the gorgons leapt up into the air and formed a massive cluster, swirling all around us overhead. It was as if they were trying to intimidate us with their size, like a swirling mass of bait fish. Baxter had nearly made it to the shelter of an abandoned car when one got him, pounced on him, and then hovered above him.

I knew what was about to happen, and I didn't want to watch; I just gritted my teeth and began to fire into the crowd of them, wherever I could see them. But the reminder was all too fresh, and I inadvertently glanced over at Baxter anyway, seeking for a spare moment to shoot it off of him. He himself feebly took aim and shot it through its chest, but three, four, six, and then nine more converged on him and attacked ferociously. These things had been driven off by us and deprived of food, and now they were *livid* and *ravenous*.

Baxter screamed "Shipley, do me! Ahhh! Do me now!" and my heart sank. But I knew what he was asking, and I knew why. They would paralyze him and eat him alive. I turned and trained my weapon on him, sending bullets flying into the crowd of them. My gunfire pierced Baxter, and he slumped over, dead. One of the gorgons turned and hissed at me before I sent it into the afterlife. I willed my ears to hear nothing else but the noise of gunfire and spent casings clinking all around us off of our tank while I grew angrier.

"Grenades!" I simultaneously shouted down into our hull. The tank rocked back and forth with the movement of the crew. All were awake now and frantically helping to mount our defense, summoning up their courage to gather extra magazines, grenades, and so forth. I was whipping my head in all directions, cursing. The sky was dotted with thick, black clumps, whizzing about and screeching, emerging and then disappearing again through the sickly mist that enveloped all of us.

If they were generating such huge amounts of their sickly mist in an attempt to intimidate us, their plan was working to their undoing: they could see us only as much as we could see them.

Ally slapped another magazine into my hand, and I reloaded. I was about to turn to my right when I just noticed one screeching toward me on my left. My Beretta rang out that way and shot it in the head.

Too late. Its dead carcass smacked into the hull of the tank and crashed into Foxy and me. My head was blasted with quick lightning as its bony cranium collided with mine. I saw stars for a moment, but collected myself and shook it off. Foxy and I heaved it off of ourselves as quickly as we could, and it lolled over the side of the tank, flopping lifelessly to the ground below.

The ground to our east was still swimming. Not for long! I pulled the pin on a grenade and hurled it in their direction, far from our tank.

Someone shouted from below us, their voice blending into a horrifying detonation. Dead gorgon bodies went hurtling in all directions over there. Some of their own seized upon this and began to feast on them. I didn't mind that one bit. *Bon appetit, fellas*, I thought. *As long as it keeps some of you bastards busy.*

Rawley had taken Baxter's place on the other tank. I could dimly make out her dreadlocks and ponytail, flapping around in the moonlight. She was cutting them down with her rifle. Joe had his back to her, and they were mirroring what we were doing, swiveling and launching salvo after salvo of rounds against the gorgons. But one landed on their tank, facing Rawley and swiping at her. She took a deep cut along her left shoulder and screamed. I carefully aimed, and then shredded the beast with my rifle, sending it flying.

I was out again. I thrust my hand down, and, like clockwork, Ally put another mag into it, and I slapped it in. I know she was doing the same with Foxy.

Wincing and crying out in pain, Rawley disappeared back down into their hull. Ollie took her place nearly instantaneously. But in his haste, and to my horror, I noticed that he had forgotten his mask! "Ollie!" I shouted to him over the din of gunfire. "Ollie! Your mask! Your mask, Ollie!" There must have been no time.

Confused, he looked over at me, and then I could see his expression change: a look of horrified recognition at what I had shouted. He just stayed that way. It didn't last long. "Your mask!" I yelled. "Mask?" I pointed at my head, looking repeatedly over at him through my gunfire. What was wrong with him? I stopped.

Ollie blinked slowly, and he stopped shooting. He just stood there. "Wha-?" I started. I traced his vision to the left of our tank, near the ground, where a gorgon had cowed him and held his eyes in the power of its paralyzing stare.

"No! Ollie!" I shouted, but then I had to turn to match Foxy's movement as he thrust to his left. "Foxy! Get it! Down there, get it!" I yelled, thrusting my head toward the gorgon that had zeroed Ollie.

Foxy caught it and mowed it down in a vain attempt to interrupt the telepathic assault. Futile. Ollie's face turned ashen, and his head lolled to the side as he slowly slid back down through his own hatch like sludge. Joe was all alone there on top now.

"Ally! Grenade!" Ally handed me another one. I pulled the pin and hurled it as hard as I could toward the mass of gorgons still coming at us from the east. *Boom.* I rapidly cast another one westward. "Joe! Grenade!" I don't know how he heard me, but he did, and he dropped back down into his hatch and closed it just in time. *Boom.*

Three gorgons descended onto his tank, ramming it in their fury. I thought I caught a glimpse of a large shadow push through the mist, to the west, away beyond his tank, and my first thought was *the cavalry! The cavalry is here!*

Foxy turned his body and was blasting them out of the sky behind me, now pointing west. I was pointing east. We both should have been pointing straight up.

Ally screamed, and I jerked my head down toward her and saw the terror in her eyes. I threw my head back up to see what she was screaming at. Just as I did, a gorgon came tearing down out of the sky and slammed into Foxy and me, knocking us back down through our hatch.

But it came inside with us.

Foxy hit his head on the shaft on the way down, and was out cold.

Ally wouldn't stop screaming. The gorgon was momentarily dazed from the impact, but soon awoke with a fury. *It was in the tank with us*. The cold, scaled-monster thrashed around, and its dangling tentacles, or limbs, or whatever the hell they were, thrashed about in every direction, whipping with the sound of wet slaps all around us.

The beast hissed and shrieked virulently. I was spattered with some fierce saliva, and scratched with what felt eerily like king crab legs. The hardened skin was slimy yet sharp with barbs. I thought back to the gorgons that I had personally encountered. Neither of the ones in the church – in the bathroom nor the hallway – had such pointed barbs. It was the same species, sure enough, but maybe a different *ethnicity* of gorgon? Who knew. For now, this one was frantically whipping around the cabin of our tank, slashing and ramming everything in its frenetic fury and desire to escape.

I had just enough wits to reach up and close the hatch. I slammed it shut and threw the ring to seal it before more of them could get in here, and almost immediately after I did so, I heard several dull thumps against the hull over the hatch.

Thank God we all had our masks on. It spasmed and flailed all around, seeking a way out, and it nipped Vetas on the hip as he feebly attempted to continue his repairs while simultaneously working to steer clear of it. He cried out in agony.

The shrieks and monstrous grunts reverberated all around us as we tried to get out of its way.

The thing smacked Simpson in the face as he shot at it, knocking his gun from his grip. Foxy, who was unconscious, somehow ended up underneath the gorgon. The thing was lying on top of him and thrashing around. Thank God he had put on his jacket before he came up with his gun next to me, or his skin would now be hanging like ribbons down his back.

I thought I felt a massive concussion outside our tank behind us. We were all now sealed back in our respective tanks, but one of *us* had one of *them* in here with us. We had nowhere to go, and all we could do was recoil our hands and try in vain to grab it somehow and restrain it. I looked desperately for an opportunity to do so.

"No…just…ah!" Ally screamed. "Get around it, Cam, and…ow!" She got whipped aside and collided with the tank wall. That just made me angrier. Ally wouldn't stop screaming as the gorgon backed up into her, drawing itself up. I could hear the wind squeezed out of her lungs as she dully gasped and strained for air. Then it lunged, rammed Simpson again, and bit him on the arm and the hand. Simpson screamed and threw a punch at it.

But a gorgon has many limbs. They were still flying around, and one of them knocked Simpson's mask from him. Another scratched me across the face with those damned barbs, and I could feel something warm dripping down my right cheek.

At that moment, our tank roared back to life. Vetas exclaimed and swore! *He fixed it!* The lights screamed into bright white inside momentarily and then faded, in startup mode, and we could all now plainly see the repulsive alien for what it was. About seven feet long, it had pale translucent skin covered in a thin layer of mucus all about, with several rippling flaps running down the sides of its head, and some down the length of its barbed and fiercely muscled back. It had long snapping arms with defined biceps. It had some kind of tail fin and dragging tentacles or limbs: I couldn't tell what they were. And it was covered throughout with those spiked barbs.

The gorgon sensed Simpson's face was exposed, and it drew its monstrous head up and stared right at him.

Simpson was already in deep shock at losing his mask and having one of them inside here with us. He screamed like a girl, while having the good sense to keep his eyes closed and his hands over his face. The gorgon grabbed his arms by the wrists and separated them outward, as if to allow for unblocked exposure to him. He screamed again.

Vetas, to his left, shouted "No! Get back, you bastard!"

I simultaneously exclaimed, "Get him!" and threw myself on the back of the damned thing, trying to put it in a headlock. I could hear its fierce breathing, and a horrible thrill ran through me as I realized that I was doing something that back there at the Cumberland I said I didn't think I could ever do: *I was actually wrangling a gorgon.* It was actually levitating, there in our tank, and I was suspended in the air above it, on its back.

Vetas leaned over and kicked it in the head to pull its attention away from Simpson, who was moaning uncontrollably. It must have sighted him momentarily before it went into its telepathy, but now the creature gasped and lurched at Vetas in revenge, while I held it steady. The rest of us somehow kept our masks on.

I could actually sense its rapid heartbeat through my left wrist while I strangled it. Its throat – if you can call it that – gurgled, and it tried to throw me off of it by going into a crocodile death roll. We toppled over, and now the wind was knocked out of me as I received the full weight of it against my chest.

My pulse pounded in my brain, and I could feel my face turning purple.

Man, they were heavy.

Thankfully, it had rolled off of Foxy in the process. He lay there quiet, but he had been shifted and looked disfigured while the gorgon had splayed him around.

My grip around its throat loosened, and it whirled in ferocious wrath and faced me, opening its jaws and pulling its head back, coiling for a strike. No longer to paralyze and immobilize; this time to bite and to shred.

I threw my hands up in front of me defensively and could just make out through my fingers a swift motion as it started to lunge, when *Chop Suey* kicked on.

Vetas had gotten the tank going again, jumped to the console, and flipped on the iPod plugged into it. He spun the volume dial to its max, and 'System of a Down' now blared throughout the cabin in high screams and throbs.

We all screamed and covered our ears. My hands reflexively went to mine, and now I could see the creature above me; its face contorted into spastic gyrations of ripping pain. Its sensitive ears were being blasted with punishingly fatal noise.

Father! Father! Father! Father! Father! Father! Father! Father!

The gorgon screamed a hideous cacophony as it pulled away from me and then whirled around the cabin, smashing its head into the walls, seeking a way out, covering its own ears in mad desperation. Ally was sideswiped by its fin and fell to the floor. My poor fiancé had been abused by this thing repeatedly.

Father into your hands, I commend my spirit!

The music continued to blare, and I looked over. Through my sweat and tears I could see Foxy dimly coming to beside me. He had a heavily bleeding gash on his forehead.

Father into your hands, why have you forsaken me, in your eyes forsaken me, in your thoughts forsaken me, in your heart forsaken…me…

Its long, pale arms went up over the flaps on its head as it flailed in agony. The DTF emitter feet away from it had started up again, and the gorgon now had that to contend with as well.

Just then, the shots rang out.

The gorgon flew back and lay still. A gurgled, foaming breath bubbled out of it, and it gasped, crumpled and deflated. I could see that its ears were bleeding.

Panting, Vetas shut off the music.

I swiveled and knelt to face him, panting in turn. There he was, with my Beretta in his hand, the chamber still smoking. The air conditioning was back on, and the smoke from the gun was swirling away from it and forming dim white *s*'s throughout the cabin. Air conditioning never felt so welcome in my entire life.

"Been wantin' to hear that song for a long time, sir," he breathed in relief.

My panting gave way to laughter.

•   •   •   •   •

We weren't out of danger yet.

I looked around the floor of the tank for the walkie-talkie. It had been thrown over by where Ally had been knocked to the floor. "You okay, Ally? Ally? Hon…you okay?" I lightly tapped her cheek.

She was phased and jarred, but she shook herself to, and looked at me. "Yeah, I'm fine. Holy crap, Cam. Just look at that thing."

She came over to me and I embraced her tightly while we both gazed down upon the hideous gorgon, keeping watch as if it might suddenly spring back to life.

"Yeah, well, there are about fifty more of that 'thing' out there still, hon." I looked her over. She looked like she would be okay. The amulet necklace swung freely and proudly from her neck.

Foxy slowly pulled himself up and covered his head with his t-shirt. Vetas helped him.

I snatched up the walkie-talkie. "Joe, Joe, come in," I said urgently, looking the dead thing up and down on the floor in front of me. There were squeals and screams outside, but it sounded as if they had reduced in volume and quantity. "Vetas, is that the Warhorse Morse? It's up again?"

He nodded quickly.

"Jet!" came the reply. "You ok? Your lights are on! Tell me Vetas got that thing runnin' again! Most of them are buggin' out!"

"He sure did," I confirmed. "Up and running. What do you see outside?"

"Well, some of them have been driven off, but others are hanging here." I looked out of our window as well. "They're stickin' around, Jet, like they're willing to take it. But something big is out there, we saw it. Since the signal's strongest closest to us, you'd think they'd bail!"

The DTF emitter was truly sounding again now, and it did appear that many of them were repelled enough by it to flee to a safe distance. But many remained, and I could see them swirling around just outside, seeking another opening.

"Hang on," Joe said. Then, he yelped, and the walkie-talkie cut off.

We heard several dull thudding sounds over there and muted gunfire in response. They sounded like that heavy concussion I had heard earlier.

Static burst. "Jet! Jet! Coming…. hatch…. we can't…coming through…"

I squinted my eyes. "Joe! Say again, Joe!"

He was holding the walkie-talkie down while he screamed. We could all hear it over the transmission. Those dull thuds. Then the sound of shattering glass.

"Breaking in!" came the next burst. "It's breaking in, Jet!" And just then, with not a moment of pause to grasp how dire our situation truly was, our hatch above us thudded as well. Over and over, repeatedly, again, again, and again:

something was ramming into our hatch. Something massive. The steel above us was actually beginning to buckle.

Whatever it was, it was going to get in, because we could all see the fragile steel circle begin to crack. I could hear dim but heavy growling outside, and it sent a sensation down my spine of pure, raw fear. I had never heard such sounds from a gorgon before. They were deeply resonant and loaded with hunger. And anger. And *malevolence*.

It was coming through.

"Joe, just hold on!"

Thud! Thud! Thud! Our hatch cracked.

"Masks, everybody – masks! Rifles up!" We all laid on the floor next to the dead gorgon and pointed up toward the hatch. Whatever was about to come through that hatch was going to be shredded by a volley of M5 pathos and vitriol.

Thud! Thud! Thud! The hatch buckled. I could see the dark sky beyond the shadow that hovered just outside.

Then, silence. We could hear the low brutish growl outside, but it seemed the creature had turned away from us.

Our walkie-talkies cut the thick silence with static.

"MS82, MS131, this is Gold Battalion Five, MS180 on point. Power down! Power down now!" came the cry over the radio.

The figure outside and above us roared in vengeance.

"Do it, Vetas, before it's too late! Cut it!" I screamed at him.

Vetas leaped over and flipped the master switch, and our tank went dark once again. The air conditioning kicked off. Our chemlights, still active, burst out anew from within, coating us in green. The tank shuddered and went silent.

Out beyond the thin, growing splinter in our hatch, a monstrous face turned and peered through it, baring its fangs at me, with a thin, sallow eye, and a look of wholly evil wretchedness. I looked at it, eye to eye, and I reckoned with it. It hissed violently, and a drabble of venom dripped from its fangs, through the hatch, and down onto my mask, sliding down in a thin, milky streak.

Only thirteen inches of steel separated us, and I wished it was more. Ain't no way I would want to meet that thing alone on a highway or anywhere else.

But just beyond it, in the night sky past its head, I saw something else, the glimmer of what looked like two tiny fireflies go sailing up into the sky. They whistled silently a thousand feet over all of our heads, suspended there for but a flicker of time while the clamor died down around us.

Many of the gorgons peeled off in all directions, as if they knew what was about to happen. They'd seen it before.

The sky exploded in white, followed a second later by a deafening explosion and dissonant noise.

The beast above us burst into red ooze with a horrible cry, spilling its contents down into our tank and onto its dead mate below. Greenish mist thrust through the splinter of the hatch and enveloped us as we all coughed and retched.

The blinding light shot through the night and lit up the world around us.

This DTF was planned. It did the job, destroying the entire enemy force within a good mile and sending everything for miles beyond that screeching off for safety.

Dozens of dull thumps and thuds sounded around us as these wretched aliens plummeted from the sky and careened into the concrete or cars off in the ditch or on the tops of our tanks.

I looked at my watch. 1925.

The cavalry had arrived.

Vetas had redeemed himself. Our tank and our hopes had been resurrected.

But we'd lost more men, which was a bitter pill to swallow. I wondered if they had family back at Base One. How long had they been in the service? Where did they come from? How long had it been since they had had any peace and respite from this war?

Baxter and Ollie were little-known members of my crew, but they were important, and they had purpose. Yet here it was happening again: more men lost on my watch.

No matter where I went, what mission I was on, where I was dispatched to, we just kept losing men. My head drooped in disappointment.

I thought back to how they had clustered close together in such a dense throng on their way to us. Could it be that they had these behemoth gorgons in their midst, attempting to conceal them from our visuals so as to preserve a surprise attack? Were they their new secret weapons? Where did these things come from? The gorgons were getting smarter and displaying signs of a higher intelligence than we had ever known.

Yes, we were delivered from them, for now.

But the clouds still lay thick over the land, and night was all around us.

8 | TRUTHS

All of it was more than unsettling to witness.

As I simmered in my disappointment, I hugged my wife-to-be, and she had a hard time letting me go. Ally was shaking. I pulled her close. "Hey, it's okay. We're all clear now." I sighed. "All clear, hon."

She nodded, but didn't say anything else, so I just held her for a while. As far as I was concerned, we could just stay like that.

We lifted Foxy up. Aside from a nasty and bleeding diagonal gash along his forehead that we were able to treat fairly quickly, he'd be fine, though bruised. He'd carry that scar to the end of his days, though. Of that, I was sure.

Simpson would recover as well. He was feeling nauseous from the close call with the gorgon, but he was going to make it.

The reinforcements helped us get the dead gorgon out of our tank using straps, muscles and manpower. It was disgusting and heavy – and it *stank*. They hoisted it up and out, letting it clumsily ricochet off the wheel well to thud to the ground, with no love lost. How these heavy beasts hovered, or even flew, was simply beyond me.

The other tank had lost both Baxter and Ollie. Rawley was bleeding badly from her left shoulder, but the three tanks that had come to our aid had brought some pretty substantial medi-kits, and medics were now treating her wound. She would be fine in time, but more than likely she was going to have to return to base or, worse, be bedridden and recuperate at Mammoth Cave. That was a pretty big gash she received, but she was alive. I counted us fortunate, as much as could be expected.

The other tanks had launched not one but *two* simultaneous DTFs and had subsequently powered down. That took care of the gorgons, and then some. However, none of us, frankly, were adequately prepared for what we would find out there lying just beyond our transports.

We climbed out of our respective tanks. Amidst the still swirling mist and the horrible stench of burnt gorgon flesh, two hulking bodies lay next to each of our tanks. Blackened and forever mummified in a disturbing semblance of rigor mortis, these were different from any gorgon we had ever seen. Not even *berserkers* were this big. They were some kind of mutant behemoth gorgon, a breed both previously unreckoned with and previously uncatalogued by us. We stared at them in horror.

Their bodies were similarly misshapen appendage-laden hulks with spines and long, gripping arms, but they were huge, thick, and terrifying, in life, and now in death.

Both had died with maws wide open, their noses crinkled, and their brows forever furrowed in vengeance, as if they wished to carry every seed of their putrescence and contempt for mankind to the other side with them. Now, frozen and upturned, they would have to be retrieved and hauled back for study.

Glad I wasn't on that assignment.

.   .   .   .   .

We were relieved to be rescued. That much was clear. Now, I had command of *four* working tanks; five, if Vetas got MS82 operational again. We weren't sure if he would or if we'd have the time. We needed to get moving up north to the cave before the day got much later.

However, in the back of my mind, we now had a much bigger problem.

Not the behemoth gorgons, although those were terrifying and altogether undocumented, yes. But gorgons had neither set traps before, nor been so crafty. They were mostly, to our minds, mindless drones. Even the berserkers would simply drift aimlessly here and there in search of food, and only when they were provoked by sound would they divert from their course or become agitated and enraged.

True, the gorgons near the coast would ward us off, so they had some form of primitive intelligence there, at least enough to distinguish their own simple objective from our desire to thwart it. But gorgons as a whole, discovering how our motion detectors worked, being led by some sort of commander, and converging upon our location under the signal, in complete stealth, shielding their approach with mist? Unheard of.

I thought back to my conversation with President Graham at the Blockade. She had said "berserkers – *and more.*" It was the "and more" that had caught my attention. Did she know about these behemoth gorgons? Had she known all along? Were they, like the berserkers, also genetically engineered?

It was a different ballgame now. We were dealing with only two possibilities. One, creatures that had apparently evolved into a higher form of intelligence. Or two, creatures that had been here all along, yet had been held back in the background for an endgame: restrained, prevented from engaging, until the appointed time, and were now set loose upon us like Rottweilers freed from their cages. It smacked of some kind of 'Phase 2' by the enemy.

The first possibility meant that we just hadn't been paying enough attention to them or hadn't been in close observation enough to witness their evolution.

The second possibility, of course, meant that the gorgons were always of a higher form of intelligence and strategy than previously suspected. That meant there was a chain of command. And where you have a chain of command, you have a Commander.

Something somewhere was calling the shots with these things and most likely had been all along. Out there, somewhere, probably out over the oceans where we'd been forbidden passage was some hive mind. And in that hive mind, there was a queen.

So, we had our queen, and they had theirs.

That could only mean one other thing on this chessboard, and it was something I had suspected all along. More was going on than we had ever been told, and calamity was overtaking us yet again. And I? I was foolish enough to believe the President and agree to serving her yet again.

I should have known better. *Graham.* Those squinting eyes that tried so hard to convince me of that which she wished: they now came back darkly to my mind, and I was filled with regret.

You know what they say: fool me once, shame on you. Fool me twice, shame on *me.*

•   •   •   •   •

While ruminating on all of this, I helped Ally and Foxy out of the tank so that we could stretch our legs. I was hungry. We all were. Luckily, the new tanks had brought some grub other than simple ration packs.

Vetas came out last. Simpson helped him out, and then, as his boots hit the ground, I asked Ally to give me a second. I went over to him.

"Hey V," I said.

"Sir," he greeted back.

"Listen, Vetas," I began. "Command isn't going to see what you did as a plus in your column. I don't know if Bassett over there will see it that way either. Give him time. He's actually a good guy. But the way I figure it, you saved us. Twice. And I want to say thank you," I assured him. He raised his head at me. "Good work getting us back up and running, soldier."

"Thank you, sir," he replied humbly. "I appreciate it more than words can say."

"I know. It's all good. Just wanted you to hear it."

"Can I start to work on the other one, sir?"

Surprised, I looked over at the other tank. "You don't have to call me sir. And frankly, V, that took about two hours to fix ours. I don't think we've got that kind of time to sit around. It's already dark, and I think all of us would prefer to be under some gun towers, yeah? You did yourself proud. You did us all proud. 82 can stay here. We'll fix it another day. I don't suppose any of their guys want to sit out here any longer than we do just to restore one tank. A bird in the hand beats two in the bush, right?" That was something my dad used to always say to me. "Let's not risk it."

Vetas smiled, though by the look on his face it was clear he was dealing with some penance issue and wanted to restore both tanks along with his name. I patted him on the shoulder. "You're good. At ease." He nodded and smiled gratefully.

I turned back to Ally. Joe and Foxy were now by her side, standing near the tanks. Foxy wasn't wearing a hat anymore, and had a nice sized Ace bandage wrapped around his mane, blanketing a white dressing.

"Well, here we are again," I said.

"Reunited, and it feels so good," Joe said icily.

"That was something, wasn't it?" I asked them. "Did you see the new guys?" My eyes widened at them. They knew I wasn't talking about the humans.

"Never seen anything like that in my life," Joe said.

Foxy and Ally just shook their heads in agreement. "I'd hate to see what woulda happened if our guys arrived even five minutes later," Foxy added. "Thanks for keeping me safe during my little nap," he smiled wryly. I nodded back at him.

"Yeah, the only thing we have to do now is to meet their queen," I said stoically and perhaps a little too loudly. I wasn't sure if my comment had unintentionally slipped out of me, or if now was the time to bring them into the fold of my suspicions.

They looked at me quizzically. Just then, one of the new guys brought us all some hastily prepared sandwiches and bottled water. I thanked him.

Lifting the sandwich, I took a bite and chewed uneasily. Another soldier came over to me with a new headset. Apparently, Stone was on it, waiting. "Captain on the com for you, sir," he said.

I took a moment, and then I waved him off with an *I'll-call-him-back* finger. He nodded. *If one more person around here calls me sir…*

I took a deep breath as they looked at me, and I looked back. Monzon was close by, but I needed to have a private talk with my own people. I noticed him glance over at us briefly.

"Let's take a walk, gang."

Ally looked at Joe, Joe looked at Foxy, and Foxy looked at each of them in turn. I walked a bit out of earshot away from the tanks and they followed me. The slow, steady, triple pulse of the Warhorse Morses were all around us, throbbing in the air, a silent repellant that kept them at bay while we prepared to move out again. But I needed to explain a few things first.

We walked a few more paces, and then I came to my point while they ate. "Alright. The way I figure it, we've only seen gorgon *drones* until now. Hell, even berserkers are just brutish drones, right? That much is clear to me now." It was time to tell them what I had told Ally.

"I need to clue you guys in on something Stone told me before he put me in solitary. It's about that berserker from the library." I looked at Ally. She nodded.

The guys stopped eating and were looking at me intently. I didn't have to ask to know that their memories flashed back to APU. To the Woodward Library. To Rutty.

"Remember the purpose of our lojack mission? To track a gorgon. Get its whereabouts, track its movements, gather intel, and hopefully see what they're doing out there over the oceans. Well, as it turns out, we were all spoon-fed a load of horseshit about our mission. Any of you remember that explosion back at Harvill while I was asleep?" They nodded. "That was a surface-to-air missile fired by someone who had the authorization, and it took down the berserker that got Rutty. That missile was locked onto the tracker that you implanted, Joe. They shot it down *only an hour* after it killed him."

Surprise and dismay passed over both Foxy's and Joe's faces.

"All along, all the rest of that day, on our way back, Command reported to me that there had been no change in the berserker's position; that it was back at the Cumberland River. That it was still alive." I shook my head and stuck out my chin. "Nope. Lies. All of them. It had been dead for hours. Stone even lied to my very face about it when we got back, as if that berserker was still alive. The whole op was pointless. At least, for us."

Everyone had stopped eating and was staring at me as they too grasped the magnitude of the deceit foisted upon us on the mission. Ally watched them. "It's true," she said.

The guys looked over at Ally momentarily, realizing that I had told her all of this previously.

"See," I continued, "the Captain told me that our lojack mission was one of several. It was only to see if any of us could actually pull it off. It was a pointless *test*."

"What?" Joe gasped. "No way, Jet. That's crazy! Why would they do something like that and make us all expendable? We'd already wrangled one and showed that we could do it. What new truths would another test give them?"

"That's impossible," Foxy breathed, his mouth agape.

Her eyes downcast, Ally didn't say anything more.

"It is crazy, and it's not impossible, and I'm telling you the truth," I uttered somberly. "He told me himself. When we're all ready to strike back, and we've driven off most of them, we're still going to have to root out the rest of them in ground incursions. Would the troops actually have the courage to do that, on the ground, man-to-gorgon? Would they buckle under pressure and fear when they came face to face with them, trying to weed them out? *That's* why we were given that pathetic mission. And it didn't just come from Stone. It came from the President. She's the queen, and we're the pawns." Meeting their eyes, I gritted my teeth and said, "I swear to you it's the truth."

Moment of silence as they wrestled with the facts.

"Well," Joe broke in, "it ain't the first time in history the peons have been sent in to do the heavy lifting under the pretense of a major threat. I mean that's why they call us 'grunts,' right? We're the boots on the ground doin' all the fighting while they sit cozied up in their armchairs, quarterbackin' everything from a safe distance. That's the way of war. Just don't ask me to like it." He shook his head in anger. "*Man,* Jet, I'm just so, *so* sorry, brother. I had no idea."

I nodded and raised my eyebrows. "See," I continued, looking up to the threatening skies above me, "they're not completely alien, you guys. Those berserkers I mean. They're genetically engineered. Don't ask me how because Stone didn't say. They're...different. Something about an attempt to infiltrate the enemy from the inside and get back at them that way, with the amped-up berserkers, and the plan failed. I don't know.

"Either way," I said, looking down at one of the two charred, smoldering husks close by, which were now being studied by a lithe soldier in camo, "I'm thinking the same thing is true about these ones here. Either they're engineered somehow as well, or for sixteen years, these ones have just stayed hidden until the time was ripe, the latter of which I find very hard to believe."

They looked at the behemoth closest to us and then back at me. None of them had taken another bite of their sandwich. Foxy was the first to speak.

"So, you think that these are engineered somehow, too, Jet? Like the berserkers? What makes you so sure?"

"I can't be certain, Foxy, but look at it. Just look at that thing. In sixteen years, we've never seen one. And look at their intelligence. Think about it.

"Not once have we ever seen them swarm together like they did when they were first inbound. Not once in any of our run-ins with the gorgs have we seen them intentionally go below an m-deck signal like they knew they could evade detection. They knew! Not once have we ever seen anything beyond a berserker. Not once have we ever experienced such a coordinated attack where they sent in the grunts first and saved the heavy manpower until they were ready to make their killing stroke. They sent in their pawns, like we do."

They were all studying me now. Ally, her eyes wide, dared to swallow her food. "You're saying it's like some chess game?"

"I'm saying it *is* a chess game. Something Pastor Rosie said to me...you guys heard it! When she came down to me at the memorial. She said I would need to be ready for when the *real* threat comes. The *real* enemy. All along we've been pawns on some big chessboard."

Ally looked at me, "So you think that they're mirroring us, Cam? We have our queen in President Graham, and we're the pawns, and you think they have their own queen somewhere?"

As far-fetched as it sounded, I knew what she was saying was the truth. It had to be. "Listen, as much as we've seen happen in just ten days, is it really so hard to believe? They're not just mindless drones. They're here with a purpose. They're draining our oceans dry."

"That I *had* heard," Joe agreed briskly. "I had chatted once or twice with Stone while you were locked up, Jet, and he did mention it. Stone," he said, shaking his head now, his eyes dropping to the ground. "Had I known he green-lighted that mission with all that balderdash at Harvill, I woulda tried to deck him too. Man," he finished angrily, gripping his fist and putting both hands on his head in a noisome exhale.

"Wait," Foxy interjected, "they're here for the water? I thought they just wanted us for food," he said. "I mean, that's what they've been doing all this time, right?"

"Right. What they want with the water, I don't know. But that's what Stone said. Maybe their planet's all dried up. I don't know. Or maybe they have some other purpose, I just don't know, bud. However you slice it, they want it all. That's why we've always been prevented from steering toward the coastlines. Whatever they're doing, it's out there…somewhere. And I need to find out where."

Ally shivered. I walked over to her, put my arm around her, and looked them up and down, saying nothing. It was clear that the burden of truth was smothering them, and they were now forced to take a pause and choose sides.

Joe said what we were all thinking first. "We're with you, Jet. I think you know that by now."

I smiled softly and clenched my lip in appreciation. *Crap, now I was doing it.* I hated when people did that to me. However, I meant it.

"I know, and I appreciate it. I'm not forming a band of mutineers here. This isn't a revolution. I'm just asking you to open your eyes and realize that not everything is what it seems anymore. Something major is happening behind the scenes, and you may have already picked up on that. You've sensed it because it's true. I've got to get to the bottom of it," I told them. "I owe Rutty that."

Rutty. At the very mention of his name, their heads bowed and nodded in solemn agreement.

"We *all* owe him that." Suddenly, I remembered Rosie's words to me, words fitting to now impart to them. "We are not candles in a wind-free world."

•   •   •   •   •

1953 hours. We needed to get a move on. I asked one of the tanks to head back with Rawley, as well as the remains of Baxter, which one of the guys had discovered in a grisly scene over by the car that he had tried to shelter against. They bagged and tagged him and then put him in MS181 with Rawley and their own driver and gunner. Rawley had been a tank gunner in her younger years, and she was stable, so if they ran into any further trouble, she could serve as backup for theirs. So, all told, there were now three (three and a half, if you counted Baxter) tanks heading back to Base One.

We had no time to fix MS82. It would stay here until a daytime mission could be attempted to repair it. For now, we were all back in 131, same crew as before. Joe and Monzon were now on board 180 and 179, respectively.

So, while I initially supposed that we might have five tanks under my command, only three would now make the continuing journey to Mammoth Cave.

I'm sure Joe was as preoccupied in 180 as we were all in 131. I figured the revelations I had shared with them would reverberate through their call of duty for long after today, as they had reverberated in mine previously.

When we finally broke, I informed the soldier with the com that I was ready for Stone, but the Captain was no longer there. *Good. Maybe I made him wait so long he gave up.* I didn't care to sit there and listen to any half-assed *glad you're okay* exhortations from him anyway.

When all was said and done, three tanks started rumbling up the highway again at 2000 hours in a wedge formation, Warhorse Morses running proudly. The gorgons wouldn't dare approach that kind of sonic intensity. We were in close formation and winding our way through abandoned cars. I just hoped we were all clear of those behemoth gorgons. I could still see that one eye and half-face scowling at me venomously through the broken hatch, eager for blood. I shivered.

Our tank was on point, and the other two flanked us behind. Scores of cars littered our path at intervals, and we had to thread our way through carefully. A lot of people had made a concerted effort to flee Russellville when the gorgons invaded sixteen years prior. Perhaps they were thinking they could get up to Bowling Green, Kentucky, and find better places to hide there. Perhaps they weren't thinking at all and were just driving and screaming in indeterminate directions from whatever was chasing them.

But this is as far as they ever got.

Twenty-two minutes later, we were passing through Bowling Green.

Whether purged from my memory from our years of long service, or something I was once told but never quite believed, snatches of old stories came back to me suddenly. Words can't describe what we saw there when we stopped briefly for a quick bathroom break, and I remembered.

Just off the highway to our north, we saw them: the fuselages of multiple airliners. It recalled to my mind the charred hull of the Alaska Airlines jet that was embedded in the soft bank of the Cumberland back home.

That was nothing. Only seventy miles to our south was Nashville International Airport, and I'm guessing that's where a few of these planes had come from, because there were several. There, along I-65, they must have come in for a landing. Either that, or the gorgons had latched on to the nose of the planes and had the horrified pilots locked in their petrifying and life-sucking gaze.

They must not have travelled far before they were assailed in midair and came smashing down into the highway here. I can only imagine the commotion in the control tower that day, trying to clear so many planes for takeoff while keeping them out of the paths of jetliners already in flight. Thus, four crumpled and blackened hulls at varying degrees of dismemberment littered the sides of I-65, their tubelike hulls dotted with tiny window holes, all blackened, all burnt.

In a few of those windows, up close, we could see blackened and charred skeletons, hauntingly peering out and waiting for all eternity for a rescue that would not come. Some of them still even had their oxygen masks attached to their faces, perpetually connected in hope to the one ingredient of life that was sucked out of their lungs.

Streaking behind one of the jets – it was hard to see clearly in the dark – were long, charred trails of skid marks from when it had slapped down onto cold concrete and then spun and skidded to a halt. Another was reduced to nothing but accordioned fragments with solid bits of the plane like landing gear, and a tail fin lying quietly on its side. A third lay capsized and cut in half. The fourth was further up over a hill. I remember at one point hearing that there were five planes, but I couldn't see the fifth. It's possible that it hit the ground dead on and disintegrated. All looked like they had been in the process of trying to land on the highway.

It was the skeletons that did us in.

When we had all gone to the bathroom and mounted back up, Ally and I remained outside the hatch, watching somberly as our tanks slid by in ghostly silent reverence for all those people – hundreds of them – that had either burned to death and were violently thrown from the plane in their respective crashes, or were frozen and then ejected anyway, and then consumed by the gorgons. But only *partially* consumed they were: as it turned out, gorgons don't like burnt flesh. Bits and pieces of human bones were scattered everywhere along the ground. I recognized a tibia and fibula on the ground next to our tank treads as we passed.

Foxy didn't want to see any of it.

It wasn't clear which way any of them had died. Whether by gorgon, fire, or impact, it didn't matter. We were threading our way not just through multiple cars now, but through a disquieting graveyard, and I was positive that the rubble occasionally crunching beneath our treads was not wholly mechanical.

We were rolling over human remains.

I commanded our tank to slow down and take it easy through here and to find the cleanest and most honoring path.

Our journey slowed out of necessity, but in ten more minutes, we had left the graveyard behind. I pulled Ally close to me, kissed the top of her head, and put my cheek to her hair. "Those poor people," she breathed.

We dropped back inside slowly and closed the hatch.

The rest of our trip was quiet, uneventful, and pensive. Foxy and Ally were lost in thought and didn't say much to me. Their eyes were downcast, and it seemed they were in forced reflection. I know I had to do the same once. If humanity didn't collectively make the right decisions to work together and in harmony with one another, then we'd all end up little more than skeletons in windows like those passengers.

I could still see that shape: sitting upright, intact, gazing hauntingly out through its window seat at me, backlit by the dim light of Bowling Green's dead city just beyond. So many victims of killing strokes. For a moment, I thought them fortunate, considering all that I had witnessed, and figured that to meet their fate in a crash might very well have been better than to be ripped to shreds by a behemoth gorgon.

We would never know, of course.

All of it was more than unsettling to witness.

9 | THE CAVE

I heard a voice speaking.

Simpson was radioing back to all of us that we were approaching Mammoth Cave and would arrive any minute.

Remarkably, I had fallen asleep. I had checked with Ally, Foxy, Simpson and Vetas, and they were all good. Vetas didn't say anything, just gave me a thumbs up.

That was 2025 hours. I checked my watch. It was now 2106, and we were finally reaching our destination after one helluva bumpy journey.

The passage had taken a bit longer than anticipated. It didn't help that the highway was littered with cars, that there was snow on the ground, and that we had passed through that airline graveyard.

But…we were now here. I was grateful for the nap, and discovered that Ally was awake next to me. I had been sleeping on her shoulder. "Rise and shine, camper," she joyfully whispered to me. "We're here." She kissed my forehead.

I yawned and stretched, wide-eyed, and smiled at her. That nap was much needed, albeit entirely too short. They always were. I shook my head in a spasm as if I had just splattered cold water onto my face and jumped to my feet as the tank stopped.

"Mammoth Cave, Mammoth Cave, this is MS131 from DN436 Clarksville at your front door, over?" Simpson said over the open channel.

The reply was nearly instantaneous. "Mobile Scout Unit 131 and company, this is DN312 at Mammoth Cave. Pop the hatch and come on in. The front door's open. Welcome home, over."

"Confirmed," Simpson said, and then I popped the hatch. Even cooler night air blew in, more frigid than the winter chill we'd become accustomed to. I looked out.

We were greeted by a few armed soldiers in the new reflective tech masks standing guard at the entrance to the yawning mouth of a large cave with a stairway descending like a tongue down into it. It banked off to the left close to us, and dropped down by several dozen steps into the underbelly of the land.

Multiple tanks were stationed nearby, all Abrams units. I couldn't count, but it looked like perhaps ten, all lined up in a neat and tidy military row.

And there, perched atop the perimeter of the cave mouth, were huge gun towers. That's what they were, though these were much more extravagant than what we had back home. The gun towers at DN436 seemed like child's play by comparison. What DN312 was equipped with left me speechless. Atop the cave mouth, there were not six but *twenty-four* defense towers: surface-to-air launchers, anti-aircraft guns, and smaller towers with M134 miniguns on rotating platforms. Long snakes of ammunition trailed out of each of them, fed into them by suspended conveyors mounted to the cave ceiling below. The rest must have been anchored from above, down through the hard granite and limestone rock, and fused with the earth. I would *not* want to be on the wrong side of these weapons. The cave mouth was imposing in so many ways, not the least of which was I felt two feet tall in front of it.

Moisture glistened off the mouth of the cave. Snow, still melting in the cool night, transforming and coalescing into tiny rivulets of dripping water that tinkled down into pools below, formed a musical salutation that reverberated in a sweet staccato melody for all of us new arrivals.

Speaking of reverberation, through it all, we heard the constant hum of multiple DTF pulse emitters, all chirping in unison and sending out their silent but vicious salvo of sonic restraint to keep the enemy at bay. I could see them interspersed between the weapons at the mouth of the cave, and I counted ten of them pointed in all directions, making up part of the twenty-four points of defense.

Just *looking* at them, I think I actually felt safer than I ever did under our own gun towers back home, and that was saying something.

Suddenly a reading of *Henry V* as a kid back in school under teacher Jackson came to me: *That's a valiant flea that dares eat its breakfast on the lip of a lion.* If any gorgons did venture boldly this way, they would be cut down without a second thought. However, ever the cynic, I shuddered, thinking, *I'd also hate to be inside that lion if too many fleas got in.* But the thought quickly passed. Mammoth Cave would surely end up proving itself as not only a massive system of endless passageways spanning hundreds of miles, but also a force to be reckoned with, reinforced with human resolve and armed to the teeth.

* * * * *

I helped Ally disembark, and the others dismounted from their iron maidens and crunched along the snowy ground, joining us at the precipice. We all gazed down into the belly of the earth that would be our home away from home for God knows how long.

At the top of the staircase, a guide met us, saluted, and introduced himself as Walker. Fitting name, since that's all we'd be doing. He instructed us to walk across a few biosecurity mats.

"Helps prevent White Noise Syndrome," he said, which was some kind of fungal disease that affects bats. I was intrigued by that bit of information. If there were any alive, down there is where they would be. I remember gorgons didn't like it underground. Maybe it was a confined space thing, which would explain why the gorgon in our tank was so desperate to get out.

If I were a bat, I'd stay down there, and I wouldn't want to be affected by White Noise Syndrome either, although the very notion seemed amusing.

"One more thing," he said. "Your masks. You can take them off and stow them for now. You won't need them down there."

We did as he said, and as we descended the staircase, I heard another voice, low, growly, in a southern twang, next to me. It said, "He lifted me out of the pit of despair, out of the mud and the mire. He set my feet on solid ground and steadied me as I walked along. He has given me a new song to sing, a hymn of praise to our God. Many will see what he has done and be amazed. They will put their trust in the Lord."

I turned to look at Joe Bassett, there beside me, probably uttering something akin to what Rutty would have uttered, as we descended the thick, long stairway into our new home away from home.

"A little bit o' Psalm 40 for ya," Joe added with a smile. I grinned encouragingly, though the psalm didn't exactly comfort me. "Relax, Jet, we're safe now," he said with full assurance. "In and out of the mud and mire in no time."

I smiled indulgingly and replied, "I'll take a preacher over a creature any day." But in truth, I was frowning inside. I appreciated the verse, but why didn't I believe him? I cast a nervous look at Ally, who returned the same look back to me.

•   •   •   •   •

"Roughly four hundred and twenty-six miles charted so far," Walker went on, leading us farther in.

I took a quick look back and noticed everyone falling in behind us, still coming down the stairwell. Except for Simpson and Vetas, that is. They were both enjoying a smoke at the top of the stairs, and I could just make out Captain Monzon making his way down from them a bit ahead with their new gunner, whom I hadn't met yet. Ally, Foxy, and Joe were close behind me.

We passed a few obelisk-looking structures on either side of the stairs on our way down – six in total – and we instantly recognized the devices perched atop them. They were m-decks with transmitters attached to them. Somewhere, in the bowels of Mammoth Cave, someone was on sentry listening for movement up top. It was a sure bet they were being overloaded with all of our signals coming down here now.

"Deepest part of the caves varies. People dispute it. Some say a hundred and forty feet, some say three hundred seventy-nine feet. Either way, it's *mammoth,*" Walker said with a wink.

I saw what you did there.

"Yep," he said, "Echo River's three hundred sixty feet below the surface, and that's about as far down as any of us like to go, so a lot of us hole up at the Rotunda before it hits Broadway, right around the Methodist Church. The rest of us are down by Giant's Coffin."

My heart skipped a beat. "Did you say *Methodist Church?*" I asked him.

"Yep!" Walker answered gleefully, oblivious to our previous foray. "About thirteen hundred feet in! Big canyon room with a ceiling about fifty feet up. They used to hold church services in there with the good Reverend George Slaughter Gatewood back in the 1830's. Got a pulpit and everything!"

Great. Nothing against the Methodists, but I think we'll skip that section. "As long as there ain't no bell towers," I said.

"Bell towers?" Walker asked, puzzled.

"Nothin," I dismissed it. I looked at Ally and then Joe, and we all rolled our eyes. I had my arm around Ally's waist, but I removed it and let myself drift back to Foxy. He was walking a bit slowly, carrying his pack and his rocket launcher slung over his back. "How's your head, broski?" I asked him.

"Better," he said, "but it still stings a bit. That one got me good. I never saw any of it, ya know. I barely looked up and half-saw this shadow slam into us and knock us back down into the tank. I don't know what I hit, but I guess I hit it hard."

"Yeah ya did," I snickered. "Looks like they got you patched up okay though. That thing was lying on you for a good bit, and thrashing around the cabin of the tank, buddy. I'm surprised you got just a scratch on your noggin. Took all of us to wrangle it again. We sure could have used you for another swift kick."

Foxy smiled and looked up at me sheepishly yet gratefully. Ally had told me that when I had passed out and Joe and the team had dragged the berserker out of the Woodward library after it had killed Rutty, Foxy had run out and kicked it hard in the side.

"Who told you?" Foxy asked.

"This fine lady right here," I said, pointing to Ally.

Foxy grinned at her. "Thanks, Lieutenant Trudy."

"Uh- Foxy. It's *Ally*, k?" she corrected him with a knowing grin.

He laughed. "Okay, thanks Ally. Yeah well, I was kinda pissed. For two reasons. *One,* I wanted to do more than stand guard at the door back at Harvill. I could hear everything coming through Preston's headset and see what little I could see of Lieut- uh, *Ally,* running up the berm at you guys, and then we saw the three of those things whoosh into the library. That was intense. And *two,* we heard what happened with your bro, Jet, and I wish I was there to, I dunno, do something. Anything. Just to do my part," he ended quietly.

He looked up at me as if seeking reassurance of his value. I never questioned it, and I never would.

"Hey, man. You're my little bro now. I mean it. You've done your part and then some. I told you I'd never forget that fellowship hall in the church, and I won't. And when you burst out of that hatch next to me and put your back up against mine, blasting away? *Whoa*. I think I felt somebody's manly deltoids pokin' into me. What have you been feeding these things?" I asked him, probing his back in mock-envy. "Hard to shoot with all that pokin' and muscle envy I was suffering through," I exclaimed.

Foxy laughed and pulled away from me. "Oh, man." He shook his head.

"You're all good, little brother. Losing Rutty," -here I looked down- "doesn't sting so much with you with me." I meant it. "You held 'em off for a good while, Foxy. We're all indebted to you."

Ally nodded, and Joe, who had drifted a bit behind us, seconded our affirmation. "I could see you guys over there, guns a'blazin,' Liam. You lit 'em up good. You're alright, kid."

I smiled at Joe. I think Foxy needed this validation. I'm not sure where it was coming from, nor did I know how long he had been at Harvill, nor who did or didn't sow into his life there. However unfortunate the turn of events was, I felt God had given a big brother to him. And a sister, and, I guess, a southern uncle in Joe. He had family again, something pretty much all of us were sorely lacking.

I squeezed his shoulder and put my arm back around Ally. We continued our slow march down the concrete walkway, and at intervals, we could see various mileposts and signs highlighting where we were with little 'You are here' markers.

We were in the Houchins Narrows, as it was called, coming up on the Rotunda. The cave echoed with the noise of humans bustling about, and along the gangways and upper and lower areas we could make out several stations that were hastily assembled, but that had tapped into the electrical lines down here. We looked at it in amazement. *There were even more down below by Giant's Coffin?* I thought. There looked to be a good hundred here alone.

Walker was in his element as he walked us past them. As we continued down, he shared about all of the activity that had happened here over the years: mining, spelunking, graffiti, exploration, and more. He told us about the lifeforms down here: bats, blindfish, crawfish, spiders, and cave crickets the size of rats. Nothing down here had any real pigment except for the bats.

I had never been in a cave in all of my life. I had hoped to see some stalactites and stalagmites growing here, trying to meet in the middle like the doors of our Blockade launch, but there were none. Apparently, they were only present much further down by Echo River. Still, the walls flickered with a dim gemmy glow like bursts of fireflies trapped in the glints of limestone, quartz, and gypsum, as they all received the light of torches and the remaining accent lighting installed long ago by the National Park Service. They lit up a world of labyrinths and palatial chambers in eerie splendor.

The walls were wet and moist in some cases, so we had to be careful ascending and descending any staircases.

There was also a musty smell down here, but it was airy too. Wafts of thick drafts mixed with strains of clean air interspersed throughout. Nonetheless, the air was close now and tight…stuffy. Silent. Air so thick you could chew it.

Sometimes, our guide told us, the lower levels were subject to back-flooding from the Green River, and that inrush of water meant a rush of fresh air through here as well. However, we wouldn't be going that low. Nonetheless, the close quarters and palpable feeling of claustrophobia slowly descended on us like an uncomfortably heavy blanket.

I wondered how long these guys had been down here, and what their communications with the above-ground folks were like. I also wondered who was close to going insane from being stuck down here for perhaps years on end, and if anyone had gone stark raving mad so far. I guess that would be Captain Vance Cardona or, at least, that's what Stone made it sound like.

We continued to march on behind our guide, and occasionally there was the sound of scattered flapping overhead. *Bats*.

Ally looked up quickly, and I could tell there was fear there. "You okay, hon?" I asked her.

"Yeah. Bats. I don't like 'em."

I laughed. "Not many people do."

"But," she breathed resolutely, "they're probably one of the last few species alive on Earth that evaded the gorgs. Probably time for me to change my mind about them, huh?" She looked at me nervously.

"Probably."

Someone was approaching swiftly up the cave from Broadway further down. Walker asked us to hold here. An officer was approaching with two minions behind him, and they were all shining flashlights at us. "Lieutenant Shipley," he greeted me, out of breath, in the dim light. I stopped and nodded.

"Lieutenant Armstrong," he said, as we shook hands. "Glad you guys made it here. Welcome to Mammoth Cave." He took a deep breath to restore his lungs.

"Thanks. Good to be here," I replied, not sure I meant it yet. "Love what you've done with the place."

"Oh, you mean the towers and the m-decks! Yeah, well, we do what we can." He laughed. "Is Captain Monzon with you?" Straight to the point.

I thumbed behind me. Monzon was still a way back, being escorted by some other Mammoth Cave personnel, but I pointed him out to Armstrong.

"Thank you. I'm sure you heard the former Captain went AWOL."

"Captain Cardona?" I asked him. "Yes. Captain Stone from 436 informed us of that prior to our departure. Sorry to hear it. Do you still have orders to shoot on sight?"

He gave me a confused expression. "Yes, we do, and we're not sorry to hear it. Well, at least, I'm not. But I'm new here. I and a few others came up last week by order of The President. Frankly, I think he was going a little stir crazy. We call it 'cave fever' here.

"There are reports that he kept talking about all kinds of nonsense like conspiracies and crazymaking talk about plots and plans and how all the higher-ups were losin' it. Well, it appears that *he* was the one who was losing it all along. Then, sure enough, he did. Up and disappeared and left all his people behind. Hasn't been seen since. So, we're still on the lookout for him."

Conspiracies. Plots. That's what caught my attention. I squinted at him.

Monzon was drawing closer, and they shone the light on him and saluted. He saluted in response. "Monzon," he greeted them with a warm handshake. "How goes the fight, gents?"

"Not too bad, sir," Armstrong answered proudly. "We're still leaderless, but as I understand it from DN436, you'll be filling that role?"

"Soon as I can, yes," Monzon replied. "As long as somebody here can show me around and point me to the men's room." He snickered. They echoed it. "Why don't you boys take me to your Command Center, and we'll start there?" Monzon asked.

Lieutenant Armstrong nodded. "Right this way, sir," he said, handing him off to one of the minions that had accompanied him, to take him back up to the Rotunda.

I guess we had passed it back that way. This place really is a maze, I thought.

We then met Larson, the new gunner who had replaced Baxter and remained with us. I shook his hand and introduced ourselves to him. Evidently, he was close with Vetas and Simpson.

"Lieutenants Shipley, Trudy, Staff Sergeant Bassett and Private Mayfield?"

We all nodded, but I cut in. "Lieutenant Trudy should be known as the future Mrs. Shipley, I'd like to add for the Mammoth Cave record."

Armstrong grinned. "Well, alright then. Congrats, you two. Let's get you all further down and settled in, and we can show you where you can bunk and wash up. We already had chow time, but we saved some for you all."

That was music to my ears. Although the thought of washing up in cold, sputtering cave waterfalls didn't really entice me, my stomach had been growling since that light sandwich we had wolfed down earlier.

Time to keep moving. Dinner was calling.

Walker guided us further in, and it was 2237 before we had finally arrived at their base, deep inside the cave at Giant's Coffin, a relative midpoint, which is where the rest of the Blockade lived and worked.

We had passed the length of Broadway and an intersection with Gothic Avenue where the cave split off in opposing directions.

I had lost all sense of direction and wasn't sure if it was east or west down here; my watch couldn't give me any coordinates.

One thing I noticed was that it was strangely warm. Either the earth's core had continued to heat up unabated with global warming, which might explain why the snow was melting and dripping into the cave so freely late at night, or all the equipment they had down here was warming things up synthetically. CPUs, terminals, fridges, cooking gear, fires, torches, and so forth, all of that may have brought it up a few degrees. Or it could just be all these people packed into this space creating the combined warmth of human connection, one of the few things we had left.

We had gone on another few hundred feet when, once again, the din of echoes of human voices met our ears.

Rounding a corner, we at last arrived at Giant's Coffin, a large open area marked by a massive slab measuring about forty-eight feet long, twenty feet high, and eight feet wide. It certainly looked like a coffin. Probably weighed a thousand tons too.

As we drew near, we could see signatures scrawled in ink and chalk all over it, all but faded: remnants of a more lighthearted time when people would head out and travel freely without care.

Walker led us to a corner of the cavern that had been hollowed out – or tunneled into, I wasn't sure which – and makeshift bunks composed of stacked cots had been set out for us. There we would take our rest, and the time for rest drew near. But first, food called our names, and we had high hopes.

Ally, Foxy, Joe, Larson, and I piled our things onto the bunks. Understandably, my future bride and I chose two that were close together. Then, Walker led us to a farther quadrant of the encampment there, weaving us through a few soldiers in various stages of undress and casual comfort. Looked like some kind of furlough, until they were rotated into their shifts, or called upon to defend the cave of course. All of them greeted us with a hearty smile. Most of them were pretty young. Reminded me of the refugees at Harvill, though they were older there. These new recruits here were greener, and they were undoubtedly who I would be training. All told, it looked like there were another hundred down here.

We reached their mess hall, which really wasn't a hall at all of course, just a partitioned off area with picnic tables clumsily stacked up on the rocks close to the limestone walls. A tiny waterfall splashed down noisily nearby.

"Wait here, and I'll grab your grub," Walker said, and disappeared around what looked like a ramshackle soup kitchen with enough equipment to serve all the grunts in here.

Soup kitchen it was. Momentarily, he came back with metal tins filled with steaming soup for each of us, along with plates of crackers, cheeses, and a flask of cold spring water, doubtless collected from the cave waterfalls, for each of us.

We ate the soup, and each of us had seconds, and best of all, Ally and I didn't feel like we had to ask what *this* soup was actually made of. The memory of that soup at the Methodist Church arguably still lingered in at least our minds. We didn't know quite what it was, but it was hearty. As for me, I felt vigor coursing through me after I ate it, like I could take on all the gorgons just by myself. And that water was the clearest, most untainted, purest form of water I'd ever drunk.

Simpson and Vetas eventually found us, and they took up a table nearby. They reeked of smoke. Where Monzon had disappeared to, no one knew. Probably back at Command and getting acquainted with their systems and layout. Larson greeted them heartily and switched tables to catch up with them. That left the four of us together again at our own table.

I checked my watch. 2252 hours. Nearly 11pm. We'd done a lot of walking, and I was ready for sleep. That soup had gone straight to my food coma zone, and I sat back and yawned.

Foxy's head was nodding, and he was about to fall into his soup. Reminded me of how Rutty would fall asleep on the toilet ever since he was a little boy. I elbowed Ally to look over at him, and she chuckled. *Kid indeed.* Joe smiled.

"Foxy, wake up, buddy," I said.

Foxy started and looked at me. "Huh? Oh, sorry. Tired." His eyelids drooped, and his head started to nod again.

"I hear ya, bro. I'm ready for some shuteye. Your head ok?"

Foxy didn't answer.

I giggled. "Come here, buddy," I said, getting up from the table as Ally and Joe watched me. I moved around to the other side of the table and picked him up, lightly lifting him over my shoulder and carrying him back to his bunk. Over my shoulder I could hear Ally breathe to Joe, "He's *such* a good big brother, isn't he?"

Her words made me smile and warmed my heart. Same thing I used to do with Rutty.

•   •   •   •   •

I had laid Foxy down in his bunk and pulled the blanket up over him. *Lightweight*, I thought and then smiled and headed back to our group. In the dim light, I could tell the crowd was thinning out, and the bunks were starting to fill up. I started to look away when something caught my eye, and I did a double take.

Toward the far wall was a soldier with a hood over his head staring at me. Though people were bustling to and fro all around him, he wasn't. No - he was completely stationary and looking right at me.

I could just make out his eyes under his hood; they were flickering in the dim torchlight nearby. He looked like his forehead was glistening wet. I cleared my eyes and rubbed them briefly, but when I looked again, he was gone.

Shaking off the mysterious stranger, I walked back to Ally, Joe, and the others, while cautiously trying to assess whether someone tangible had actually been standing there, or if the light and my fatigue were playing tricks on my mind.

At long last, I gave up and sat down. Probably some worn-down recruit regretting what he signed up for and hating being stuck this far down below the surface of the earth.

Ally was yawning.

"Let's hit the hay, everybody," I suggested. "Probably going to be a long day tomorrow. What day *is* tomorrow anyway? December 13th? Man, the days just kinda blend together." I shook my head and rubbed my neck.

Just then Walker returned with Captain Monzon. We all rose and saluted.

"At ease, everyone. I know it's late, so let's get some rest," the Captain instructed.

"We, uh, were just thinking of that," I replied.

"Good. We'll wake at 0900, a nice late start for once. No more of these senseless God-forsaken early risings, right? Not if I can help it," he said, tossing a team-player smile our way. "I figure we've got enough ammo and manpower now to afford us a little breathing room, and I daresay we deserve it after the highway incident.

"So, Shipley, at 1030 hours, we'll have everyone gathered down here for an initial briefing, and then you take them up top and do some patrol training. Lieutenant Trudy and Staff Sergeant Bassett, you'll be educating the science folks about what the gorgons can do, the insides and outs, and about what you've learned from that one you have in captivity back home. I'm going to continue to make the rounds and familiarize myself with the personnel here, right?"

"Sir," we confirmed in unison.

"Right. Good night, folks." He started to turn away, and then stopped and turned back to me. "Oh, Lieutenant Shipley, I had a transmission come in from DN436 from someone in Halcyon, said he couldn't reach you. Beckinsale, Pete I think was his name."

I leaned toward him. "Yessir," I confirmed.

"He said you asked him to let you know about any change in the oceans, sea level, stuff like that. He said, 'minus twenty-three inches since the initial invasion.' Mean anything to you?"

Minus twenty-three inches. Good Lord. The sea levels weren't rising from global warming and glacier melt as Pete had suspected they would. They were in fact *dropping*, and dropping dramatically.

The gorgons were definitely taking our water. How were they getting it off of the planet? And what were they doing with it once they did?

"Lieutenant?" the Captain repeated.

I turned my attention back to him. "Uh, no, sir, just science nerd stuff," I said and grinned at him.

Monzon scanned me for a moment, flicked his eyebrows up, and turned away, moving briskly down the hall back towards Command.

I looked over at Joe.

"Sea levels were supposed to *rise* four inches every decade," he said to me grimly.

I nodded. He was in that conversation, and he remembered. The gorgons were definitely stealing our water. I thought back to all the times where there had been reports of them at the edge of the Cumberland or elsewhere and how they had been partially submerged. I thought back to the times where I'd heard so many reports about how viciously they drove us away from the coastlines. Was it to keep us from whatever was robbing Earth of its precious natural resource? That had to be it.

But it would have to wait. We needed sleep badly.

•   •   •   •   •

We retired to our bunks, and I fell right away into an uneasy sleep full of bizarre dreams.

Dreams of being inside a gorgon again and Rutty being there. Rutty being a gorgon. Stone being a gorgon. Gorgons everywhere.

Skeletons leering out at me hauntingly from airplane windows. The mystery soldier here in the cave. That frightening behemoth gorgon just inches away from me outside our tank.

Endless ranks of human soldiers willingly enlisting in a battle that would claim most of their lives. And all of them chanting something in unison, something scrambled and indecipherable at first.

I strained my eyes and leaned in closer. What was it? Closer.

I tilted my head to hear them.

And then, all of their voices merged together in their dissonance, blending into a single sonorous speech and coalescing into one unknown human staring at me with deadened eyes and stern lips set in a clenched jaw.

"Time is running out," I heard the voice speaking.

10 | TRAINING

It was the derelict, Captain Vance Cardona.

It wasn't the voice I had heard in my sleep, but that's who I awoke to: his picture, at least, on a slightly crumpled printout that had been placed beside me in my bunk as I slept. I looked around suspiciously as I rubbed crusty sleep out of my eyes, and blinked. Very few other people were awake in here. The cave was silent now, except for the slow tinkling of the waterfall across from us, random snoring, and the occasional flitting of bats from one corner of the cave ceiling to another.

I looked at my watch. 0619 hours on December 13th. *Never ceases to amaze me.* I was so trained by this time to report early, and so conditioned to be an early riser that I just couldn't find it in me to slumber.

I glanced over at Ally, who was lying on her back and breathing heavily. Joe was just past her, dead to the world and most likely dreaming of Maureen. I turned the other way and saw Foxy's messy blonde locks sweeping down from the back of his head toward me, the other half of his head still concealed in a bandage. We should have changed that dressing earlier, but someone would see to it in the morning.

I looked back at the picture. Who had placed it there? I thought back to the mysterious soldier I had espied hours earlier across the cave. Maybe he *was* real. Maybe my eyes weren't playing tricks on me after all. Time would tell.

The man pictured before me was in his fifties, like Joe Bassett, with a shaven head and a strong black beard. His face was either incredibly dirty, with grime creased into those wrinkles, or his features had just developed that way so as to highlight the subterranean strain he was under as he went crazy just before going AWOL.

The name VANCE BRENNAN CARDONA was printed in large bold letters below his picture, and in smaller letters below that, "ABSENT WITHOUT LEAVE" was emblazoned in red print. It looked strangely like a modern-day wanted poster. And below that?

"SUBJECT CONSIDERED ARMED AND EXTREMELY DANGEROUS. SHOOT ON SIGHT."

Appalling. Was he really that bad? And who put it here on my bunk and why? This wasn't some random leaflet just dropped onto my bed in the middle of the night. I thought perhaps Monzon might have done it to familiarize our crew with the derelict, but then, none of them had his poster anywhere near their bunks: I was the only one.

I looked around the cave again. *Not a creature was stirring, not even a mouse*, I heard in my head, which only made me think of Christmas, which, of course, conjured up an image of a tiny tree in a small, quiet room in my mind, and then I was back there in Harvill with Rutty once more.

Weird being stuck in a world full of gorgons with no 'fa la lalla la...' he had said.

I missed my brother. No matter how many days ago it was, the memory was fresh, and the loss was still acutely felt by myself *and* our team.

We were drawing close to Christmas, and I would miss spending it with him. Then, I remembered the optimistic words of the President, back there in our Blockade.

"Let's all hope we can get this all done by December 25th, and we'll give everyone a merry Christmas, yeah? I'd call it the best Christmas in sixteen years."

I wondered briefly if Vance Cardona would play a part in Christmas somehow. But I wondered even more what this random poster was doing sitting on my bunk with me, placed there surreptitiously by some mystery person in the middle of the night.

Uneasily, I stared at it until my eyes couldn't prop themselves up anymore, and I fell back into a merciful extension of sleep.

∙　　∙　　∙　　∙　　∙

Someone tapped me lightly on the shoulder. I emerged slowly through the fog and heard myself snort out of my snoring. Groggily, my eyes willed themselves to open, and I looked over, blinking. I could wake up to that face any day.

Ally.

Those sea-green eyes, those wells of beauty, deeper than the bottomless pit of Mammoth Cave. I smiled at her. "What time is it?" I yawned.

"0900," she answered sleepily, and lay back down. She was still in her bunk beside me, propped up on her elbow, her brown tresses flowing down her chin and perfectly framing her soft face. My future bride was before me, and I thought back once again to the silly, pig-tailed interloper from Alpharetta that had showed up in our Blockade only a week and a half earlier. Always blows my mind how things work out, but they were definitely working out for both of us.

She was stunningly beautiful. And she would be mine. *How did I get so lucky?* I wondered.

I looked around. Something around here smelled fantastic. It was coffee coming from the mess, and it had an aroma I'd smelled somewhere before. Macadamia nut?

Joe and Foxy were nowhere to be found. Vetas, Larson, and Simpson were a stone's throw away in some other cots closer to the wall, and they were still snoring. They must have been burning the midnight oil and gone up for a few smokes.

Foxy came walking back with Joe. "Top of the morning, Jet!" His bandage had been changed, and he looked bright-eyed and bushy-tailed underneath the new whites, which blended nearly perfectly into his blonde waves beneath it.

"Mmm, mornin' buddy," I said, sticking a finger in my eyes and sitting up. He handed me some water.

"Time for some grub," Joe said. He had a mug of coffee in his hand, and *boy* did it smell good. "They put on a hearty cup of, well...me!" Joe snorted. "Seriously, this is nearly as good a cup of coffee as Maureen puts on."

He smiled, but I could tell his words belied the fact that he wished he was home with her. I appreciated what he shared last night about Maureen's eyes and the life behind them. I felt the same way about Ally's eyes.

"That sounds good. And it *smells* good. Wow. Just let me splash some cold water on my face. How's that noggin of yours, Foxy?"

"Oh, good, man. Thanks. It was a doozy pulling off the old bandage; it kinda stuck to me," he laughed sheepishly. "But they got it off and smeared some ointment on it. I'll be alright."

"Do they have showers here?" I asked.

"Just what you find in the little waterfalls around the corner in the Wooden Bowl Room. There's also a tiny pool there."

"That's good enough for me," I muttered, getting up and stretching. I was ready for coffee, breakfast, and a cold shower. Ally joined me, and I put my arm around her. "How'd you sleep, sweetheart?" I asked her as she melted into me, and I smelled her hair. Joe smiled at us as we embraced.

"Okay, I think!" she chirped optimistically. "Better than the inside of a tank or a Subway restaurant, that's for sure."

"I bet," I replied, scratching my head. "Well, Joe, how's your Psalm 40 now? You still got a new song to sing? You puttin' your trust in the Lord?"

Joe nodded. "That I am, Jet. I'm puttin' my trust in Him even *more* after a decent night's sleep. *Joy comes in the morning.* Psalm 30:5. That one's for free." He winked at me.

I laughed. "Man, you would have given Rutty a run for his money in quoting the good word, Reverend."

Joe laughed and slapped me on the back with a warm grin and a noisy, hearty sip from his mug. I couldn't wait to have my own.

We strolled back to their mess area. Walker, who had been sitting and eating, noticed our approach and got up to get our food. He must have been assigned as our guide *and* maître d. "Mornin,' crew!" he greeted us enthusiastically. "Hold tight."

We sat, and he brought over plates of what were obviously MRE packs. Meals ready-to-eat, stored in freezers to far outlast their normal shelf life. I had high hopes we'd get better, but what more can you expect in terms of breakfast served in a cave?

But the coffee! Oh, *man,* did that hit the spot. It was bags of Hawaiian Lion macadamia nut coffee, ransacked from who knows where. They ground them in here and heated up water fresh from the cave. The combination of fresh spring water and delicious coffee was more than enough to offset the disappointing breakfast. I thought back to the imitation eggs and crappy coffee we had back at our own Blockade, and decided this ranked better.

Walker informed us that they had hydroponics here as well, somewhere down below, and soldiers tilled them with care, growing basil, peppers, herbs, cucumbers, spinach, strawberries, lettuce, celery, oregano, broccoli, and beans. Some of those graced our plates, including some peanut butter spread for the celery.

And where there is peanut butter, life goes on.

We sat and talked for a while on the edge of ruin and resolve without a care in the world. I wondered if Joe was remembering his days in the service before the invasion. Chumming around with fellow soldiers on missions far from home, but reveling in comradery.

That's exactly what we were doing, and it was a nice change for once, especially after that ordeal on Highway 68 with those behemoth gorgons. I wondered if it would last and if one day we'd be free of all of this, to sit and laugh at old grief together.

•   •   •   •   •

We finished our breakfast and headed down to the Wooden Bowl room to shower. Several soldiers, young and old, were down there already, in various stages of undress. *Lots of tasty, naked humans down here for gorgons to feast on, and no clothes to get in the way,* I thought. *Morbid.* I hoped it would never come to that. Reminded me of several classical paintings I had seen in school of nude, helpless humans being cast into the pit of hell. The only difference was it would be freezing cold down here, especially in that water.

I smiled approvingly, however, when Ally looked at me and disrobed, eyes on me the whole time, and then lightly skipped over the rocks like a cave nymph to the shower at the wall. I looked back at Foxy and covered his eyes. All that was left was his smile underneath my fingers, which he tried to scoop aside. Joe, ever the gentleman, looked away.

We all showered and sputtered in the frigid waterfall, and felt our breath get sucked out of us stepping into the stream, but it was refreshing beyond compare, truthfully.

I stood in front of Ally to shield her from view, even though I was shivering. We were all quaking and laughing in our nervousness.

Toweled off and redressed, it was now 1015 hours, and time to head back up to the Rotunda inside the cave for the 1030 briefing. We were refreshed and ready for a long walk, and now I had another mug of coffee in my hand to power me forward. Ally walked beside me sipping hers. Could life get better? I think not.

Halfway up, we were met by Armstrong again, toting a flashlight and shining it at us. "Lieutenant Shipley, how'd you sleep?" he asked.

"Fine," I said, waving away the light. "Thanks for the grub and the shower."

"You're welcome! Captain Monzon is already up there and ready for your troops."

"Fine."

He nodded and returned, his flashlight sweeping across the ceiling and sending bats scampering for a new location.

We made our way up to the Rotunda, arriving just shy of the 1030 start time, and connected with Monzon. He looked like he had had a long night with very little sleep, if any at all. His right eye had a slight muscle spasm to it that he was fairly obviously trying to hide. He smelled like a *lot* of coffee. I didn't envy the officers that gave up so much to ascend the ranks and forfeit sleep. His gray hair was evident in the cave light, and his lumpy face looked even lumpier after no sleep.

We gathered nearby. Personnel were filing in from all directions in front of us and behind us. Captain Monzon took up a position on an elevated rock berm against the wall, across from an illuminated historical information podium for visitors. Beyond that was a recessed section of the cave, flanked by walkways, that you could hop the bars and drop down into.

The rest of us gathered around him on all sides, filling the walkways. He looked at his watch, and I looked at mine. 1029. He was probably going to start on the nose with military precision.

As predicted, he did. 1030 on the nose.

"Folks, gather 'round please," he said. "Squad, ten-hut!" he greeted. Everyone stood at attention and saluted, including us. And then, as was our custom, he dropped his salute and raised both arms palm upwards. He was being installed here today, and both he and they needed to receive it well.

Thankfully, they echoed it. He seemed like a decent man, and as they were leaderless, I think they welcomed him. We did too.

"At ease, soldiers. That's the last time we'll do that. I'm about as informal as they come." Murmurs of laughter echoed throughout the cave.

Good thing Monzon was up on that berm. He was ripped with muscles, but he was short and stocky, and people in the back were looking over soldiers in front of them just to get a good look at him.

"I'd like to introduce myself. I'm Captain Miguel Monzon, and I've been dispatched by the President to fill the void left by my predecessor here, Captain Cardona. Word is there's still no sight of him. Keep looking. We'll find him, hopefully before the gorgs do.

"Now," he continued, "some of you may have heard that we ran into a bit of trouble on our way here last night. You also may have heard of some disturbing rumors of a new and previously unclassified type of creature. It's large, loaded with muscles, rippling with purpose, and dangerously strong. Please allow me to take a moment to dispel any myths or embellishments you may have heard. I am not this new creature."

The troops erupted into laughter. So did Monzon. He was definitely large, but neither mean nor nefarious. His muscles would help, not hurt. Always good to see a senior officer connect with the rank-and-file.

Monzon paused, and his smile faded a bit. "But, yes, in truth, we ran into some trouble, and were very surprised to encounter what we are now referring to as 'behemoths.' They appear to be far more dangerous than the berserkers that many of you have undoubtedly encountered before today. Thankfully, however, they also are equally susceptible to the technology we possess in order to disrupt them and send them packing." The crowd murmured.

"I'll say this because at the culmination of our encounter last night, our rescue squad from DN436 in Clarksville detonated not one but *two* large-scale DTF devices, which destroyed the gorgons nearby, including these new creatures. They will be studied and catalogued shortly.

"Accompanying me on the journey," -here he motioned over to us- "are Lieutenant Cameron Shipley and Private Mayfield from Clarksville, as well as Lieutenant Allison Trudy and Staff Sergeant Joseph Bassett from Alpharetta. I believe you've heard of them." At this introduction many necks strained over to see us. The crowd of soldiers around us swam and jostled for a peek: the President had said that they had heard of us.

Monzon continued. "They have been on some heavy missions over the past two weeks and have come face to face with the gorgs. Additionally, we have several personnel from DN436 who are part of their tank crew, and they will be assimilated into the ranks here with you as we all co-labor to reinforce this Blockade.

Reinforce this blockade? From everything I'd seen, this was the most reinforced Blockade I'd ever heard of. Monzon continued.

"We're going to split into teams. I'm continuing to get to know you and your Blockade, and to integrate known protocols into your current operations. As many of you are new recruits, Lieutenant Shipley, assisted by Private Mayfield here, will be training us on ground incursions and recon operations. Lieutenant Trudy and Staff Sergeant Bassett will be educating our science team." He stopped. "Uh, where are you, science team?"

We looked over as a small group of about ten soldiers on the other side of the cave acknowledged him with a wave.

"Ah, yes, thank you. They will be educating you on what they've learned from the gorgon they have in captivity in Alpharetta."

Again, astonished murmurs floated throughout the cave at the news of the gorgon they captured. A soldier standing next to me breathed to his buddy, "See? I *told* you it was true that they caught one. Whoa."

Monzon paused for emphasis and then, pursing his lips, looked down. He crossed his arms at his chest and then looked back up, his sleeves bulging out so far at his biceps that I thought they would split.

"This is the big time, boys and girls. For those of you who are new, this is where it all begins. You've done a tremendous job protecting this Blockade, one of the biggest and best in the world. Here is where we train for the counteroffensive. Here is where we prepare to strike back. May God be with us. *Vaya con Dios*," he finished, lifting his arms outward, palms up.

There followed a deafening cacophony of *hoorah!* and *oorah!* and *hooah!* and *hooyah!* blending together and representing all branches of the military joined into one. The more seasoned ones, the vets and those longest in service, just nodded somberly and mirrored Monzon there, palms up. It was a joyous and appreciated moment.

I've been told that there was great division in the armed forces before my time. Before the invasion, that is. The more rank-and-file Army and Marine grunts disdained the navy boys and the flyboys, and vice versa. But here we all were, joined together by common purpose, and sects no longer existed. We were the United States Armed Forces, united against a common enemy, and we were preparing for battle royale.

"It's now 1045 hours. We commence at 1200 hours. Those with Shipley meet topside at the main entrance. Bring your masks and weapons, people. Those with the science team, meet in Com here with Lieutenant Trudy and Sergeant Bassett. Other officers with me in my quarters. The rest of you, at your assigned stations. Get some food in you. It's going to be a long day of training.

"Dismissed," he concluded and stepped down into the crowd where he was immediately swarmed by soldiers saluting him and wanting to greet their new leader.

Momentarily, he strode back over to us. "Nice speech. Short and sweet, Cap'n," I said, and saluted him.

"That's the way I like it," he said, grinning back. "Thank you, gents. Ah– and lady. *Permeso*," he said, falling back into his own tongue and bowing slightly. "Excuse me." Trudy smiled and mumbled something incoherent back to him. "I also didn't get a chance to congratulate the two of you. I'm very happy for you both," he said, clapping each of our shoulders as he pushed us further into each other. "The gorgons may have taken everything else away, but they will never take away love, nor honor. *Nunca,*" he said. I knew that one: *never.*

"Now, Lieutenant," he added, seemingly, as an afterthought, "did the President tell you anything about what she's planning for her, shall we say, decisive resolution? Did she happen to share that with you?"

My eyebrows went up, more out of surprise that he would ask me that question out in the open. "Uh, yessir, briefly, sir – though, I-" I faltered and trailed off.

Monzon studied me. "Lieutenant?"

I couldn't hide my distrust of the President. Not here, not now, and especially after the behemoth gorgon and the subsequent talk with my friends. I cleared my throat and looked down.

"Sir, I don't know if it's my place, but-"

"It is your place. Go ahead, Lieutenant," he interrupted me. "I want to hear it."

I studied him momentarily. "Well, I just-" I stammered out, not sure how to grease the wheel. "Sir, I'm not entirely sure I trust the President on this one, nor my own Captain. After all, it was on their orders that we took on a suicide mission on our last outing, and I lost my brother." I could feel Foxy look over at me. "I-" I trailed off. "I just don't know what to say, nor why you would ask that now. But I'll fall in line with you, sir. We all will. We'll all do as we're told," I said, but I had to add an addendum, "as long as it makes sense, of course. It's just that a lot has happened that has kept us in the dark, and all of us here think that something bigger is going on that we're not being told about. Makes us a bit uneasy, sir."

Monzon regarded me gravely. "I have heard of your loss. My sympathies. We don't need to discuss it now.

We'll have time. Keep your wits about you and take these guys' training wheels off up above, and we'll talk after, yes?"

I slowly nodded. That oddly felt like some kind of probe. I wasn't sure I was looking forward to the rest, because I knew he had been installed here by the President.

Monzon grinned again. "It's all good. You may speak freely around me. You have what you need? I trust you guys. Just show everybody what you know, yeah?" He handed me a folded-up printout. "Roster. Here's names, ranks, and brief descriptions of length of service for each. I think you'll find they're all faithful."

Faithful? Weird word to use, but whatever.

"Roger that," I said, taking the roster and shaking his hand. He shook hands with the rest of our team as well. *This* Captain I liked. It would be nice to sit down and enjoy a nice mug of Lion coffee and learn more about where he came from, how long he had been traveling with the President, and if he had family.

"Good luck," he said, and then he was off.

•　　•　　•　　•　　•

1152 hours. We had grabbed a bit more food to carry us through the day, and after hugging and kissing the future Mrs. Shipley, I squeezed her and sent her off with Joe to train the science guys in Com.

Foxy and I grabbed our packs and headed back out and up. I had my rifle, and Foxy had his rocket launcher. *He and Rutty and their rocket launchers, man.* I would never understand, but I shook my head and smiled.

A *lot* of guys were headed up with us. Dozens. Their ages spanned late teens to early forties, I guessed, mostly in the former category. There was one walking beside me, a female, who looked like she was about twenty. She had long tresses bunched up in braids and tucked neatly under a hat. She walked with a proud and resolute gait toward the top, seeming not even to be remotely out of breath.

Another one looked like just a boy, maybe no greater than fifteen years old, but that couldn't be. Surely, the military wasn't conscripting juveniles in these missions. I wasn't about to check IDs though. *Let 'em train,* I thought. If they lost a parent to a gorgon, who was I to stand in their way? They were most likely all firmly committed volunteers resolved to do their part.

I looked back and saw our guys as well: Simpson, Vetas, Larson, and a few of the crew from the Abrams squadron that had rescued us last night.

It was a longer hike than I remembered back from the Rotunda, but I think that's just because it was all uphill, and then the stairs to the precipice. The chilly air above was throbbing with the sound of the emitters at the cave's mouth. Thankfully, the tanks were turned off. I didn't even know if we could stand the combined pulses of all those emitters at the cave mouth *and* the ones coming from thirteen tanks. Thankfully, the audio frequency was quite high and were more *felt* than heard, but it was a continuous and subconscious rhythmic audio assault that we had to nonetheless acclimate to. It subtly assailed one's equilibrium more than one's actual sense of hearing.

Being able to walk freely out in the open was still so weird. It would take a while getting used to that.

Foxy and I reached the top of the stairs and donned our masks, hung a left, and assembled at the top on the trail just past a wooden fence. A few of the guys were there already, waiting for us, all masked. We greeted them and introduced ourselves.

Most had heard of our mission to APU and Harvill Hall, and of Rutty. They expressed their condolences. I thanked them. One of them mentioned the church. I shook my head and said, "Yeah, wasn't that something." That's about all I could muster. I was more inclined to dismiss it and get to training. I felt strangely like a celebrity. I think Foxy was eating it up, because they had heard how he saved me. However, most of them wanted to talk to me.

"Heard you got sixty on your own there," someone said.

"I heard it was closer to eighty," said another.

I laughed. "Actually, it was thirty-three, or so I'm told." I looked down, humbly, but apparently my legend preceded me, and no reduction in count seemed to reduce me in their eyes. "Alright, alright, you guys, enough of the hero worship. Fall in line."

They smiled and fell in with the rest of them.

When it was clear that everyone was all here, Foxy gave me a count. Fifty-six, including us. A few of them were nervously looking around through their masks, watching the skies, and shuffling their feet. Despite the arsenal of protection around us, it would appear their faith in their fortress was as fragile as a spider's web. If I were truly honest, I would say mine was still fragile as well. *So,* I thought, *let's all work on our faith together.*

"Alright, ya fuzzy patches," I began, "let's shake off some dust. I'm Lieutenant Cameron Shipley, and this is Private Liam Mayfield, but you can call us Jet and Foxy, if you want. I guess it's our callsigns." I shrugged and looked at Foxy. "Why don't you guys tell me what you know about gorgons. What's the Number One Rule?"

"Never look directly at a gorgon," a few of them said in unison.

"Close your eyes," said another.

"Run, and don't look back," said one more.

"Good, good. That's right. What else do you know about 'em?"

"They're fast."

"Sneak attacks."

"They thin out during the heat of the day."

"They bleed just like everything else," said a young voice. It was the girl I had noticed earlier with the tucked-in tresses.

I smiled grimly. "I like that answer." I moved closer to her. "What's your name, Private?"

"Private Janine Pullman, sir," she spoke up, sticking her chest out, "but most everyone here calls me *Neener*." The corner of her mouth curled upward in pride, and there was some scattered but subdued laughter.

"Why do they call you that, Private?" Foxy piped up.

She turned to him with a playful grin, and there was more there than acknowledgment, because she blinked at him slowly. *Looked like love at first sight to me.*

"*'Ja-neen-er',* she enunciated. "Ya know. *Neener neener?* It's because I get everyone back if they mess with me, sir. So, people don't try to prank me or mess with me. And I'd love to get the gorgons back too. *Neener neener,*" she breathed seductively toward him.

Foxy laughed and said, "You don't call me 'sir.' I'm a private like you, Neener."

She smiled at him and then turned back to me.

"Well, now that you two have met," I noticed that she smiled and blushed at Foxy again, "let's cover a few of the basics.

"Everything you've said is true. And you're right, Private Neener." I couldn't restrain a laugh. Neither could the troops. "They *do* bleed. You could say I reached a bit of a tipping point after the murder of my fellow soldier at the church that you've heard of. I had to steel myself and man up. And that's what you've got to do. That's what we're all going to do here today.

"But, as usual, there's more." Some of them looked at me intently, hands behind them at the small of their backs and looking way too intense and formal. "We've all known for some time that there are two kinds of gorgons. The regular drones, and the berserkers. The berserkers are generally bigger and act like a crack addict. They jerk around a bit, whatever, like a synapse misfire or something's not right in their head. What you probably didn't know is that the berserkers are genetically engineered hybrids, cultivated by the United States government in an effort to destroy the enemy from the inside. An idea, which, as we have since discovered, failed miserably."

Many of them were astonished at this news. One of them raised their hand. "How did they do that, sir?"

"I don't know. I don't think there are many that actually do know. Probably hush-hush. And, well, as Captain Monzon said earlier, last night we discovered something even more terrifying, and that's that we came under attack by a *third* variant of them, never before seen. An even larger and more terrifying breed. We call 'em 'behemoths' because that's what they are. They're big and nasty, and if you take a gander at our tank over there, the one with MS131 on the front, you'll observe how they desperately wanted to be invited to our party inside. One of them nearly smashed its way in. A little one, a regular drone, actually *did* get inside with us."

I watched as many of them strained their necks to get a better view of the top of our tank, dented and misshapen. Eyebrows went up and mouths went wide as some of them began to imagine how they would have reacted had they been in our shoes.

"Yeah. That was a scene, alright. None of us knew anything about them until last night. We were attacked on US 68 just past Aurora before the cavalry came and detonated two DTFs." A hand went up. "Yeah, you," I pointed at him, a youngish male soldier.

"DTF? What's that?" There was some mocking laughter from some of the more seasoned enlistees who evidently regarded the question as rather elementary.

It was elementary, in a way, and my eyebrows went up in surprise. "You don't know what a DTF is?" He shook his head.

But then I remembered that these guys had never been attacked here, which made me both pity and envy them.

"Well, look behind you at all that stuff perched at the mouth of your cave. Those are DTF emitters. DTF stands for *Dissonant Tidal Flood*. It's like an EMP based on audio technology that incorporates the gorgs' own technology, uses it against them, and channels it into super-high-frequency audio waves that they can't stand.

"That throbbing pulse you hear anytime you're up here comes from those mini-DTF emitters. But our tanks have projectiles that shoot a much larger version that radiates outward for miles, dissipating as it goes and leaving one helluva wake for those things to flail around in. I envy you for both not having been attacked here and also that you haven't had to use them, because they're *powerful*. Foxy and I have sat through *four* of them now: one in Clarksville outside the church that some of you appear to have heard of, and three on US 68 last night."

Another raised his hand. "Sir?"

"Go ahead." I just shrugged at all this 'sir' business.

"These behemoth gorgons, as you call them, any idea where they came from?"

I shook my head and sighed, thinking of an answer that might suffice. I genuinely didn't know.

Foxy spoke up. "No, man, we don't know. We were all on a break when we looked east and a huge cloud of gorgs was swooping in. Our gunner launched a DTF, but we didn't shut down in time, so, it saved us, but it also shut *us* down pretty quick," he said, looking at me sadly. Neither of us looked over at Vetas; no sense in further shaming him. "We were running point on sentry, posted up on our tanks, and they actually snuck up on us, silently, crawling along the road."

"*Crawling?*" the young soldier asked incredulously.

"Yeah, man," Foxy said. "Or slithering. Or floating low. Hell, who knows, but it looks like they figured out that our m-decks – those are the motion detectors that we have – put out radar pings wide and high, but not down. They came in *under* the m-deck signal. It's like they figured that out. They're getting smarter, I swear."

At that comment, several of them breathed out low gasps of amazement. Some even turned around as if to study their own emitters and determine if their respective signals were low enough to the ground. Neener was looking at Foxy and she was obviously concerned, biting her lip. Foxy clenched his lips in empathy at her.

I scanned the crowd. "Alright everyone, just relax. We made it out. You will too. Your Blockade has got to be the most reinforced one I've ever seen or heard about. You'll be fine. Now, here's what we need to do, and this is our assignment.

"You guys all have your masks and your weapons. The President informed me, before we left, that there's some special plan being formed to lure the gorgs in, pin them all in a few geographical areas, and then blast the crap out of them with DTFs. Where that will be is anyone's guess, but these gorgons are everywhere. And now we're learning of a new species. So, what that means, unfortunately, is that it's going to most likely come down to ground assault and incursions into known nests to completely weed them out from wherever the remainder of them are lurking. And to do *that*, we need forces that are trained and ready, brave, and equipped. That's why we're here. That's why *you're* here.

"We've been in close proximity to the gorgs, and we've performed daily recon operations for years now, back at DN436 in Clarksville. My brother and I, that is. Foxy here is new, but he's a damn good soldier, and was himself a rescue from Austin Peay University. He turned into one of the finest soldiers you could ask for. And if I can do it, and he can do it, then so can you."

Foxy blushed at my affirmation, especially in front of Private Neener.

"So that's enough of the briefing. I want you to get to know each other. We got fifty-six of us up here. I want you to break up into teams of four each and introduce yourselves. Find out where you come from, your ages, your favorite flavor of guano. Hell, I don't know. Just get to know each other. You won't be a complete unit until you know how to function as a family, because family is all we have left. If you're going out into the badlands in search of gorgs to root out, you're going to need to lean on the man or woman to your right and left and call them family. Is that clear?"

"Sir, yes, sir," they all echoed.

"Alright. See to it. Foxy and I will come around and check on you guys after ten minutes and see how you're doing. Then we'll break for drills. Beat it," I said, and then rolled my eyes in my head, realizing I had inadvertently repeated something Captain Stone always said.

They all broke up, awkwardly looking around themselves and grouping up with the three others nearest each of them. Some of them buddied up due to past service together, such as Simpson and Vetas.

Foxy and I put some distance between us and them in order to chat while they met each other. "Nice work, bro," I encouraged him and put my hand on his shoulder. "You're better at speeches than I thought you were. Especially to interested parties of the female persuasion."

He laughed. "You saw that? Neener's pretty, isn't she? Seems plenty tough too," he said, casting a look back to make sure he knew where she was. I chuckled to see her and Foxy lock eyes for a moment as he searched for her.

I had Ally. Foxy deserved someone nice as well.

"Yes, she is, and yes she does. I'm glad for ya, brother. Think these guys can handle this?"

"Shoot," he sneered. "I'm a refugee who was stuck in a university dorm hall for fifteen years, man. If I can do it, so can they."

"Only fifteen? You weren't there from the outset?"

"Nah. My mom and dad and I were visiting my uncle who had just enrolled and was about to start his first year at APU."

"That's right, you were just a toddler."

He laughed. "I was. I still had a pacifier even. At *three!* I had a picture back at Harvill somewhere." As he spoke, his words were loaded with both memory and grief, and I guessed that he had lost it at one point. His smile faded.

Foxy with a binky. Now that's a picture.

"I never heard your story, brother."

"Hmm, not much to tell," Foxy said. "We were on campus to see my uncle when the gorgs went live, and my mom and dad took me into one of the buildings. We hung out there for a while." He shrugged his shoulders and popped in a stick of gum, chewing furiously as Rutty used to.

"They got my mom first and then my dad six months after that." Foxy stared off into the distance. "I didn't cry much for a baby, but one time, they told me I was bawling. And that's what drew some of them in. Dad told me not to feel guilty about it after they got Mama. I was so little, but I remember him saying that. We just hid, but they got him too, eventually. Then I just got passed around, you know. Adopted out." Foxy's voice shook, and I could see his eyes were welling up. He was looking away from the troops, up over the hillside. He nervously looked at me and then downward. Gulping hard, he said, "I don't wanna talk about this, man."

I felt like a jerk. As with Ally back at Harvill Hall, I just had to pry, didn't I? Their stories were their own, and their stories were laden with grief. I choked up. "I'm sorry, man. I don't know why I do that."

"What?" he said, passing his fist through his eye and sniffing.

I sighed. "Ask. I don't know why I ask."

Foxy shrugged his shoulders again and set his rocket launcher down. "Hey, man, it's all good. You're human.

We're family. You do it for the same reason that you just asked the troops to get to know each other. We're all we have, right? Stories matter."

Foxy chewed his gum hard. He was right: stories do matter. He just wasn't ready to tell his, and I sensed a deep longing for a mother and father he never got a chance to know, and a future he was robbed of. *He was such a little guy when it happened,* I thought.

"I'm gonna go check on the groups," he said. I nodded and watched him trudge off, holding his torpedo shooter proudly and looking everyone else over. Such a short time he'd been in service, but he had turned every bit into a soldier, and I was proud to serve with him. Foxy met my felt yearning for my own brother with grace and healing.

I pulled out the roster that Monzon had given me and looked it over. Various names. Some of them too young to have even been alive when the gorgons came. Some of them almost as old as Rosie. One of them was a Sergeant. I would need to connect with that one.

I started to flip the page, when movement caught my eye. Something down the trail, creeping slowly in and out of the foliage. My head cocked, and my eyes squinted. Too big for a rabbit or a squirrel – if there were indeed any left. I swung my rifle around and stared off down the winding path, advancing. "Foxy," I called over my shoulder. "Contact!"

I couldn't see or hear Foxy respond, and I didn't want to lose the target by looking back at him. If it was a deer, we needed it badly. Even a lone rabbit would provide some good food for a few of the troops if we could catch it and skin it.

I advanced down the trail and noticed a shadow dart behind a thick tree up ahead to my right. I thought I smelled a brief whiff of cigarette smoke, which confused me.

Suddenly, I was upon it. It was behind that tree up ahead on the right, whatever it was. I could hear and feel Foxy behind me. The troops, all holding their breath, fell silent behind us as we approached.

That's when I heard the recognizable *snick-chick* of a few guns cocking behind me, stopping me in my tracks. A youngish voice said, "Hold it right there, Lieutenant. Private, you too. Drop your weapons and turn around slowly please."

Foxy and I froze, totally confused. My brows furrowed. "What the hell is this?" I muttered. We complied and dropped our weapons and turned around with hands raised. It was the fifteen-year-old boy, with his gun trained on me, and Janine, with her gun trained on Foxy. I narrowed my eyes in disbelief at them.

"What are you guys doing? What's the meaning of all this?" They kept their guns firmly fixed on me. Behind them, the rest of the troops stood completely still. I searched for Vetas and Simpson. There they were. But they were being restrained by other soldiers, held in place with guns to their own necks.

I shook my head. What was going on here? We had just met these troops. Had they all gone mad?

Foxy and I kept our hands up, staring at them with faces clenched in confusion.

Twigs cracked behind me. I could hear footsteps.

Keeping my hands raised, I slowly turned back around to face whatever it was. Foxy did the same.

There he was, stepping out from behind the tree and turning toward us. A man, about mid-fifties, shaven head, with a thick black beard adorning the lower forty of his face. His mask was pulled up over his dome and resting on his bald head. He was dressed in fatigues and carried no weapon except a sidearm holstered on his hip, but in his right hand he took a long drag of his cigarette before his arm fell back down. He exhaled a strong, steady plume as thick and vaporous as gorgon mist.

That's when he looked at us: squarely and grimly, undaunted. I already knew who it was.

He stood before us proudly, with his troops sandwiching us on the other side and holding us at bay.

My mouth was agape, and my eyebrows fell in disbelief. Here before us was none other than the target our own Blockade had said was AWOL.

I looked at him, and he looked at me.

It was the derelict, Captain Vance Cardona.

11 | CARDONA

There he was: filthy and sweating, but I knew it was him. I was incredulous.

"Captain Vance Brennan Cardona, if I'm not mistaken," I said with my hands behind my head, and not without contempt. "AWOL, in dereliction of duty, and yet," I waved a palm at him up and down, "here you are. Mind telling us just what the *hell* is going on?"

Cardona said nothing. Just took another drag of his smoke and blew it our way.

I briefly tried to calculate how quickly I could draw my Beretta and gun him down in obedience to Stone's orders, but I'd surely be mowed down in the process.

"Down on the ground!" Private Pullman ordered.

I heaved a sigh and bowed my knee. Maybe that's what they all did once. Maybe that's what he wanted. I could feel the boy's gun trained on me as I stood there and weighed my only options.

"For every twelve, there's a Judas, right?" I asked him, sighing. The edge of his mouth curled up in a knowing smile, and he clicked his tongue twice.

He took a few steps toward Foxy and me. "You think I'm a traitor? That I should be named Judas because I *allegedly* abandoned my post?" he asked me grimly. "Hardly complimentary, soldier."

Why did he emphasize 'allegedly'?

"Well, that's what I would have thought before your beloved privates here demonstrated the utmost hospitality and trained their weapons at us," I said smugly. I was truly confused, but I must admit I was more amazed at the specter of him walking around so freely when all I had heard up until now was that he was officially AWOL.

Foxy slowly turned back around to Janine. "Yeah, Neener, what are you-"

"Shut it, Foxy!" she ordered, turning him back around as she jerked her sidearm toward him.

"Okay, okay," he stammered.

There was a moment of silence while we all acknowledged the gravity of the moment. If Cardona hadn't really gone AWOL, why did Stone say he did? And if he *had* gone AWOL, why were none of his troops surprised, and why were they now holding us at bay, seemingly at his command? And if none of the above were true, what fresh hell had we stumbled into?

I stared at Cardona, and he stared right back at me. If I didn't know any better, he was assessing me. Sizing me up. Same with Foxy. He took a final drag on his smoke and then dropped it between his legs and crushed the butt of it into the forest floor.

Cardona looked back up at Private Pullman. "Easy, Neener," he said. "Put your weapon down. You too, Jenkins."

They slowly complied. "Sir."

He approached me and looked me over slowly. Though he was over twice my age, there was a force wrapped around him that I wasn't sure I could contend with. Grizzled through long testing, basted in pure raw animal instinct and marinated in proven survival.

"Good thing you weren't wearing your headset, Lieutenant Shipley." He had a thick New York accent, and I could smell his heavy smoke breath. "Or this may have turned out much differently. You too, Private Mayfield. Can't have such communications on an open channel with Command."

I tilted my head at him. "What does that mean?"

A thin wisp of a smile appeared at the edge of his lips. "I can imagine how perplexed you must be. Come. Both of you. Let's go inside and have a nice chat, shall we? I think we all feel safer under the gun towers."

Foxy looked around in confusion. "Wh-what about the troops, and the training?"

Cardona looked over at him with a cocky bob of his head. "Oh, Private Foxy," he breathed. "I can assure you my troops have had all the training they'll ever need."

•   •   •   •   •

I didn't get it. *No one* was surprised to see him. We passed several soldiers on our way down. *Every single one of them* saluted Cardona. The first time it happened I looked at Foxy with my mouth wide open. What the hell? It's like he hadn't been gone a day, and no one was surprised at his return. Then again, he was slithering among the crowd of soldiers in the dark last night. Perhaps, he had returned from his dereliction before we had even arrived and had made amends. Perhaps all was forgiven by his Blockade, and now he would co-captain with Monzon.

And just then, the truth socked me right in the face. I actually let out a light laugh of understanding as we rounded the corner at the top of the cave mouth and began to descend the stairs back inside. *Of course!* No one was surprised to see him because everyone *had* seen him.

This guy hadn't gone AWOL at all. There could be only one truth, and that had to be it.

"That was you I saw last night, wasn't it? In the crowd. Staring at me from under your hood."

Cardona said nothing, just smiled.

"I suppose I can also thank you for the nice leaflet you left under my pillow last night?"

Again, silence. He was smug, but it wasn't a patronizing smugness or a cocky arrogance such as I had suspected of Bassett early on. No. His was more of a confident magician who had just performed one of his greatest tricks and wanted you to know how it was done by leaning into you and waiting for you to receive revelation.

"Boy, do I have questions right now. *So* many questions, Captain," I said, shaking my head.

He smiled at me. "And believe me, you shall have answers to them. I promise you. The first thing to know, of course, is that there is only one version of the truth, and sometimes wolves masquerade in sheep clothes."

I looked over at Foxy and frowned. He looked back at Neener, who still smiled at him, but it was more of a reinforced smile of one who had just had a jolt of renewed confidence coursing through their veins.

Whatever they weren't telling us, here we were again, kept in the dark about something. I gritted my teeth in frustration. I didn't like this withholding of the truth, and I wasn't about to stand for it again. My chest seemed to heave a giant exhale entirely of its own accord, as I looked down into the dark of the cave mouth.

Our gang was going to flip when they saw this. I wondered what Monzon would think. I wondered what Ally would think.

I wondered what Stone and the President would think.

·   ·   ·   ·   ·

"Brother Cardona!" shouted a voice up ahead. There were bright lights shining toward us from some equipment in operation at the Rotunda, but I couldn't see clearly who it was. However, it wasn't difficult to discern that Mexican accent. Out of the light strode the short, stocky figure of Captain Monzon as if he was ready to hug an old friend.

Without acknowledging me or Foxy, he went right up to Cardona and gave him a high shake as they pulled their chests into one another and gave each other a hearty pat on the back before they separated. "Hoorah," growled Monzon as he took him by the shoulders, and Cardona echoed it right back. "You been okay? Mission success?"

"Mission success," Cardona answered with a smile.

Foxy was watching this scene unfold with the utmost of disbelief. "Alright, would someone tell me just what the hell this is all about?" he yelled, and it made some of them around us jump. His eyes were wide.

The two Captains turned to him nonchalantly.

"At ease, Private Mayfield," Monzon said. "We can and will explain. Come with us please. Your colleagues are already waiting for us at Giant Coffin."

It was a lengthy and silent stroll, except for the occasional mumbled ramblings I could hear Foxy chanting beside me. Ramblings of *you gotta be kidding me*, and *we come all this way for nothin,'* and *what the hell is going on?* and *AWOL my ass*. That last one had me stifling a laugh. I was surprised and confused as well, but never in the same way as I felt on our last mission up to APU. Something just didn't smack of sinister in all of this, and I couldn't quite put my finger on it. However, I suspected that around that last corner up ahead, it would be like cold water splashed on our faces, and then we would suddenly feel the bite of knowledge and wake up.

At least, that's what I hoped for.

We made it to Giant's Coffin, walking behind Cardona and Monzon, who had been talking easily a few paces ahead. We were still weaponless, and Private Neener and Jenkins were walking behind us. The rest of the fifty-six had dispersed or resumed their posts at the Rotunda, except for Vetas, Simpson, and Larson; they were coming behind us.

Ally and Joe were there, standing by the giant coffin slab, and she walked up to me with a big grin. "Hey, hon," she said, curiously optimistically, with a shade of surprised joy. "Make sure you're ready to sit down for this one."

Confused, I looked at her, and then at Joe, who was shaking his head with a giant smile plastered from ear to ear. Walker had been there talking with them, and then he left.

I wondered where Armstrong was in all of this.

No one here was surprised by this development. But Armstrong had appeared disapproving of Cardona, and I was eager to hear his take. I truly believed that he was not in the know, but it sure seemed like everyone else was. This whole AWOL account no longer had legs to stand on, and that meant that Stone – and probably the President – had once again lied to me.

A group of picnic tables from the mess had been pushed and clustered together, and we were all invited to sit down. I sat next to Ally, Joe and Foxy were across from us, and Vetas, Larson, and Simpson sat at an adjoining table.

Cardona and Monzon were up front talking quietly, and Cardona had shared some kind of joke. Monzon laughed heartily and nearly doubled over. I turned to Ally and said, "Would you believe this? That's our AWOL Captain, as if it never happened."

Ally smiled at me. "Just wait," she said with a wink.

Monzon composed himself and cleared his throat. "Alright, troops. Welcome to Part B of the intro speech. I'm truly sorry we had to proceed out of an abundance of caution, but Mammoth Cave Command here needed to ensure where your hearts were."

I watched them curiously. He had said something about the faithfulness of the troops earlier on. I wondered if that's what he meant here.

"Lieutenants Shipley and Trudy, Private Mayfield, Staff Sergeant Bassett, and Privates Simpson, Larson and Vetas, I'd like to introduce you to your," -here he made overdramatic air quotes- "*AWOL* Captain, Vance Cardona." Monzon then stepped aside and watched with a grin as Cardona took his place front and center for us.

Cardona was a big, thick man, with that shiny chrome dome and close-set eyes under a Cro-Magnon brow that you wouldn't want to receive a headbutt from, and he had the shave nicks to thicken some aggression to boot.

His lower jaw was covered in black moss: a thick beard that made him look like a pirate, or some kind of renegade at least. He kept his thumbs in his pockets as he spoke, except to occasionally gesticulate for added effect. All the while, those beady eyes poked out at us, above half-moons of eyelids that seemed to regard the truths he needed to express with pity and sympathy for those who had, up until now, believed otherwise. He was in the know on something big, and it was his turn to share it.

"Folks, I'm here today to tell you that you have been reduced to pawns in the biggest chess match this planet has ever seen," he began.

That I had pretty much already suspected, but I was more than eager to hear what he meant by it.

"I'm going to direct most of what I say here to you, Lieutenant Shipley, because I know you've spoken directly with the President. Staff Sergeant Bassett, I know you've talked a bit with Captain Stone at DN436 as well, so some of this might ring true for you too. The bottom line is that you've been lied to, albeit clever lies that have taken on the guise of truth.

"You were told, Lieutenant Shipley, that the President has construction crews working on undisclosed locations for massive counterstrikes against the gorgons. This is a lie. You thought those behemoth gorgons were never seen before. Not true. You were told that nukes were off the table. Another lie. You were told that the military has been given plans to destroy the gorgons with DTFs that will knock them out permanently. This was only half true.

"We have known of the existence of the behemoth gorgons for some time. We know the locations that have been planned for the counterstrike. We know that it's not just with DTFs that they're planning on sending these things packing."

"And how do you know all that, sir?" I asked rather skeptically.

"Because I served with her, Lieutenant. Up until three years ago. Then I," he smirked, "apparently started asking too many questions. Found myself reassigned here."

He looked us all over. "I know you've had your doubts. I know about your distrust with what's been going on. I know about the operation that killed your brother. I know about your little roadside chat after the attack on the highway last night."

Monzon. He was nearby. He must have been listening in and told him of our skepticism. That was probably confirmation enough for both of them of our potential allegiance, but they had to be sure.

"Before we could let you in, we needed to test the waters, so you'll pardon us for not being more forthcoming. We're the only Blockade who knows the truth, and we intend to keep it that way. Not even your precious Stone, who is apparently in Graham's pocket, knows the real agenda.

"That's why we had to preserve my AWOL status up top, Shipley. Your Command and the President cannot know that I'm back here, nor can they know what we're about to do."

"And what's that?" I asked curiously.

"Fight back. We're going to stop the President and her advisors from doing something absolutely horrible and absolutely irreversible. Her reassigning me here, and not just flat out having me killed, may well prove to be her undoing.

"Now. Let me take you all on a little stroll down memory lane, if you'll indulge me. Then, everything should be clearer. Thomas Jefferson once said, 'On matters of style, swim with the current, on matters of principle, stand like a rock.' All of us here are standing like that rock, and we're not getting down until it's safe to swim again."

•   •   •   •   •

We settled in. Cardona had taken a long pause for thought.

"It was the spring of 2026. I was thirty-nine, and a well-regarded advisor to the Secretary of Defense for international affairs. I had been so after having been promoted up through the ranks for my early work in the Air Force, and then switched to a Seal Team and covert ops in Afghanistan after the Taliban came back to power. Injured my back in an op and had to settle for desk jockey.

"I had been on staff with the SecDef for six months when the invasion happened. We watched and waited for those three months while the gorgs just hovered there, wondering, like the rest of the planet, what they were and what they would do. We used drones, and got up close to several of them, trying to ascertain something – *anything* – as to why they were here.

"Then, as we all know, they activated, on September 3rd, 2026. Every one of us scrambled, which is pretty much what everyone *everywhere* did. Thankfully, we were aboard Air Force One at the time with the previous President, members of his cabinet, and the Secretary. We landed in Nashville due to reports that the gorgons were paralyzing pilots and dropping planes out of the sky. We didn't know what the hell to do. No one did. *Paralyzing? How?"* He held up his arms in helplessness. "None of us knew what the hell was going on or what the initial reports meant.

"We had been watching what was happening on the ground, and if I remember correctly, we were cruising at fifteen-thousand feet, low enough to see explosions down below...throngs of them attacking our people...chaos. We were ordered down by our F-35 patrol. We'd had them cover us since the aliens arrived, out of an abundance of caution. Thankfully, they were there. They deployed chaff, they enacted countermeasures, but they just weren't enough. We had to dive, and we had to land, and land hard. Once grounded, we had to remain in the plane as we saw the chaos unfold around us. Some of them came at the plane and attacked the windows, trying to look in, but it didn't look like their vision was all that good. They took down our F-35 Lightning and F-22 Raptor patrols, and those poor pilots crashed.

"Well, thankfully Air Force One has a pretty reinforced hull, as you may guess. The plane has been in Nashville ever since, on the northwest runway, toward the outskirts of the NIA airport. We watched with binoculars through the windows as they terrorized Americans there. Everyone inside Air Force One was on their phones, on the tube, on the radio, listening to reports coming in from all over the globe.

New York. Los Angeles. Singapore. Riyadh. Pretoria. Kyiv. Pyongyang. Seoul. Cairo. Hong Kong. Luanda. Mogadishu. Rome. All of 'em...under attack.

When they were done there, they fanned out across the land. That's why it didn't take long for them to reach Clarksville, Shipley. Or Alpharetta, Sergeant Bassett. Hell, you can take one good look at our planet at night and see where all the bright lights are coming from and decide easily where to strike. And strike they did, all over the globe. There was nothing we could do.

"We couldn't stay in Air Force One forever, and it looked like they had moved on. The hull is reinforced, but we had no more air cover. The damned things were faster than our jets.

"Secret Service had radioed ahead to our Nashville branch, and they had Suburbans coming up Highway 40. They were prepared to crash through the fence. They just had to run for it." He laughed grimly. "No one really knew yet how sensitive the gorgs were to sound. So, foolishly, an entourage of Secret Service escorted the President in a thicket of automatic weapons, *at Graham's behest*," he enunciated. "'Get the President to safety first,' she said. And they ran, shielding him with cover fire. All that gunfire only drew the rest of them in like a dinner bell." He paused, looking us all over. "I think you all know what happened next.

"Well, Graham was sworn in momentarily thereafter, with the President's corpse lying thirty feet outside the plane. Thank God we were able to get the door closed fast enough. But she effectively had a sitting president assassinated, and then feigned horror at his demise. We all saw it. We just didn't see it for what it truly was at the time."

I had never heard this account, but now it was clear how exactly Graham had come into the Presidency. That information still didn't bring us any closer to what was going on now. Cardona had a long way to go still.

"We informed our allies that Graham was now the POTUS, and briefed other militaries on what we knew. We all stayed in that plane for three more months, too terrified to leave. It stunk in there, and supplies ran low. We'd had communications with some pilots who managed to take shelter in the airport and some that were stuck on the ground in their own planes with their own passengers. Our pilots were still flight-ready. We hadn't lost them.

"Every one of us had seen what the gorgons did to the President and the Secret Service, so we blocked off the windows, sealed off the cockpit, and just waited. Over that time, we observed that the gorgon population tended to thin out during the day, which we all know now to be standard. They don't like the heat, and it was still fairly hot for mid to late September. And we could clearly tell they were attracted to noise.

"There were different reports from all over the globe. Some said they had different abilities. Some said animals were immune to them. There were even reports that blind folks were immune. That stood to reason, we figured, because the blind can't actually *look* at them. But the blind also couldn't see where they were going to make a run for it, or even how they were going to fight back. So much conjecturing early on," he said and then lowered and shook his head.

I thought back to Rutty keeping his eyes shut and shadowboxing against that thing in the library. I winced, cleared my head, and tried to listen.

"The President had a decision to make, and she would need our help. Graham proposed two choices: either we all run for it in opposite directions and let the chips fall where they may, or," he paused, "someone takes the hit so the President can get away. *America needs a President,* she said. And she was right. We did need someone in charge, and we couldn't afford to lose two in only a few months. There would be no hope. America could not afford to be leaderless.

"So, Graham proposed a solution. Five planes would simultaneously take off and lure the gorgon population away so that we could escape. The only planes left and ready to fly were those filled with Captains and their passengers. They had been waiting on their own tarmacs for those three months as well, trapped in their planes out of the same fear that gripped ours. They were closer to the airport terminals."

"Oh, man," I breathed. I knew where this was going. "Those were the planes we saw outside Bowling Green, weren't they? The planes were all there, filled with corpses inside. Tell me that was them."

Cardona locked eyes with me and nodded grimly. "They were given direct orders by the President of the United States of America to take off. She was patched in to Air Traffic Control herself through our pilots, talking to all five of theirs. But not only that: she told them that the skies were clear, and that daytime would be best, since the gorgs tend to thin out then. So, believing our President to be charitable, maternal, honest, and the leader we so desperately needed, they complied.

"You should have seen her on the call with them. So convincing. So cheery. So drippingly saccharin-sweet. The consummate preacher. It was *all's fair in the sky, you're free to fly*," he mocked.

"Oh, we all dissented to her plan. *All* of us in Air Force One dissented. That would be a death sentence for all of those planes, and all of those souls, and we knew it. She even allowed a vote after attempting to further convince them. Some folded. Eventually it was 32 nay, 16 yea. But she held veto power, and she overruled all of us.

"There was screaming in our cabin, until those remaining Secret Service loyal to her pointed their weapons at the dissenters and quieted them down. No matter how you sliced it, everyone in *there* wanted to live. It was an impossible choice. In order for us to get away, this *had* to be done. It was *sick*.

"A few of us threw up right after her phone calls, as well as up until the very moment those poor planes launched, and we waited, watched and prayed for their deliverance as we listened in.

"We watched them all launch, one by one. It was December 7th. Last week marked sixteen years since five planes climbed into the sky on the orders of the President, and we made ready to escape across I-40 into the Embassy Suites north of the airport, for more space, accommodations, food, and communications. That would become, for all intents and purposes, our new White House."

Cardona sighed heavily and cleared his throat. "It's something I will forever regret. We said a prayer for those planes. We watched and waited, most of us uttering a silent 'please' to God to allow at least one of them to escape. It didn't take long. The gorgs zipped by overhead and then thinned out over us, zeroing in on those jetliners. And," he paused, "we ran, and we ran, as through tears we watched every last one of them plummet from the sky far beyond us along the horizon. I don't know how we did it, but the rest of us made it, and we threw ourselves into that hotel, and there we stayed. But the planes…well…as you know, they're mostly now sitting outside Bowling Green on Highway 68. One of them banked hard left and was downed over Clarksville, just shy of the Cumberland. I've seen it with my own eyes, as I'm sure you have."

I *had* seen that plane before! That was the burnt-up chassis embedded into the soft banks that we saw on our way into C-Range with Rutty, Ally, and Joe.

"All those people…" he ended in pensive reflection and a shake of his head. "There was nothing we could do except run. And we made it, and that hotel became the new executive mansion.

"Every last one of us, over the next few weeks, wrestled with grief and anger at the President *and* ourselves for not being strong enough to dissuade her. We couldn't look at one another, much less her. But at least we were alive. And being alive in the face of annihilation has a way of persuading you to accept every last compromise that you make as merely another instrument of survival. You begin to pat yourself on the back for making it another day, though that day had someone's blood on its hands." He shook his head.

Cardona's lingering grief was powerful, and he had my pity. I could do nothing here but think of Amos and that church once more. What Cardona just described is exactly what Amos had done.

"Well, eventually, her silver tongue and faux compassion assured us there was nothing else we could have done, and we relented. She rallied us and coaxed us back into some shattered semblance of unity. Though the very notion of acceptance was detestable, we grieved, made our peace with it, and decided to move on, choosing to channel our anger at the gorgons instead of Graham. We were Americans. We were going to survive.

"So, over the years, we planned, and we deliberated, and we commiserated. And as you can guess, we assisted with the construction of the Blockades, maintaining communication with whatever leaders we could, nationally and internationally. Most of them had perished of course. We got a new satellite network up and running out of what we all decided to call The Green House, mostly because of the Embassy Suites logo, but also because we wanted to preserve the Earth and win her back. We communicated and ran everything from there. How we weren't attacked and destroyed there as well, I don't know. But I do have my suspicions that Graham made it so that the gorgs were provided, shall we say, 'tempting distractions,' in order to divert attention away from her location.

"Anyway, we began the long, slow fight to reclaim. We found out about the amulets and discovered them all over the Earth, apparently discarded by the gorgs after they got here. Maybe they didn't anticipate any resistance. Maybe they were just careless. Who knows. But we started researching what they were and what they could do. One of our own guys, an intern at the Department of Energy was with us, and *thank God* he survived. It was he who discovered their power, and realized they could be channeled. We began to deploy them on a small scale for concentrated locations. None of us had any clue at the time just how revolutionary and indispensable they would prove to be.

"In the meantime, we had to contend with illness, disease, lack of supplies, cities being overrun, power outages, and natural disasters as well. It became too much, and there was complaining and dissension in the ranks. We all had cabin fever. It wasn't unexpected. You just can't provide for everybody left if there's not enough humans and provisions to get it to them.

"Graham began to close off, to over-delegate, because she wanted no part of the actual hands-on rank-and-file work in the trenches. She stayed holed up in that embassy and never left. She gathered counselors around her that she could trust, fending off the constant requests for aid or supplies and farming them out to other people, whether they volunteered or even had any experience. She sent men out on recon missions from our hotel, just as you all do. Many of them didn't even have weapons. We were still learning about the gorgs. A lot of them never came back. Her own son was an intern with us on that plane, and she made the mistake of sending him as well. We never found his body. He was only twenty-five.

"Well, that *broke* Graham – the death of her only son – and she became harder and harder to gain access to. Believe me, I tried. And then the SecDef got sick and developed cancer. There weren't any viable doctors around. We lost him a few years later. Graham appeared unremorseful. That hurt. The SecDef was a good man." Cardona cocked his jaw to the side in disapproval and then quickly gathered his breath once more.

"Time passed. I was ultimately promoted to a sort of SecDef *pro tem* position in 2030. I was in on the meetings that she began to hold, sometimes in secret, during all the construction of the Blockades and networking throughout the years. We felt like we were slowly regaining ground.

"One of her military guys came up with the berserker initiative, to target them with guns that had a sort of meth ammo. She heartily approved it and signed off on it. We had been trying everything, but nothing was working, and we were hungry for innovative new ideas. She thought that might just make them crazy enough to attack their own and kill them from the inside. A *Trojan Gorgon*, if you will. Create savages. That sort of thing.

"Anyway, we set a trap over by the airport and lured them in with wild hogs we had caught and sedated. They made such a racket when they awoke. Well, the gorgs did what they do. They heard it, they swooped in, and we unleashed a volley of sniper fire: darts loaded with meth, anabolic steroids, isotretinoin, interferon-a, and more. You should have seen it. Got every damned one of them.

"But," he paused, "in retrospect, I wish we had missed, because the evil things that came out of that trap didn't do what we thought they would; we just made them meaner to all of *us*. They became psychotic. It is yet another thing that I will never be able to undo. And for that, Lieutenant Shipley, I owe you my deepest apologies and beg your forgiveness."

I swallowed hard, but I nodded. *Rutty was killed by a monster that Cardona helped create.* But another thought arose in me. *He was a pawn too, but the President had green-lit it. Remember the real threat.* I had to battle between the two opposing voices while he continued.

"So, then we had to contend with berserkers as well. They didn't do the job, and we couldn't fight the gorgs without any special technology. The masks came way later. With the passage of time, the President's science team suggested they try again, only this time by creating an abomination. An even more dreadful creature. Take berserkers and engineer them with DNA from some of the world's worst animals.

"There were laboratories nearby that had such biological preserves in cryogenic freeze. Honey badgers. Gorillas. Pitbulls. I don't know what the hell they concocted in that lab, but they had special snipers shoot those darts at the berserkers at long range so as not to arouse the wrath of the local gorg population, and those berserkers got a *lot* bigger and a *lot* meaner. *Rabid.* And super strong. A side effect of the gorilla and pit bull DNA, I suppose." He hung his head low and blew out of his nose.

"I just wish my voice of dissent had been louder all that time. I think everyone figured that they would be so uncontrollable that they would just destroy any gorgs around them, and, well, we had gotten so good at hiding. And there were only eleven of them, if memory serves, so if all else failed, we could take out those last eleven when it appeared that the rest of the general gorg population had been killed off." He heaved a massive sigh and shook his head again. "Wrong yet again. Now we have to clean up that mess too."

"Anyway, with all of those cumulative failures, Graham was losing it. She still is, though she pulls off 'normal' like you wouldn't believe. Like they say, 'You can put lipstick on a pig, but it's still a pig.'

"Inside, she was flying off the rails, like some of those trains out there. Some of the propositions she made were not met well by the international community, and she began to feel ostracized. Polarized. North Korea, Iran, and China all had leaders filling the bellies of the gorgons, but she had literally just started to make inroads with China in May of '27, so she had an alliance there that was improving. Then a gorg got him. And she did *not* like his successor. He ate her up, chewed her down, and spit her out like a gorgon. So did Iran. And North Korea, well, same old story: they just simply wouldn't ever play ball with us.

"She closed ranks even more and formed her own Illuminati. She actually called them that! The Canadian and UK Prime Ministers. Australia. Germany. Israel, although they were still recovering from the Gaza war of '23-'24. That war really ripped them apart from the inside, but they collected themselves and joined. And Mexico too. It was a consortium of seven, and Graham called that a holy number. I was no longer part of those meetings, but the Embassy Suite wasn't secure, and I had been charged with Hotel Security as part of my pro tem SecDef duties. So I snooped. And I snooped.

"And one day, I heard them. In conference with each other, on a video call. It was September 3rd, 2037. The eleventh anniversary of the attacks. Graham had been closed off more than usual and stayed in her suite all day. She said she was not to be disturbed. I went down to my office and listened in. Unbeknownst to her, I had installed a wire. Audio only, but it was at least something. She had her Illuminati on call with her, and she had a proposal, one that she said they should desperately consider.

"*For too long,* she said, *we've dealt with enemies on multiple fronts. Centuries. Millenia even. We will never be able to purge this threat from our planet unless we are absolutely unified. But unity does not always come from diplomatic negotiation and petitioning; sometimes it must come by stronger means and through the systematic and uncompromising eradication of persistent obstacles.*

"*Obstacles.* I'll never forget that word, nor the rest of her speech, as long as I live. Made my skin crawl. She was about to offer up something terrible. She continued. *So, I propose the following: in secret, we create three large zones with lures so irresistible to gorgons that they will have no choice but to converge there, and then we take them out. All of them*, she said. I listened closely.

"The three zones were the Azadi Lake in Tehran, Iran, the Kyŏllyong-jŏsuji lake in Pyongyang, North Korea, and the Kunming Lake in Beijing."

My mouth dropped, and a tremor ran through me. Every hair on my arms and neck stood up. "Iran. North Korea. China. Her enemies. She's going to lure the gorgons there and then nuke the whole area."

Cardona nodded soberly. "Why kill the gorgons when you can take out not only them, but your enemies as well, and start the planet off fresh? *This is my proposed final solution*, she said to them. *An end to this menace, and my strongest proposal in order to give the Earth a fighting chance. We will kill two birds with one stone, as it were, ridding ourselves of multiple menaces, and restore the sanctity of Planet Earth anew. United.*

"Her precious Illuminati nodded emphatically to those same words that have been spoken before by the likes of Adolf Hitler.

"These three regimes have long been thorns in the side of policymakers and diplomats. She wants to cling to power, and this is just the panacea she needs to do that. If you can do that, and rid yourselves of a few naysayers, well, you'll eliminate dissent and be in power forever. You'll be a dictator, sure; but everyone will know not to mess with you, and your country will be secure in the knowledge that it's the undisputed leader of the free world - forever.

"And, folks, it's already in motion. Her consortium of seven all voted *yea*. It was unanimous. They've been developing this for the past five years, and they've bought off local officials to look the other way while their slow-moving freight gets in there. They've got a lot of DTF emitters set up already in two of the locations, most of them, encircling the lakes.

"We know the gorgs are drawn to water, so those are obvious lures. But there's no real local security to stop them because they've got dirty politicians in their own pockets, and most of the local population is gone anyway. There's no one to sentry against her. She's made deals with up-and-coming heavyweights who are ready to take over the country in the absence of the leaders she doesn't like. It's sinister and unthinkable, folks. With the local populace gone and in hiding, hardly anyone sees what's going on."

"You said *hardly* anyone," Foxy questioned.

Cardona looked at him solemnly. "Anyone who does see, you must understand, cannot be allowed to disseminate that knowledge. So, they're caught between a cruel fate. Look the other way from the gorgons, or look the other way from your own human race. Either way, you're cooked."

"Shit," Foxy muttered and shook his head.

"It's collateral damage on a global scale. Take out the gorgons and your enemies in one fell swoop. Problems – *plural* – solved." He shifted his feet and looked uneasily at Monzon, who had been silent the whole time, listening intently. "Well, I couldn't let slip that I had heard her proposal or their agreement to it. I was horrified. I started asking questions, quietly, secretly, of those who I thought I could trust. Shrouded questions that didn't give away what I knew. Probing questions.

"But I made the mistake of thinking the new VP was still honest, and I couldn't find anyone not completely allegiant to Graham. He was incredulous and told me I better stow my suspicions post-haste. I could tell right away he wasn't safe. Then, he caught me poking around for answers and any intel I could gather on when or where they would carry out their plans, and he had me reassigned here. That was three years ago now.

"Since that time I've done everything I could to establish an underground network, traveling far and wide, connecting with former associates, finding out who's still alive and sympathetic to our cause. And believe me, folks, there are many. *Many* who support us and are ready to take her down. If for no other reason than the fact that she's long overstayed her welcome, and here we are, still, with gorgs steering our planet and Earth being drained dry. The military brass knows. And they know Graham hasn't lifted a finger to stop it; she's just padded her own pockets and placed insulation around herself: everything a dictator does to stay in power. There is a growing resistance ready to take her down, and things are now underway to that end.

"Well," he said as he slowly stretched, and then sat. "That's my story. That's where we're at, and we're all in for one helluva ride. Your Commander and the President knows how allegiant my Blockade is to me. Because I knew all of this, friends, you were most likely sent here to assassinate me. That's the cold, hard truth."

The real threat is before you. Rosie was right. The President was the real threat. She was willing to do whatever it took to hold onto power, and she was guilty of inconceivable atrocities committed thus far in that pursuit.

"That was one of our directives," I confirmed.

I looked around. Everyone was letting it all sink in. There was no way this could stand. You don't just nuke your enemies because they disagree with you. Sure, the gorgons had killed off eighty percent of us, and natural calamity had taken another five, but there were still survivors out there, pockets of survivors, such as those at Harvill Hall, who needed to be protected, integrated, and rebuilt into family.

Humanity was *barely* starting over, teetering on the brink of extinction since the gorgon attack. To detonate nukes in those cities would cause massive fallout for years to come, rendering them inhospitable graveyards for over a century, much more than they already were.

I had read a little on the potency of nuclear weapons. The yield today from a nine-megaton warhead, composed of up to nine million tons of TNT, could be up to *six hundred times* as powerful as Hiroshima. The effects would be far-reaching and devastating. Three of them would *level* those countries and bring about a nuclear winter. I thought it pure cowardice that Graham wouldn't provoke Russia. She knew their counterattack would wipe us out as well, if indeed anyone in the Kremlin was still alive and had the nerve to launch against us. *Coward.*

My heart was racing at this news. I looked over at Monzon. Joe must have been reading my thoughts because he piped up. "What's your read on all this, Captain Monzon? When did you join the resistance?"

Monzon laughed subtly through his nose. "Resistance is the right word. Graham doesn't know her own troops. She doesn't get down that low, and she's too preoccupied with seeing this through. I doubt she even remembers me. Rawley and I were stationed out of Fort Campbell and came up to your blockade on a sub, up the Cumberland from Nashville. She was on it, but as usual, locked in her quarters. The acting Captain didn't really have any interaction with her.

"But word has been spreading, and cracks were forming in her foundation. Some people split off, and those that did, it's because of rumors of what Cardona here started. Then, they saw requisition orders for military shipments to those three places, as well as personnel being shipped off in secret there. It doesn't take a genius to put two and two together. Word is spreading, and there are rumors of entire bases defecting. She's watching everything like a hawk…but a hawk *consumed* by paranoia and unable to fly."

Monzon looked back over at Cardona. "And there has been surprising but small consent in some circles, as well. Some have even posited that this 'panacea,' as you called it, Captain Vance, could actually rid us of the gorgons. And if it took out our political enemies, well, it would be a small price to pay, they figured. Well, it just might, but none of us could live with the collateral damage and the ensuing fallout, because those things would create our own mutants, lasting decades to come. We'd never emerge from the fog.

"Our planet is already decimated nearly beyond repair. There must be a better solution, and we're trying to find it. This *scorched earth* policy of theirs must not be allowed to succeed," he concluded.

In the echo of that cave, all of us sitting there, we knew that we were the last Blockade on a frontier of war, and something ugly was coming. Something vast and dramatic, and we had to form plans on how to fight back.

Standing there, I regarded Cardona and allowed what he said to sink in. I regretted calling him 'Judas' a few hours ago. Far from it. He seemed now to be so much more of a messianic figure to these people, and rightly so.

If he hadn't spread the word, Mammoth Cave would be a very different place right now, and its personnel would be blindly following orders to the detriment of several million innocent lives. I wondered what kind of messages they had to bring down here to inform all these people and shine the light of the truth into their eyes.

All of them had banded together on common purpose, united in the belief that humanity was worth saving, and you don't flush the baby down with the bathwater.

Of all the moves that Graham was making, the ones she was planning to make – that *all* of those seven world leaders were now planning to make – were absolutely and wholly unconscionable.

I sat there in thought, and my mind went back to Amos at Madison Street United Methodist Church. What *he* did was unconscionable. But there was a difference.

Amos killed to survive. Graham would kill to eliminate. Amos killed here and there because he had to. Graham would kill thousands because she wanted to.

Neither was thinking straight, and both had suffered from some measure of cabin fever and insanity. The pressure of choices. But they made their beds and slept in them. On some strange level, I couldn't help but feel sorry for Amos now, killing stray wanderers just to have protein to survive.

That's what he had said as he slid down that bathroom wall. *Protein.*

In both cases, all of Amos' victims and all of Graham's victims, had been reduced to just one thing:

Meat.

I shook my head. Ally noticed and turned to me. "What is it? You okay?"

I exhaled noisily and looked at her, taking her face in my right hand and stroking it. She smiled gently.

"I've never told you how beautiful you are, have I? I've told you that I'm glad you're here with me and that I wouldn't have made it through Rutty's death without you, but I haven't told you how beautiful you are, how much I love you, nor how much I can't wait to be your husband. In light of all of these revelations, Ally," I paused, "in light of what we're all going to need to do, I just want you to know that I'm here for you and I love you."

She breathed a gracious laugh and tilted her head, resting her hand on mine on her cheek. "I know, babe. I feel the same way. I love you."

Cardona had just started talking about us grabbing some food after that long account. I looked at my watch. In the dim light of the cave it was nearly 1400 hours, when we all heard a sound.

Again, the cocking of a weapon.

We turned around in a reflex, along with everyone else, to face it. There he was, with his sidearm pointed squarely at Cardona.

He was filthy and sweating, but it was him.

12 | ESCAPE

I didn't know what else to do, and my heart was in my throat.

It was Lieutenant Armstrong. He stood there alone, pointing his gun at Cardona, but the Captain didn't flinch. "Armstrong. I had a feeling you might remain unconvinced, my friend," the Captain muttered.

"Oh, we're not friends, *Captain*," he hissed with utter disdain. "You call yourself an officer. Look at you. Lying and spreading your own propaganda for your own personal gain. The President was right. You're nothing more than a lowlife scumbag that couldn't make it in the upper crust and decided to drop down where there would be less of a challenge, right? No one up top wanted to deal with your *savior* complex, so you figured you'd come here and delude a bunch of kids instead!"

"Yes, I'm sure you're right," Cardona agreed sardonically, slowly starting to walk around the table.

Unfortunately for Armstrong, his voice had carried, and now a mass of soldiers, faithful to Cardona, was starting to gather, seeing their beloved Captain held at gunpoint by this new, *un*-beloved addition to their team. Armstrong had only a sidearm. No way could he hold them all at bay.

"Lieutenant, put down the gun," Monzon ordered.

"I don't answer to you!" Armstrong spat back. "I don't answer to either of you! I answer to the President of the United States of America," he said proudly.

"Lieutenant, you're sweating, you're nervous, and you're not thinking rationally," Monzon said, hands up and trying to reason with him. "Let's talk this over."

"We don't need to talk anything over," he insisted. "We all heard it straight from the horse's mouth. You're guilty of treason. Both of you. In fact, *all* of you are," he hissed, and in addressing all of us he became aware of a soldier sneaking up behind him. He spun, and shot him in the heart. The dead soldier clutched his chest and fell backward. I didn't know his name, but there was one less soldier to contend with Graham. The rest of the soldiers behind him recoiled.

"Armstrong!" Monzon screamed at him. Ally and I stood at the crack of his gun.

These soldiers all seemed like enemies less than an hour ago. But *the enemy of my enemy is my friend*. It had taken a bit of convincing, but all was clear now. Why couldn't Armstrong see that? He backed away and put distance between himself and both groups that were now sandwiching him.

"Armstrong," I said. "Listen to me. Please. You're in the minority, all alone down here. I know. I get it. I've been there. Just put the gun down please, before anyone else gets hurt." Ally put her hand on the small of my back, but I could feel her also tugging me to sit back down.

Armstrong didn't say anything else, just creased his mouth into a smile and breathed out through his nose while shaking his head confidently. Just then I noticed he was wearing his headset. "Command, Armstrong, come in?"

My eyes opened wide in horror. He was going to alert Command of Cardona's return! If he did that, what was to stop the President from sending up a brigade to shoot an EMP right down our cave mouth or to rout us out with her infantry? Or worse, what if he already had alerted her, and she already knew?

"Armstrong, don't," many of us pleaded, putting our hands up.

We could all hear his headset scratch.

He opened his mouth. There was nothing left to do. "Command, Armstrong, did you hear all th- *ooof!*" he exclaimed, as the wind was knocked out of him from the side. Armstrong turned as the other soldier tackled him, and he fired down into his brain. Ally screamed.

Another faithful soldier down as Armstrong pinned him, and fired yet another shot into him. He landed with a tough thud on the cave floor, with the dead soldier on top of him. His headset flew off of him and landed a few feet away. He was now screaming in desperation and trying to form an intelligible sentence as he fought off multiple recruits who now leapt upon him, all of them creating commotion and din to drown out his yells. Another shot fired amidst the crowd, but I didn't see if it hit anyone.

"Armstrong!" I shouted. "No, wait, just get back, here, give him room. Get his gun, and just-"

A tremendous commotion sounded from the cave's mouth, rolling down the cavern toward us. I knew that sound. It was the M134 miniguns and other guns at the front. But what were they shooting at? Surely if the President or Stone had received Armstrong's transmission, they couldn't have gotten here by now. *Maybe they were already here.*

The guns were going wild, and call me crazy, but there were strange noises mixed into the whirring of those miniguns. They were strafing at something. I could hear soldiers yelling to one another frantically. A few of them eventually ran our way: the youngest of them, most likely just trying to escape. But they were frantically putting on their masks. Why were they putting on their masks? They said we wouldn't need them down here. That could mean only one thing.

Gorgons.

The din continued, fusing into a crescendo that culminated in a loud series of tremendous *booms*. We covered our ears. The rumble continued down through the tunnel beyond us. Additional cacophonies sounded, like huge chunks of metal dropped off a building or thrown into a pit. Armstrong laughed hysterically, but it was obvious he was frightened. "See? You brought this upon yourself, *Captains!*" he sneered again. A soldier standing near him kicked him in the face, and he was out cold.

Then the lights to the cave shut off. Something colossal shook the earth beyond the Rotunda, and I could feel my legs involuntary quaking from the vibrations as I glanced down at my feet and the ground below me.

The Giant's Coffin slab suddenly made itself seem like an imposing presence now, looming over us: an impenetrable block of solid rock leaning over us in the pitch blackness.

"Shhh!" shouted Monzon.

"Quiet!" shouted Cardona at the same time.

Straining our ears, we all listened. That's when we heard them. Humans, wailing and screaming, but far away, mixed with dull thuds that continued to resonate and reverberate past us and bouncing off the cave's walls. Then growls. Shrieks. Something was approaching, and it wasn't singular. There were *many* somethings approaching.

The shrieks grew wilder and nearer.

Multiple chills ran through me. Ally felt blindly in the dark for me as I fumbled for a chemlight. She wrapped herself around me and whimpered nervously, "Cam…" Multiple chemlights sprang up around us: little green flickers springing up in the dark like candles.

You are not a candle in a wind-free world. Well, Rosie, here are the candles, and here comes the wind.

"Shh, it's okay, baby," I said. "Where's your rifle? Neener! Jenkins!" I whispered to them. A voice sounded to my right as I kept feeling for chemlights in my pockets. Found one! "Where did you lay our weapons?" I breathed somewhat frantically. I snapped my chemlight into action as I checked my straps for grenades. I still had three of them attached to my vest.

Our guns, next to the table: my XM5 and Foxy's rocket launcher, along with our Berettas. We armed ourselves as quickly and silently as possible. Everyone else did the same. Our own bunks weren't far from the picnic tables. I could just make out Ally and Joe scurrying up the broken rocks to their bunks to retrieve their weapons. It was remarkable how quiet everyone was being, but I could hear the constant snick-chick of hammers being drawn back and guns being readied.

Foxy lifted his pack, which had extra torpedoes in it, and loaded one in his shooter.

"This way, people," Cardona said sadly. "There's nothing we can do about all of them up there. I'm sorry, but there just isn't." He looked around quickly, trying to see in the dark. "Monzon, I'm guessing we have about sixty of us here, all told."

Horrible sounds of smashing and screaming further up the cave corridor. *Sixty people. Less than half of all those here,* I guessed.

"Then let's move. Come on, people, the party won't wait. Masks, everyone. Put them on right now," Monzon breathed to them as he softly clapped in urgency.

Then we started running.

We were holding out our chemlights in front of us like bobbing will-o'-the-wisps. Foxy mounted his to the front of his launcher, and I did the same with mine. I could hear myself breathing in my mask, echoing dull, panting dual-tone respirations in my own ears.

Where was Ally? There she was, keeping pace with me to my left. "Ally, Foxy, Joe, if we get separated, make a short double staccato sound, like this," -here I tut-tutted for them like a snare drum- "and we can find each other. Got it? *Tut-tut,*" I repeated. They nodded.

We filed down through the passageway. Bats scattered as we approached.

I could hear some of the soldiers behind me swearing. In their haste, they had forgotten their masks, or they never had them on that day to begin with. This Blockade, like so many more of them, had gotten cavalier and comfortable, despite their knowledge of our deadly situation. When would we ever learn? You don't take off your mask. You don't leave it behind.

For the rest of us, our faces were ovular and lit up in the bobbing reflection of our own chemlights stretched out before us. An eerie scene.

All of that machinery, all of those tanks, the DTF emitters, the miniguns. All of them were nothing compared to the gorgons. I just knew they had a behemoth with them, and probably berserkers as well. They had probably been circling far overhead, deciding that their front ranks should go forward and take the hit as they knocked out our defenses. They were expendable. They had reserves. They knew we were no match for them. They had probably sealed off the cave too, preventing escape. That was the sound of all of that machinery tumbling into the cave mouth.

I swallowed hard. I didn't know how we were going to get out of this one, and I couldn't help but keep looking back. All of these shaved heads bobbed behind us, many of them holding up their green lights that barely lit up anything; all of them repeatedly looking back over their own shoulders as well.

Cardona was strangely calm, although panting, and he was briefing Monzon. "I've been all the way through," he whispered. "A few of us have. We need to split up. We've gotta give them less targets and ensure survival for as many as we can. About three hundred feet more and we'll reach Wright's Rotunda. We can send several that way, through the Cataracts and out through Violet City Entrance. That's one. After that, about seven hundred feet from there is an elevator to the top at the Pass of El Ghor and some tree cover above.

"Some can take the elevator, hide, and wait there. Still others can head down the stairs to the Snowball Room where they have restrooms, and then follow that through Cleaveland Avenue out to the Carmichael entrance. That's two and three. And four, the rest of us can take the longer, harder road through the rest of the cave, past Boone, Kentucky Avenue, and Mount McKinley until we reach Grand Central Station and the Frozen Niagara entrance at the other end.

"Everyone, just relax. We've prepared for this contingency," he added solemnly. "Any Star Trek fans here?" he laughed back at us. I furrowed my brow. "Well, get ready. We're about to embark on the Kobayashi Maru, the no-win scenario."

What did that mean? I wondered.

We ran on, and the noise of screeching and thudding receded into the distance.

•   •   •   •   •

We had gone on blindly in the dark for another half-hour and were drawing near to Wright's Rotunda. Thirty minutes, but the time seemed interminable. A moment of choice lay before us there. We were all in a cold sweat in the dark, in terror, and our masks were fogging up from our panicked respirations.

All this time, I was fearing falling into some unknown crevasse, but Cardona apparently knew these passageways well, and he led us faithfully.

I couldn't imagine what those poor soldiers faced back up there at the Rotunda. All I had ever heard about gorgons and underground was that they didn't like it, so it was odd that they would even try to come in. It wasn't too drastically warm though, once you left the Rotunda or Giant's Coffin, I remembered. They were probably desperate for food, and *angry:* we had killed two of their behemoths. They were getting smarter, and more vengeful, all this time.

The thunder had abated.

Cardona held up a hand and had us stop as he looked back. As we *all* looked back. There was no further sound coming from back up the tunnel. Maybe we had escaped them.

Those last to enter Wright's Rotunda turned and formed a defensive perimeter as we waited to catch our breath. I could hear several people gulping amidst their breath, choking back the fear. Those with masks on slid them up over the tops of their heads. It was admittedly harder to see in the dark with the masks on.

"Alright, folks," Cardona whispered. "We need to split up. Get those masks back down. I know we all want out of here, but those of you who know me know that I laugh in the face of a no-win scenario." He turned to me and winked. "Kobayashi Maru.

"So, you know what we do from here. We need a few proud souls to hold the line here and fend them off, to give the rest a chance to get to safer ground above. We only need a few. But we need air, we need water, and we need to get out of here. I need members of *my* crew to hold here, and when you see them, you know what to do."

Five of those soldiers volunteered instantly, and bravely. As to what he said they knew to do, we were clueless, but I suspected they had booby-trapped the caves for a contingency such as this. He had mentioned something along those lines as we ran. I looked around and could barely make out Foxy and Joe in the dark. Joe was really breathing hard. Ally was panting at my side.

"Alright. Good on ya. Stand your ground and then bank to the right here, and then you make for Violet City after the rest of these guys." They nodded. He held up a chemlight to his own watch. "It's 1442. Get to the top. We'll rendezvous at Frozen Niagara at 1800. Stay alert. Get some water if you can, and keep your wits about you. Hoorah."

"Hoorah," they echoed quietly and then replaced the defensive perimeter. Cardona unstrapped something from his bandolier, and counted the numbers off in the dark. "Checkpoint One," he breathed and handed a small cylindrical device to one of them.

"Alright. Let's give them less targets. Ten of you, split off that way toward Violet City. I don't care who. Remember: Frozen Niagara at 1800. Go. Move."

Several of them awkwardly looked around trying to decide if they should go. Some started and then stopped after realizing a mate was staying behind. Maybe some felt safer down here and weren't sure what they would meet up above. Or maybe they knew what the Captain had planned and were placing all their faith in him. I didn't know. Eventually, ten or so split off just as he had ordered. We were now down to forty-five men.

We went on another ten minutes or so before someone insisted that they would pass out without water. As luck would have it, we were coming up under what they called Double Cellars Sinkhole, and there were a few falling freshets of water against the moist cave walls. We had to hug the walls and literally suck the water from the limestone as it trickled down, but it did the trick for our parched mouths, dried from panting and fear.

Our troop was drawing near to the Pass of El Ghor and two splits there: one for the elevator, and one banking right toward Cleaveland to the Carmichael Entrance. We didn't know which one we should be taking; it was never assigned.

Just then a shout went up behind us and a horrid yell that stopped us dead in our tracks. "Shhh!" I hissed. Our hearts pounded, and we listened with our eyes.

The muffled cries stopped, and we could faintly hear one of them yell "Do it! Now!" One second later, a horrible unearthly blast shook the cavern walls around us, followed by the sound of sliding stones and the grinding of boulders through rubble. Dust dislodged and floated down from the ceiling around us. As I suspected, one of them had detonated a booby trap blast, most likely cutting off the rest of the gorgons behind it. There were muffled concussions following that. They were still trying to break through!

"Go. Go!" barked Cardona, pushing people in front of him in their back. "Ten of you split off that way. Go now! Five of you can fit into the elevator. Remember! Frozen Niagara, 1800. Go!"

A tremendous bellowing roar rolled down the passageway behind us, and we *felt* its thunder. Mixed into that roar was the sound of screams. Right then, I didn't think those poor soldiers at Wright's Rotunda had put enough distance between themselves and the gorgons before the Violet City entrance.

Indiscriminately, we all split apart. Two of us broke off toward Cleaveland, running and stamping loudly. The youngest of them was whimpering. I could almost feel the visceral terror running down his spine as he fled. The other one of them was looking over his own shoulder and should have watched where he was going. He lost his footing and went careening against a side of the cavern wall, scraping and scratching himself up in the process. "Ah!" he screamed feebly as he grabbed his leg. He must have broken it in his fall. "My leg! My leg!" His buddy desperately tried to silence him and get him back on his feet.

At that moment, the tunnel back by the Rotunda shattered into dust: a great screeching roar went up and filled the cavern around us. We could hear – and feel – it getting closer as it smashed down the passageway to our six.

I covered my ears and quickened my pace. Another chill ran through me.

"Go! Go! Move!" Cardona screamed, pulling at his vest. In the mayhem, we couldn't see who was whom. Five of us broke for the elevator: Ally, Joe, and I, and two soldiers who I hadn't met yet then threw themselves in with us. One of their guns jabbed me in the neck as we slammed inside the elevator.

Where was Foxy?

Thankfully, the elevator still had power, though I didn't know how. It must have been on its own circuitry, and the rest of the soldiers' gear was on generators and tapped into other circuits in the upper half of the cave.

The door hadn't shut yet, and the creature was thundering down the hall toward us. "Foxy!" I yelled desperately down the hall and poked myself out of the elevator door frame.

There he was! Foxy was kneeling down in the middle of the cavern, and I could see him there, a tiny figure, bending down with his rocket launcher suspended over his shoulder. It was happening all over again. I envisioned Rutty bending down in that library and taking aim right before that berserker smashed into him.

Foxy took aim. He fired. A stream of white flew out of that tube, and the cave wall beyond him detonated along with something else.

A horrendous explosion threw him backward, and I saw a large shape wreathed in smoke and ruin go flying past the elevator entrance and into the wall beside him. Foxy leapt out of the way as it landed next to him. Shrapnel flew all around. It was a behemoth, sure enough, and it lay there twitching and flapping in agony. Then, it was still.

However, noise was still coming down the hallway.

A huge sound of massive shrieking and hissing was speeding toward us. Floating out of the corridor Foxy had just blasted came the dreaded mist. There were a lot of them inbound. A *lot*.

At that, we heard the humming again.

What I wouldn't give for a tank with a giant DTF right now, I thought. *Screw the threat of the President, now we actually* need *someone to fire one right down Mammoth Cave!*

"Foxy, we've got to go!" I yelled to him.

Foxy looked over at me. He couldn't get to me, and they would be on him any minute. He would have to crawl over the behemoth and run like hell down Cleaveland toward the Carmichael exit. He started to climb, madly, throwing his rocket launcher over his back, but the skin of the behemoth must have been extremely slimy and hard to get a grip. I could see his chemlight reflecting off of it: it was glistening, and I could see him slipping. He grunted and tried with all his might, and then he whipped around and stared back at the corridor entrance through his mask. I could almost see them in the reflection of his mask.

The mist always precedes the gorgons, and now they slowly filtered out, baring their fangs and bobbing their heads, their arms outstretched toward him. Their prey was right there, and it didn't have anywhere to go, so they didn't need to rush it.

"*No,*" I hissed through clenched teeth. I started to run out toward him when big fierce arms yanked me back into the elevator. As they did so, one of the gorgons whipped around and looked our way. The damned door still wasn't closed!

I couldn't see Foxy. Where was he? Had he made it over the behemoth yet? Would he get away in time?

Bassett hissed at me. "Are you nuts, kid? You've got Ally right here." Then, he softened and leaned into me. "Save *her,* kid."

Joe looked at me good and hard and said something I'll never forget. Because he *himself* said he would never forget it from back there at Harvill.

"John 15:13: *Greater love hath no man than this; that a man lay down his life for his friends.*" He smiled tenderly, gripped me solidly by the arms, and patted them. "Tell Maureen I love her and that she's the best thing to ever happen to a scoundrel like me. Tell her she'll always be my Ace Queen." He lifted his mask up over his head.

"Joe, don't…Joe…" was all I could mutter, as I clenched my teeth.

And before I could stop him, he ran out with his XM5 and began to shoot wildly at them. Multiple hisses sounded from around the corner in the clearing above the Snowball Room. They were hissing at Joe now, and he was drawing their attention away from Foxy, buying him time to escape!

Spent cartridges ejected from his rifle as he took them down and flew all over the alcove where he stood.

I couldn't see Foxy. We could only see Joe, and the four of us stood there knowing the inevitable was about to happen to him. His mask was off, allowing them to seize fully upon their prey. I could see the lightnings from his gun reflecting off of rivers of tears flowing from his stern eyes.

Then, his guns stopped. His trigger finger no longer obeyed his mind. Ally and I saw Joe slowly tilt his head toward us, while his eyes were locked with a gorgon's; as our door began to close, his color turned a pallid pale. Somehow, he was able to wrench only one eye away from the gorgons that held his gaze, and give us a sincere goodbye. One of sacrifice, of boldness, and of no greater love. His smile turned statuesque, and he moved no more, a frozen testament to sacrifice: one eye on the enemy, and one eye on us.

"Joe!" Ally pleaded helplessly amidst her tears. And just like that, Staff Sergeant Joseph Bassett was gone, as the heavy aluminum slab door slid between us. Our card-talking, country-drawling gentleman had just gotten his royal flush.

We turned away in horror as our door finally closed and clicked fast. There was a tremendous thud and repeated smashing of large brutes into that tiny elevator pocket just outside. One after another, they were smashing and rending something in their fury. We knew it was Joe.

I could hear growling as they fought over his carcass.

We couldn't cry. I knelt down, grabbed Ally, and covered her ears, and she covered mine. We just watched each other, drowning out the noise of what lay beyond the elevator doors. The other soldiers stood transfixed, their rifles trained upon the doors beyond us, breathing hard with eyes ringed in horror.

Suddenly, we were lifting. Rising. Heading to the surface and out of that hellhole. Not twenty feet up, a massive detonation heaved our car off its rails, and we tumbled back to the corridor floor, right back where we had been, smashing down into the bottom of the elevator shaft.

A huge inferno roared outside, and fire leapt through a small crack in the elevator doors, which had been knocked cattywampus in the plummet. The gorgons screamed at the noise.

Captain Cardona had just detonated Number Two, and we were alone.

•　　•　　•　　•　　•

It was 1520. We didn't dare to move. We couldn't afford to. That fire was still roaring outside, and who knew if the corridor was stable enough to let us crawl out.

Roughly a minute after the first detonation, we heard faint shouting, then another explosion, and then a thick sound of falling stone that rumbled and shook the very bones of the earth. It sounded like the rock wall had been riven in two, and large amounts of gravel were being poured into a pit. Then, silence.

It was pitch black except for our two chemlights. No one spoke. If the gorgons were truly getting smarter, then they were listening.

Jolting us back into fear, yet another detonation exploded further on down the passageway about ten minutes after we lost Joe. Cardona had said something about Boone, Kentucky Avenue, and Mount McKinley, and then Grand Central Station and the Frozen Niagara exit. He must have detonated Number Three down Boone somewhere.

Poor Joe. Poor Maureen. Poor all of us.

We didn't know where Cardona or Monzon were. We didn't know where Foxy was. Not knowing drove me crazy and made me incredibly anxious, more than the rest of them. We didn't know where anyone was anymore, and we were trapped in this elevator shaft.

I was holding Ally against my chest, and we both had our guns drawn and our masks on. The other two did as well, but they had slumped down against the floor to rest their aching feet.

Ally was shivering. And not just from the cold. "You okay?" I whispered in her ear.

I felt her lightly nod. "It...it just reminds me of being in the dark under that car after the Subway. So dark, and trapped, not sure where to go," she whispered back.

"I hear you, hon. We'll make it." I hugged her.

My face was trained toward the elevator door this whole time. I could only imagine what fragments of Joe remained outside that door, and none of us wanted to see them. So much evil.

Joe had sacrificed himself for us in the face of that evil, with no regard for himself. What was that verse? John 15:13? I would have to look that up and share it with Maureen if I ever met her.

The weight of it all crushed down upon us.

I hoped to God that Foxy was alive. I wasn't much one for prayer, but perhaps now was the time.

"Hon," I breathed. In the darkness, she turned her face toward me. "Pray with me. You guys too. What are your names?

In less than a whisper, they shared their names. *Antone. Hofstetter.* One very young girl, maybe 15 if that, and one older guy around mid-twenties.

"Pray with me."

They bowed their heads. I didn't quite know where or how to start, so I tried to remember how Rutty prayed.

Dear Jesus, I began, like Rutty would. *We don't know where we are, or what's going to happen next. We don't know where Foxy is. But you do. Man, Lord, we want to get out of here. Can you just- would you, uh, please just get us out of here and keep us all safe? All of us. Ally and me, Foxy, and Antone and Hofstetter here. Please. Uh, thanks, Jesus.*

I lifted up my head, and then quickly bowed it again. *Oh! Amen.* I could see Ally smiling at me in the dark. "That was nice, Cam."

"Thanks, Lieutenant," one of them mouthed quietly. I smiled humbly and then took a deep breath.

I looked at my watch again, as if 1800 would suddenly creep up on us and catch us at unawares. 1530. Time was crawling by. I let my head fall back against the elevator wall, looking upward.

Through the grate in the top of the elevator cube, as a tiny pinhole in the distance, I caught a few rays of light stretching through the dust far above us in the elevator shaft. Blinking to make sure I wasn't seeing something that wasn't there, I slowly started to stand. Ally stirred and said "Wha-?"

"Shhh, it's okay. Hold tight," I said, looking down at the three of them. I held up my chemlight. The hatch of the elevator was intact but loose. The questions now were could we get it off? And, was there a hole in the shaft allowing access to the Pass of El Ghor outside where Joe had died? If even a tiny fragment of the rock wall of the elevator shaft had collapsed and opened, the gorgons could enter through that and follow us up.

We can't stay in here forever, I thought as I dropped back down quietly. *We'll miss our rendezvous with Cardona and the rest of them.*

"Okay. We can remove the hatch to the elevator and climb up the shaft. We have to be absolutely quiet, but I think we can climb up the shaft to the top. We just have to pray there aren't any holes in the wall outside the shaft.

"You see that light up there?" I pointed through the grate. They all jostled for position to see it. "That's our way out. From there, we're up top again, and we can hightail it over to Carmichael and Violet City to meet up with the others before we all move down to Frozen Niagara for the 1800 rendezvous. We can't stay here."

"Oh, yes we can," said Hofstetter. Antone, the girl, looked at him. "They'll send a rescue. And the Captain will come for us," he insisted. "He'll come for us!"

I crouched down in front of Hofstetter. "What's your first name, Hof?"

"Robert."

I looked at him. "Robert, we were sent here to assassinate your Captain on orders from the President. We just didn't know it. No other Blockade will come here to rescue us now. What's done is done. Those gorgons could have been driven here by other DTFs for all we know. The Captain gave instructions for all of us to meet him at Frozen Niagara at 1800. That's what we're supposed to do. No one will come back for us, and I'm not going to let any of us die in an elevator shaft. We're soldiers. We fight. Now how 'bout it? Can you help us get out of here and stop the President?"

He looked at me in amazement. The news of the assassination plot took him by surprise.

"If you want to see your Captain again, *we* have to go find *him*. There's no other way out of here."

In the dim light of the shaft, I could see the resolve building in him. He looked away from me and up the elevator shaft, then sighed, and finally he looked back up at me. "Okay."

"Okay," I said, patting him on the shoulder. "Now, who's the lightest?"

•   •   •   •   •

"Most of all, you've got to keep *quiet,*" I instructed them. We hoisted Antone up to the ceiling of the elevator, and not daring to breathe, she slowly pushed open the hatch. Mercifully, it had come loose and didn't need to be pried out. The elevator had shifted as it fell, and the shape buckled, causing the grate to loosen.

We all held our breath as she slowly slid it aside and then gave us the okay to lift her further.

Antone looked to her left and then paused. She quickly then motioned for us to wait, and then she turned her head and looked down at us with fear in her eyes, beckoning us to bring her back down.

She grabbed the hatch and slowly set it back in place.

"There *is* a hole just outside the shaft. It's not big, but they could probably force their way through and widen it if they needed to. I saw flicker of flames through it," she breathed haltingly.

"Okay, okay. Well that's not terrible news. We just have to pray that only the *fattest* gorgons are still out there, right?" I laughed nervously. "As long as we remain quiet."

As long as we remain quiet. Story of our lives for the past sixteen years. That shouldn't be anything new.

As she was poking her head out, I could survey the shaft above us a bit better beyond our lift. We'd have to grab onto the poles aligning the walls, and they would undoubtedly be slick here and there. So would any indentations for our footing, but it would be possible.

"I'll go first. I'm heavy, so lift hard. But…slowly," I urged them. "Antone, you keep watch and look sharp." I donned my mask. "Hofstetter, get that mask on. If any of you have gloves, now's the time."

Hofstetter pulled his mask down over his head and took a strong tug on his canteen. Maybe it was liquid courage.

Ally put her mask back on too, and she and Hofstetter made a catch with their hands. They took my boots, pushing me up. Thankfully they all had gloves. They strained and grunted, but quietly. Antone stood armed and ready in case we had visitors.

I pushed the hatch grate aside again as inaudibly as I could, and my mouth creased into an open O as I watched the shaft hole like a hawk. No trace of mist. Hopefully, they had either moved on or been burned up.

The good news was that the elevator was mostly intact and on the ground floor. We wouldn't have to deal with any loosening, jostling, rocking, or plummeting. For a split second, the thought occurred to me that Jesus might just have heard my prayer.

I lay down, still watching the hole, not daring to creep too close to it, and reached down into the cavity below. I silently pointed to Ally. She slung her rifle over her back, took my hand, and the two soldiers hoisted her up. Now there were two. Ally and I reached down and helped Antone up, for she would be an easy three. She was lithe and felt like a feather.

Antone knew what to do when she got to the top. She instantly resumed her defensive posture and trained her sidearm on the hole in the wall.

Hofstetter had just put his hands up when we heard a sudden noise outside. I put my hand up to tell everyone to hold, and swung my M5 around. My training kicked in again, and I remembered our standard ROE to wait a full sixty seconds before movement again. That was a long minute. If anything did rear its ugly head at us, it would have been demolished instantly, but five more would have taken its place. I thought about dropping a grenade through there, but what if it was Foxy? And a grenade burst might harm us at close proximity as well.

No one was tut-tutting outside.

I turned my attention back down to Hofstetter, and squatted at the hatch while the others kept the hole at bay. I stretched as far as I could to grab him up myself. Our hands met, and I lifted. Up he came.

The sudden sound was deafening, and it threw my eyes into wild confusion and anger. I almost dropped him. I heard Ally gasp and cry "What was-?"

Hofstetter's canteen had fallen loose from his belt and was smashing around the floor of the elevator!

I could see it below him, ricocheting around wildly, finally lying still, as he swung between me and the floor. I gritted my teeth at him and pulled him up as hard as I could. My back twinged from the effort.

Hofstetter was up. I scowled and shook my head at him, grabbed his gun from his holster, and slapped it into his hand. Then, we both trained our guns on the hole.

Another minute went by. Nothing.

I scanned all of them and gave them the all-clear to begin the ascent. It looked to be every inch of a one-hundred fifty-foot climb. I looked at our shoes. Thankfully we were all wearing boots with strong treads on them.

The rails and cables were old, but they held fast to the wall. There looked to be a shelter up above the elevator shaft, so thankfully there was no rainfall or snowmelt in here, or they would have been rusty and perhaps snapped off.

Fortunately, everyone here had gone through enough drills to ascend a vertical wall with little grip. *God bless you, Basic Training*, I said to myself.

We were slow going, but I could see the rays of light growing stronger and solider as we neared the top. The thought ran through my head: *Please God, don't let anyone have anything else unsecured to their belt or vest. And no sneezing. Our masks would help with that.*

I was nearly there, and sweating like a pig. Ally was right behind me, and then Hofstetter, followed by Antone.

I had about twenty-five feet to go.

It was getting lighter up top. A smile was even growing on my face, full of assurance that we were going to make it. I looked down to see everyone's progress. In the dim light far below, I could barely make out Antone.

But below her, something was moving at the bottom of the elevator shaft. I squinted my eyes. A distinct but noticeable blueish-green mist was swirling far below her. I held my perch and leaned far out from the pipes so everyone could see me, breathing out "Hold...hold!" Antone kept climbing. "Antone, hold!" She looked up.

At that moment a dark shape thrust itself through the small breach in the shaft wall below her, sending concrete bits flying. Spindly arms were gripping through, trying to heave a bulk through the breach. A shrill shriek went up. We had been seen!

Antone looked down in horror. A gorgon was trying to stick itself through the hole, wriggling and writhing as it scratched itself up against the concrete wall. It tried again and again to breach the hole, but it was too big, and the hole too small.

"No!" she screamed back up at us.

I could dimly make out the gorgon below, ramming itself through the breach in fury, each time creating new cracks in the concrete wall and flaking off small fragments of the aperture, slightly widening it each time.

The elevator shaft began to fill up with the infernal vapor below. I dared not look down. We were going to get to the top, gorgons be damned, even if there were gorgons above us to damn as well.

"*Move! Climb!*" I roared back down at them. "*Climb, damn you!*" We threw caution to the wind and made as much noise as we had to in order to get up to the top quickly. I could hear the scuffing and heaving of all of us as we desperately tried to ascend the shaft.

Smash. Smash. The gorgon had broken through! Concrete and dust were sent flying below. It pulled back and then launched so fast that it had rammed the other side of the elevator shaft and was temporarily dazed. It wouldn't be long before it came to, however.

Antone screamed in fright. "No! No! Please don't leave me down here, help! Someone help me!" She was climbing but not grabbing onto anything solidly enough, so she was slipping down the slick elevator rails. "*Help me you guys!*" Antone grabbed up and clutched Hofstetter's ankle above him. He slipped down a few inches.

"Ow, no!" he screamed at her. "Get off. Get *off* of me!" He flailed his ankle as he desperately tried to shake her off and remove her grip on his leg.

I reached the top and pulled Ally up behind me. We clung to the exterior elevator door and pried it open, me pushing one way and Ally pushing the other. Ally lost her balance and nearly fell back down the shaft, but I grabbed her belt, pulled her back in, and held her close. We both turned around and looked back down in horror.

Hofstetter was shaking his leg violently to release Antone.

Far below them, the gorgon slowly came to and composed itself. It raised its head and looked up at them. *Movement.* Hofstetter saw it, but Antone wouldn't let go.

Hofstetter held onto the rail with this right hand, drew his weapon from his belt with his left, and shot down at her. Multiple times, through Antone's head, neck and shoulders. Fortunately, he had the sense to fire at the gorgon as well, and it fell dead.

Antone screamed something unintelligible, fell silent, and dropped straight down onto the gorgon below, her blonde hair swirling up around her as her dead eyes stared up into the abyss. She landed with a hard thump below, but others were already sniffing the hole and surging through. The vapor enveloped all of them, and she disappeared into green fog as another gorgon started to squeeze through in order to consume her.

"Hofstetter, you bastard! She was just a little girl!" I screamed at him. Sissy ran through my mind. Nevaeh ran through my mind. The little girl from Harvill ran through my mind. Neener ran through my mind. Even Ally as a young girl, trapped in that Subway with Holt, ran through my mind. All of these little girls deserved to be loved and cared for. Protected. Not cast off as a diversion to facilitate a coward's escape.

Surprisingly, he turned and shot at us too. The shaft echoed with gunfire. Anger raged through me. "Stop! Robert, stop! We'll help you! Climb! Climb!" I yelled. He was panicking. So was I. My stomach was in knots, and I revolted at the thought of helping him up.

Hofstetter climbed. There were more shadows emerging through the vapor and swirling through the mist down there. They must be all over Mammoth Cave by now.

Hofstetter climbed: frantically, and with purpose. He was dripping with sweat and fear, but he was almost to us.

More gorgons burst through the hole down below! They looked around, shrieking and hissing in venomous fury, slithering around each other, all of them jockeying for position to get at Antone's corpse.

I unwillingly lugged Hofstetter up. He hugged me and thanked me, but he was crying. "I had to do it! She wouldn't let go, and I was going to fall back down there with her," he practically whimpered into my shirt.

And then, I suddenly felt like I was hugging Stone. Hugging Amos. *Hugging Graham.* My eyes flared.

An unexpected heatwave passed through me, and I wrenched him off of me. "I know, I get it," I said, as I reached into my top pocket and pulled out a small ovular capsule. "And that's why I have to do this." I punched him in the gut, and he instantly doubled over, his mouth agape and his eyes popping out of his head. I ripped off his mask and fisted the cyanide capsule deep down his throat, and then gave him a swift uppercut with my knee, forcing him to swallow.

Ally shouted "Cam, what are you do- no!"

His eyes widened at me in terror as Ally reached for him, as if to pry the cyanide pill from his mouth, but she missed.

There was only one thing left to do. I side-kicked him back into the shaft, and his convulsing body smacked against the side wall. He fell flailing like a spaghetti noodle on top of the pile of gorgons waiting there: the sippy was already doing its poisonous work. There was wild hissing and screaming below as writhing and shrieking noises enveloped all of them together.

"Don't worry, hon. He doesn't have long," I said, as I retrieved a grenade from my vest and pulled the pin. "Fire in the hole," I breathed calmly, and let it fall. All went quiet.

Ally dove out of the way beside me. I could see the tiny explosive plummet downward, passing a few gorgon bodies that had just literally lifted off the ground. Too late.

Boom.

A horrible fireball filled the lower chamber and rose toward us rapidly. The elevator shaft shook, and I had to steady myself against the side of the wall next to me. Wild, angry flames came rushing up to greet me, and my hair flew back in the gust. Antone was gone, killed by Hofstetter. Hofstetter was gone, killed by me.

"Cam! Cam, come *on!*" Ally murmured at me, dazed. She grabbed my arm. I was smoking from the flames which were seeking a way out for fresh oxygen outside that shaft. They had enveloped me momentarily. Suddenly, I was in a coughing fit. It took us a few minutes before we got the smoke out of our lungs and could carry onward.

I just hadn't known what else to do, and my heart was in my throat.

13 | FATE

"Enough of this, I've had enough!"

Ally coughed and retched. "Cam, how could you do that?" she spat out. "How could you *do* that to Robert? You murdered him! He was just trying to survive as well!"

It was raining up above, and we were now being pelted by strong drops of water from angry afternoon clouds overhead.

"Yeah, well so was Amos," I coughed back. "So are all of us. But there are lines that you just don't cross, Ally! Lines that separate us from the gorgons, and even worse, lines that separate us from *ourselves*!" Our voices were carrying, but I didn't care. "Lines we can't cross, or we're evil. Just like Hofstetter! Just like Amos! Just like *Graham!*" I counted loudly and firmly off my fingers as I said their names. I could feel the veins popping out in my neck. But Ally didn't back down.

"And you didn't just cross one yourself?" Her eyebrows shot way up at me. "Cam, in giving him that sippy and throwing him back down the hole, you *become* evil. Who are you to mete out justice against someone like that?"

"I don't know, Ally. I just- I- I don't know! But you can't stand back and watch people do stuff like that, can you? I've had enough too, you know."

"N-no, Cameron! No!" she stammered, I guess seeking an additional argument. "What would Rosie say? What would she say to this? Or- or-," she paused, and I knew whose name she was about to invoke. "Wyatt! What would he say to what you did, Cam? Would he approve?"

"Leave Rutty out of this," I breathed, firmly, checking the skies, my eyes blinking in the rain. We were both shivering after the cold of the cave, and our sweat was now freezing rivers on our bodies. I grabbed my rifle and checked my things. "I want to find Foxy. Are you coming or not?"

Ally looked at me sternly, but then she looked down and softened. "Cameron, listen to me. *Listen to me!*" she insisted, when I paused.

I turned my head. She walked slowly over to me.

"I love you, dammit! You know that. We've been through a lot together. And I'm going to be your wife. But you can't just cram a sippy down someone's throat because they did something unconscionable, Cam! That's what Graham is doing. You do that, and you're no better than her! We're all part of the same team of pawns on *her* chessboard. If Rosie were here, she'd remind you who the real threat is. She would have wanted Robert to face *justice*, not revenge."

I looked at her standing there in the rain. As we were being pelted, something in me eventually softened. She was right, of course, though I didn't want her to be through my angry panting for both breath and sanity. After all, not for a moment did I ask myself, "What have I done?" Had I become Amos when I executed Hofstetter? In so doing, I *became* Hofstetter. I was becoming Amos. I was becoming Graham.

That wasn't justice. That was *revenge*, and I still didn't recognize the difference. Graham was proceeding on a path of revenge because her conscience was seared. That was not my path, and my conscience was still intact.

"I'm-I'm sorry," I found myself finally muttering, staring past her.

She looked at me with full sincerity and didn't smile. Instead, she reached up and touched my cheek with her palm. "That wasn't justice. Justice is us going to get Liam."

I slowly nodded. There was more to be said – and probably unsaid – but we grabbed our masks, put them on, and started running. I was surprised at my level of energy as I felt vigor coursing through my legs in the rain. We ran toward the Carmichael exit. It was a ways up ahead, and we couldn't see any of our own waiting there. I could only imagine what was happening down below me in the passage of Cleaveland Avenue. The ground ahead of us looked somewhat sunken, so we went around. We didn't know if Foxy and those two others were alive, unconscious, or dead.

There was a large structure ahead, with stone columns and huge overhanging rafters with blackened fittings, a covered area of some kind. Following the ground, I guessed that the Carmichael entrance was beyond it.

We made it and dropped down a bank into a soft, muddy trail with a huge slab of concrete greeting us that had an overhang at the top. The heavy steel doors met in the middle and were locked. I took the butt of my M5 and shattered the lock after a few blows. But a realization stopped me in my tracks. Why was it locked? If it was locked, that meant that they were definitely still inside! A chill ran down my spine. *They had never made it out of Mammoth Cave.*

I opened the door, but surprisingly, Ally hesitated. "Hon, come on, let's go. He's in there."

"I want to, I-I just, I dunno," she stammered. "I thought they'd be right here. Why aren't they here? What's come over me?" She looked around in all directions, hoping against hope that we'd find someone hailing us from afar. There was no one. They were still in there, which meant we had to go back inside. "The thought of going back down in there again...something's just off in me," she trailed.

I was moved with pity. She was remembering being stuck under that car again as a little girl: trapped. "Hon, it's okay. You stand guard here. Wait at the entrance and see if anyone else shows up. We know no one else came this way, so it's probably safe to assume you can wait just inside the door here. You stay right here, hon, and I'll be right back. I promise."

Looking deep into my eyes, she nodded quickly. I kissed her and said, "I'll find him. I'll bring him back. *Justice.*"

She nodded again, smiling this time. I remembered back there in Harvill when I took her in my arms, and her lip was quivering. She had to conduct a suicide run, and she was terrified. Yet here she was now, terrified still, and *I* was the one conducting the suicide run. My heart ached to stay with her, but I had to find Foxy, and she was already safe here.

I gave her one last kiss and then burst through the door. Standing at the top of the stairs, I looked down to what might be my doom, and plunged into it. I took a stiff breath, and let the air fill my lungs as I checked all my ammo. My XM5 was loaded, and I had several extra clips at my side. My Beretta was cocked and ready, and additional magazines were strapped to my vest. I still had two grenades. Chemlights. *Ready.*

I descended the stairs and started running, taking only one short glance back at Ally standing up there behind me. I whispered, "I love you. Keep your mask on!" I couldn't hear if she replied, but I saw her wave.

I mounted my chemlight on the tip of my M5 and proceeded up Cleaveland.

•   •   •   •   •

"Foxy. Foxy," I whispered. "Foxy, it's Jet. I'm here, bro. Where are you?" Then I remembered. *Tut-tut, tut-tut,* I clicked my lips. *Tut-tut.*

Nothing.

I had been going on for ten minutes, looking down and up, down and up with that blessed chemlight and making sure no sudden crevasses had opened up at my feet.

Far up the passageway, I dimly noticed a small dot. I stopped and tried to slow my breathing. My heart was thudding. Were there any other ways into this passageway? There had to be. Did the gorgons know to fan out into those and completely cut us off? Who knows. I couldn't be sure.

The light bobbed faintly in the dark, and I hesitated.

Tut-tut, I clicked.

Tut-tut came the near immediate answer. My eyes went wide, and I quickened my pace. *Tut-tut,* I clicked one more time. I felt likè a bat using echolocation or something. *Tut-tut* came the answering click up ahead.

And before I knew it, I was there. "Jet!" he screeched happily, and then crouched down as if the echo of my name would come around and clobber him in the back.

I could see him or, rather, the silhouette of someone hunched down with a long cylindrical object, his yellowish-white hair backlit by a sickly green behind him.

It was Foxy. He was *alive.* Two other soldiers were crouched on the corridor floor amidst some rubble. All of them were masked, alive, and appeared to be relatively okay. We'd need to get the injured soldier some medical treatment, and, as Foxy and I had done with Joe on our previous mission trip home, we'd have to help him hop his way back.

"Oh, *man,* am I glad to see you, bro," he said. "Tut-tut indeed!" He let out a genuine laugh of relief. The others smiled, though one of them looked like he was about to pass out from exhaustion.

"We were all too terrified to move. I went all the way up to the exit, but it was locked, and I couldn't get out without making a huge racket and banging it down. I also couldn't leave these guys behind. They're brothers. That's Knick and that's Knack. I don't think that's their real names, though, ha! Don't ask." He seemed unnaturally jubilant and full of things to say. I grabbed him and hugged him tight. "Is everyone okay? Where's Ally? Did the others make it out? What happened about about twenty or so minutes ago?" he muttered into my collar. "Another explosion down by you guys?"

I laughed. "Which one should I answer first? We got out of that elevator eventually. Me and Ally. She's fine. I don't know about Cardona and the rest. But let's get out of here, yeah? So good to see you, bud." I ignored the question about the explosion from my grenade in the elevator shaft.

He laughed nervously. "Yeah, sounds good." He turned to the two soldiers who were with him. "You guys good to go?" They nodded.

"What are your real names, guys?"

"I'm Weston Racey," said the injured soldier, "but I go by Knick. And the other one here, who apparently has flat feet and likes to pinball off of cave walls," he said in mock accusation, "is my brother Bridger. But he goes by Knack." Bridger waved.

I chuckled. *Knick Knack.* "Odd nicknames. Why do they call you guys that?"

"Our dad called us that because we were apparently useless around the house. At least, that's what he said," muttered Weston. "Useless knick-knacks." He shrugged.

"Well, we're all about to make a real dent in someone *else's* leg: the *President's.* I'd hardly call you useless. Good to know you. Come on, we gotta move."

They nodded and smiled.

I turned to Foxy. "Did you blow the roof back there?"

"Yeah," he laughed, proud of himself. "Ol' Faithful," he said, slapping the turret of his rocket launcher. "I figured you guys were heading up the elevator, and the rest took off towards the other exit. So, when I didn't see you follow, I turned, loaded another one, and caused a cave-in behind us to seal us off so we could get out." He paused, and his countenance fell along with the tone of his voice. "We lost Joe, didn't we? You don't have to tell me. I know it."

I breathed through my nose. "Yeah, we did, bud."

Foxy was silent for a bit as we trudged along, him holding up Bridger around his waist, Weston doing the same on the other side.

"I could just make him out beyond the flames and the gunfire," he said quietly. "And the gorgs of course. Man, I thought that was it. Thought my number was up. But then someone was spraying gunfire at them from over where you guys were, and they all spun away from me and whipped around at him. I didn't wait. Just threw myself over that big sonofabitch and hauled ass to these guys. Then, I turned, locked, loaded, and shot. He did it to buy me time, didn't he?"

"Yeah, he sure did, bro. But he quoted John 15:13 before he died. Something about *no greater love*. You and I have to look that up when we get topside."

He nodded. "I already know it well," he said, and his words came out as a solemn vow. "Thank you, Joe," I heard him breathe quietly.

We continued back up Cleaveland to Carmichael. Thankfully, there were no sounds behind or in front of us.

In ten more minutes, we reached the base of the stairs. I looked up, but didn't see Ally at the top. That concerned me. We had made it up four or five steps, Foxy and I were trying to stabilize Bridger, when she appeared through the door again. She was trembling in the cold but unharmed. Thankfully, her mask was on.

Ally looked at us and laughed softly, but it was one of joy and celebration. She clapped her hands. "You guys made it! Hey Foxy!" The light dimmed behind her for a moment. She must have found Cardona and the others, and here they came!

Ally lifted her mask up over her head to breathe freely, and perhaps so we could hear her better. It was hard to see in the caves through our masks because they had a darkening effect to a certain degree.

"Get up here, I think I saw Cardona and the rest of them down below, Cam!" she shouted, holding on to the rim of her mask. I tilted my head. If Cardona wasn't with her, then what was that light dimming behind her a moment ago?

Suddenly, everything seemed to slow down. Her very words seemed to drop in pitch and turn into thick mud rolling slowly down a hillside. I had smiled at her and then looked over at Foxy who was smiling and waving as well, glad to see her. But his smile faded and was replaced by wide-eyed fear as he stared back up at my future bride.

I turned back to Ally. "What?" she asked slowly.

The Carmichael entrance had opened and closed, and something had come in behind her.

Looming up at the top of the step, between us and the exit, was a gorgon. It hovered there, its arms fanning out, jetting out a thick, huffing mist that pushed all the oxygen away from us, sealing us in a vaporous capsule of dread; the thing was large, looming, and dripping with venom. It hissed once and then silenced, eyeing her. Ally's expression warped, and her eyebrows went up as she whipped around, bringing her mask back down over her face and fumbling with her rifle.

"Hon, no, NO!" I heard myself yelling, and I tore myself from Bridger's grasp, reaching for my M5. *"No!"* I screamed. "Ally, just back away! *Get down here!"* I bellowed at her.

There was no sound. Or, whatever sound *was* there had been stolen from us, swallowed up in mist and unyielding, uncompromising terror. Foxy tripped going for his sidearm. He couldn't shoot; Ally was in the way. Neither could I.

Ally jerked and raised her rifle at it. The thing was only six feet behind her and growing larger. And without warning, it seized upon her, hissing and howling, trying to grab at her and restrain her. What was it doing? She was trying to free herself from its clutches. And then, somehow, in the struggle, Ally's mask got knocked off of her head. My eyes widened. *No!* The thing had knocked her mask clean off of her face, and here it came: tumbling down the steps toward us.

And then…the gorgon hovered, bobbing its head…*humming.*

"No, no, don't look! *Don't look!"* I heard Weston yelling beside me. Bridger collapsed and covered his face. "Ally, duck!"

She didn't hear him. "Cam, where are you, I can't see!" she shouted, batting the air, and coughing amidst the vapor.

The gorgon clawed at her and she was trying to push it away from her with every ounce of her being, trying to loosen its grasp of her, all the while keeping her eyes tightly shut as they whirled around together, bouncing off the walls at the top, wrestling for control.

She freed herself from its grasp, but whether through trying to get her bearings before coming down the stairs or through sheer accident, she did precisely what none of us are ever supposed to do. It was only a flicker of a moment, but she opened her eyes narrowly, peeking through to see where she was. It was enough. The gorgon flew into her view and matched her vision in a heartbeat, locking eyes with her with a chilling hiss.

And then…it calmed. The gorgon had found a mark.

I tried to lunge up the steps toward her, feeling every one of my bones springing into action through the creaking horror. Endless waves of fear rippled down my neck and out through my legs.

Ally's rifle discharged, but it was aimed at the ground. Her mind somehow could not will her bones or sinews to raise her arm the rest of the way and fire back at her own mark.

She stared at the gorgon, and it calmly stared back.

The recoil from her rifle involuntarily jolted her backward; her muscles had turned to putty. It shot her arm backward and dislodged itself from her hand, clanging to the steel grating at her feet while her head stayed trained on the gorgon.

I don't know what I said. I don't know what I did. All I knew at that moment was that she was falling, and I was stumbling through hot tears to get her. *Falling.* Backward, reckless, nothing to stop a catastrophic plummet head over heels down the stairs to certain death below.

What I didn't know then was that she was already near death, locked in the poisonous stare of the gorgon's lethal telepathy.

Suddenly, time flew back into action, and every piece of me crawled with horror. I only just managed to grab her as she fell, taking her into my arms roughly as we collapsed together against the stairs.

We slid down the steps in each other's arms. Gunfire erupted over my head as I cradled Ally to me. Her breathing was slowing. Her veins were blue, and her skin tone had paled; yet in that moment, as with Joe, she slowly willed her eyes over to me. I felt every labored breath as she clung to life. She was quite the fighter, just as Joe had said, and I knew it. *Come on, Ally...fight. Please.*

There was a massive collision and thud above me. The gorgon flew backward through the entry doors. Another took its place...and another. They were no match for Foxy, Weston and even Bridger, who had summoned up the courage to defend himself. Bullets raced over our heads and around us as I tenderly stroked her hair.

Oh, Lord, hon, no, no, no was all I could breathe while her deadening eyes locked into mine. Her pupils were dilating. *Stay with me. Stay with me!*

Ally's breathing quickened for a moment. Her human heart desperately wanted to pump blood. Her brain desperately wanted to send synapses to the rest of her body functions to just keep going; to push through. But now, the pulse and meter of them were dropping. There was more space in between the pulses, and that space was increasing.

Guns. A spray of anger, defiance, and utterly hot rejection flew overhead as our guys mowed them down above. But they kept coming.

"Hon, look at me. Look at *me*," I breathed. "You're not looking at a gorgon, sweetheart. You're looking at me, the one who loves you. It's Cameron, honey. I'm here, baby. I'm here. Don't go. *Please* don't go," I cried. Hot, thick tears raced down my cheeks, and my vision blurred. Her face doubled in my view as she kept looking at me; the pace of her quick, short breaths slowed to a crawl.

My fiancé was dying in my arms, and there was nothing I could do about it. Ally kept looking at me, her mouth frozen open forever in shock.

A terrible explosion rocked the passageway above, and fire and rock flew down at us. Someone had thrown a grenade. Ally and I slid down one more step. Ash and dust coated us and settled upon her open eyes, and she didn't blink. The gunfire continued. But I heard none of it. I gritted my teeth and clenched my jaw. Everything in me tightened in revolt.

"Lieutenant Allison Trudy," I growled through gun smoke, "I *order* you to stay with me. I *order* you to stay with me, hon. Don't go!" But she didn't hear me, and she could not comply.

The gunfire stopped, and there were no more explosions. The shadows above had either retreated, or been punched back. But the damage had already been done. Thankfully, the entrance hadn't been sealed off.

Ally's chest sunk, and there was a long trailing high-pitched wheeze that escaped her blue lips. Those staccato breaths with long gaps filling the horrible space in between: gaps filled with memory and *ache*. Filled with longing for a future that would never be, and a tomorrow that she so desperately craved, yet was denied her. I smoothed back her hair and called for her quietly. "Ally?" I waited. "Ally?" Nothing.

"Ally, I'm here. I'm here, baby. You're alright. You're alright. I'm here."

Nothing.

Ally Trudy was dead.

How could this be? We were out! We had escaped! We were alright...weren't we? She was supposed to be safe. Why had she looked? Why the *hell* had she looked, even if it was only to look away? That was a gorgon hovering there, and many more outside. There was no way we were all going to make it out of this war, and that was my reality. I always knew it.

That icy reality now mixed with hot rivers of agony pouring down my face, as growl of agony met groan of anguish, welling up from deep within my gut and pouring out of my lungs. I smashed her into my chest and quaked with anger as I pressed her into me amidst my guttural choking cries. Then, I could take no more.

I lifted my head up and roared in defiance at this war, at Graham, at the gorgons, at everything. I'd had *enough*. I held Ally in my arms, my dead fiancé, the love of my life who would never be my wife. And I would never get to be her husband. We had shared so little time together, yet I had known that she was the one.

And now, here in this damned cave, she was *taken* from me.

Foxy sprang to my side, as did the others. Even Bridger tried to stifle my cries, as they had in the library. Gagging yells tried to make their escape from the center of my lungs, only to be reflected by hot, wet palms over my mouth. My eyes were frightening half-moons of insanity, spilling tears over all of us and washing the grime from Ally's face.

Foxy had been crying too. He held me back and covered my mouth, and I was surprised at his strength.

For some reason, I observed through my grief the two young soldiers who were trying to help him. Two brothers, here with me intact and alive, but another searing reminder of another painful loss.

Rutty.

I couldn't take it. I deserved to scream and rend the universe with my sorrow. My own cries would be the DTFs that would evoke terror in the hearts of every gorgon and send them flying in distress and panic. My roar would puncture their ears and crush their skulls in.

I tried to fight the guys off of me, but I felt something else renewing in my heart, as if Ally was calling to me from beyond, imparting a deep-seated desire to see it through. Welling up in the very center of my sorrow, I paused.

I probably wasn't thinking straight or clearly, but I choked back my cries, wrestled myself out of Foxy's grip, and gently laid Ally on the stairs, off of my lap, setting her head down gently on the cold rock. Her hands fell to her sides, palm upwards.

I stroked her dry hair, reached behind her hardened neck, and unclasped the amulet necklace I had given her: the one Rosie had given to me. I turned it over.

DELIVER US FROM EVIL.

I turned it back over in my hands, kissed it, ran my hand down her cheek, and then clasped it around my neck. Her beautiful pale skin looked and felt wooden now.

Bridger and Weston then took her body gently and slowly back downward.

I suddenly felt a panic: a sense of impending doom surged through me. Without warning, I whipped myself around to Foxy and clutched both sides of his blonde head in my hands. His face was affright at this sudden change, and he was panting heavily as he put his hands up.

"Jet, wha-" he winced.

"You listen to me. And you listen good, do you hear me?" I roared.

"Yeah. Yes!" he quaked.

"You will *not* die, soldier. Do you hear me!? I won't lose anyone else. I just lost the love of my life and my future bride, and I will not lose you, do you hear me, Rutty? I will *not* lose you too! You're all I have left! You can't leave, bro! You *must* stay alive and see this through with me - that's an order. Do you hear me Private? An order! Acknowledge!"

I was squeezing his head on both sides, and with each statement I pressed inward on his temples. His eyes were wide under furrowed brows. Had I continued, I might have accidentally crushed his skull in. Yelling through my agony, my face completely wet with sorrow, I couldn't see his face clearly, though he was inches from me.

"You have t-to l-live," I choked, trying to calm down through the hiccups of my cries.

Foxy looked at me and nodded. He was crying, and his eyes squinted. "I will, Jet, I promise. I will." Then, he dropped his voice to a whisper through his tears. "My name's Fox. *Liam – Fox – Mayfield.* You- you called me Rutty."

I tilted my head at him in confusion. No, I hadn't. I certainly hadn't. I knew it was Foxy in front of me. Why would he say that? I slowly pulled my hands away from his head, and his breathing returned to normal as I watched him. He heaved a lungs-clearing sigh and wiped his eyes.

I turned away from Foxy and looked down the steps at the two brothers sitting there with my bride-to-be. As I did so, I suddenly got a heart-wrenching picture of a family that would *never* be.

Two brothers and the bride.

Me. Rutty. Ally.

A future riven in two…destroyed.

I looked back up at Foxy and choked back an apology. "Foxy, I'm so, so sorry. I know your name. I know your name, bro," I said, collapsing once again into tears as my eyes swam. "I know your name," was all I could say as I fell into his chest, and he held my head as I sobbed uncontrollably.

·　　·　　·　　·　　·

I don't know how long we stayed down there. I didn't know what time it was. Nor did I know how we had made it back up to the top. All I remembered was sliding my fingers down her eyes and closing her eyelids. And now I was carrying her in my arms, her cold body resting against the warmth of mine as I plodded through the rain. One of them had placed her mask back over her face, giving her some dignity, and someone had offered me mine, but I refused. Right now, as in that church bathroom, I just wanted to die. I wanted to be with her. But somewhere inside me I knew that my dying wouldn't solve anything or give me the revenge I desperately craved.

Foxy must have helped Weston carry Bridger the whole way, because I had lost track of where everyone was.

The rain was pouring now, and we must have looked like a ghostly procession as I carried the limp lifeless body of Allison Trudy down the hill toward Frozen Niagara. I don't know how far we walked, nor how long we waited there, but somehow we arrived and waited in complete silence.

It was a small, nondescript, concrete square carved into the hillside and set back from a fenced-off concrete pad stretching out from the side of the hill. We turned and waited. For us, it was the end of Mammoth Cave, in all of its reinforced but false sense of safety, its tremendous and ultimately useless armament, and its proud and dangerous hubris. In the end, it just didn't matter. They got us anyway, and they took from me what which was most precious.

It was Ozymandias all over again.

1800 was drawing nearer, and the skies overhead were getting darker. We waited. I could tell they were looking at me and watching Ally closely, as if she might suddenly spring back to life with a gasp. I didn't want to sit, I just wanted to stand and to hold her. To remember her. To look at her beautiful ashen face.

Finally, Foxy spoke up. "1800 now," he said.

No sooner had he spoken than there was a cannon blast to our left. We all glanced up. And there was another. And then one more.

Four tiny, familiar dots went shooting up into the sky, whizzing over our heads. We watched them tickle the sky with their light, illuminated against the rain as water splashed into our eyes. I looked down. I knew what was coming next.

The sky once again lit up with lightning as four successive DTFs burst in close proximity to each other overhead. Then, the waves hit us, followed by the slow roll of thunder. The combination was horrendous, and I felt the wind knocked out of me, but I took it. The gust nearly knocked us all backward. Somewhere far away over the hills there was the sound of shrieking and odd yelps of dismay, as gorgons either fled Mammoth Cave to outrun the blast, or were enveloped in high-pitched agony and imploded, their brains demolished.

With a clenched jaw and grim face, I took it in. I'd seen it all before. This was nothing new.

I looked down at Ally and wiped some decaying winter leaves from her body that had blown onto her lifeless form. Every time I looked at her, it was a death knell to my heart, knowing that she was truly gone.

Then they came rolling into view up the greenway. Four tanks. Why was I not surprised? Except…something was odd. The tanks hadn't shut down. They could now be seen rolling up the hill even before the DTFs had burst. What did that mean? I squinted at them, though my mind was in multiple places. Had Cardona figured out a way to enhance RF shielding on tanks?

Of *course* Cardona had backup tanks down here. In all likelihood, they had been retrofitted to be shielded from any kind of aerial surveillance. At least, they had DTF projectiles and emitters. I could see the familiar black domes on the backs of the tanks as they came rumbling toward us.

And then we heard noises to our right: more stragglers coming down the bank toward us from multiple points. Other survivors who had held back until the appointed hour of the rendezvous. I counted eight of them.

The tanks stopped at the end of the path to Frozen Niagara. None of their hatches opened. Their turrets were pointed straight at us, and I could tell they were looking at us. Someone inside those tanks was registering how few of us there were, realizing that one of them was dead. They were probably figuring out what to say – *and what not to* – before they popped their hatch.

Foxy started walking over to them, his rocket launcher over his shoulder, checking the sky for any sign of them, despite the DTFs. He looked like such a man now. He was a little kid just over a week ago at Harvill Hall, a kid in a baseball cap, waving to me from across a clearing.

The hatches finally popped, and there he was: Cardona. And there was Monzon as well. The third and fourth hatches popped open, and a few others emerged whose names I didn't know. Neener and Jenkins were there, as were Vetas and Larson. I didn't see Simpson.

Most everyone was here, alive and well.

Except Joe.

Except Ally.

All of them stared at me with sympathy and grace.

At least, I think that's what it was. It was hard enough to see through the pouring rain, let alone the pouring sheets of water flowing from my eyes. I didn't realize I was still crying in my silence.

•　　•　　•　　•　　•

I sat in my tank: stoic, brooding, disconnected from life, my eyes closed, holding my dead future bride in my arms. I vaguely remember someone saying something about a burial right there, but I shook my head and wordlessly took her to the tank with me. I don't remember getting inside, nor do I remember them handing her body down to me or what was even said after they closed the hatches.

All I knew is that we were driving now, though I wasn't certain where we were even headed.

At one point, I felt a hand on my shoulder, and I slowly felt my dried eyes crackle and blink over to Foxy. He was looking at me with a regard full of understanding and pity. He said nothing, just squeezed my shoulder. Dust was mixed into my sweat and colliding with my tears; my face felt arid and weathered. I turned away from him and looked ahead through the window.

Past the heads of the others in our tank with us, I could see the road scroll by underneath our tank.

Where would it lead? Where were we bound?

My last big conversation with Ally was about justice versus revenge. Was there really any difference? Who cares, as long as the objective was accomplished and the evildoers paid for their crimes, right? I tried to remember everything she said, but in my mind's eye, she sounded muffled and muted, and I could already barely make out her face. Instead, I closed my eyes once more and saw her lying beside me, close up, on my bunk back at the Blockade. Before any of this had happened.

In the brief two hours that we had together yesterday morning, we had loved each other enough for a lifetime. I choked back some grief and tried to remain composed.

I wondered where her spirit was now. Was it in Heaven? *Heaven. Jesus.* I had prayed to him to get us all out of this safely. And he had. But then he took it back. As with Rutty's death, I felt a profound sense of anger welling up inside me at the injustice of it all, the injustice of *everything.* I was unable to think straight; all I could see was the color red.

I blamed God. I blamed the gorgons. I blamed Graham. I blamed everything that started with 'g.' But most of all, I blamed good ol' Cameron Shipley.

I should have insisted that she come with me. I should have made her come down into that tunnel and told her it wasn't safe to be up there by herself. I should have warned her more firmly not to open her eyes. She knew it, but maybe if I had said it with more fervency, more volume?

Regret and blame coursed through me as I stared dead-eyed through the cabin. Then, I simply became more and more angry at her.

Dammit, Ally, why did you leave me so soon? Why did you look!? You said you would absolutely *be my wife – so why did you leave me? Why, oh why did you look, Ally? Why, after all we'd been through? Why??*

I gripped her tightly to me, holding both her and my breath until eternity exploded in rage. I finally took a deep breath and softened my grip. No anger, rage, or revenge would bring her back. *But,* I thought, *it might just make me feel better in the end, despite everything she had told me.*

No. I had to think clearly. I shook my head and tried.

Graham. It was always Graham. She had started this whole thing.

She sent the President out to his death.

She sent those planes off as a diversion, killing all those passengers so she could escape.

She commissioned the berserkers *and* the behemoths.

She ordered us to lojack that gorgon that killed Rutty.

She had us sent up here to unknowingly assassinate Cardona, who was yet another of her threats.

She was going to nuke her enemies and call it collateral damage under the guise of killing the gorgons.

And for all I knew, she probably drove those gorgons up here after us, back at Mammoth Cave.

Her offenses were many, and she was clearly guil-

I stopped and opened my eyes again. *Wait. What was that thought?* I rewound the tape in my head.

We obviously had the technology to drive off the gorgons: DTFs. They always fled *away* from the signal. But what if the DTFs could be harnessed? What if they could be focused and channeled, unidirectionally, to send the gorgons where one wanted them to go, like a fan to water, or a broom to dirt and dust?

Then, it hit me. Of *course* they could be focused and channeled: that's *exactly* what she said they were planning to do with the three geographic nuke targets. She was going to steer the gorgons there with focused DTFs: like guides, ushering them where she wanted them to go, herding them into those areas with her. Not just some erratic, expanding circumference spreading outward and then dissipating; no: essentially, sweeping the entire planet of gorgons, funneling them all into three dustpans. And then, nuking each one. The blasts would be close enough to each capital cities of her opponents to reduce them to hopeless ash for decades to come. Certainly beyond her own years.

But they would rise again. People always do. And they would know who did it and seek recompense. Graham didn't care. All she cared about was her own lifespan and preserving herself and her power. She didn't want to just rattle sabers; she wanted to stab, impale, and gouge all those damned idiots who dared cross her.

And then I saw the truth. The truth was that she had needed to test the effectiveness of steering gorgons to a target, and she had just practiced that very thing *on Mammoth Cave.* Hell, I'd even said something similar to Hofstetter in the elevator before we climbed!

She had sent those gorgons there, to see if it could be done, and if in the process she was able to take out both Cardona and Monzon – who I'm sure by now she figured had flipped sides – then so much the better. *You can't make an omelet without breaking some eggs,* she had said.

But how? Something on the ground would be only as effective as its signal strength. They would be stationary and could only manipulate as far as the terrain around them would allow it. Something *mobile* on the ground then? Tanks? No, no. Too small. And it would require a massive coordination of *many* tanks moving in unison. They were slow. They would also have to worm their way across an Earth littered with abandoned cars, buildings, and so forth. And some of the bridges had been blown up intentionally so as to allow passage of the naval vessels, they said. They could only go so far. Beside all of that, that would only bring them to our Eastern seaboard. The target areas were all in Europe. I was thinking two-dimensionally. No. *Think.*

I was certain the signal would be sent from the air. Perhaps, in tandem with the buildup of the tanks and ships, they had also retrofitted airplanes and jets with these DTF emitters? Would their signal be powerful enough?

I remembered something that the tank gunner said to me on our way back from the Methodist church. *And Sabre Airfield northwest of here, up at Fort Campbell? They're about to get their remaining jets retrofit with these babies too. We should be able to mount an aerial defense coming up here soon too.*

My gut roiled, and my hairs stood on end. She was double-crossing her own military, playing them, concealing her true objective. And they, too, were unwitting devices of her master plan. This was for no aerial defense! This was a sadistic *offense!*

As the road scrolled by underneath, I knew in my heart that I was dealing with a devil. A villain. A narcissistic dictator who had to be stopped, and I would not stop until she was. President Graham was going to pay for what she'd done, one way or another.

I had been filled with resolve before, after taking that swing at Stone, lying there in the brig. Then, I had actually met the cold-hearted snake herself a few days later. She seemed so dignified and resolute, queenly and leaderlike. And I, like everyone else, had believed her, falling under her spell. But no more. This was a woman who had clearly planted Armstrong up at Mammoth Cave, and she was willing to let him get killed in the crossfire. She was altogether sinister and remorseless.

It was up to all of us to help save all those people and thwart her plans for nuclear annihilation.

Not revenge. It would *not* be revenge. It would be justice. Pastor Rosie's words came back to me.

Revenge never leads to receiving. Revenge only ever leads to dead-ends. Your path goes out, Sergeant Shipley. Justice knows no shortcuts, and the wheels of justice have only ever turned slowly. But always remember this: the only way out is through, Cameron. The only way out is through.

I would have to go through it.

And now, I was also a murderer. I had murdered Hofstetter in cold blood. In revenge. I would have to keep that a secret, and I would have to learn from it. Rosie would tell me it was the wrong thing to do and a despicable act, if she found out what I had done. I would be court-martialed. I *should* be court-martialed. But that would have to be dealt with later.

I looked around. I could feel my senses reeling, and I let out a deep and labored sigh. Foxy turned to me when he heard it. I spoke to him under my breath.

"How many of us are left?"

He frowned. "Twenty-two. Five or six in each tank."

Twenty-two renegades against an empire.

"And both captains are with us?"

He nodded.

"I have to stop her, Foxy. I have to stop Graham from killing all those people. I can't do it alone. I need your help." I stared at him.

He gulped, looking around at the others, who were all silent and facing forward. Foxy turned back to me and nodded. "I'm with you, Jet. Always have been." He smiled sadly and then looked down again.

A blurry memory came back to me of being in the tunnel with him. On the stairs. Foxy had been crying. He said I had called him Rutty. I bit my lip. I had been so lost in grief that everything was warped and hazy, but now I saw it clearly.

"Liam Fox Mayfield," I said to him.

He turned back to me. "What?"

"Liam Fox Mayfield," I repeated. "That's your name. *Foxy.*"

Foxy smiled faintly at me, but I know he knew what I meant and that I was trying to undo my slip-up in the tunnel. He took a deep breath, and I put my arm around him.

My eyes were summoned ahead through the window once more. We were on the edge of night now. My guess is that they had disabled any trackers on our tanks to ensure Halcyon, or any similar departments allegiant to the President, wouldn't be able to monitor our movement. But where were we headed? That I didn't know. I wasn't even sure if Cardona or Monzon knew.

It was a foregone conclusion that Cardona probably had a pre-appointed destination already worked out prior to us fleeing the cave. But he had spoken of contingency plans before, and I wasn't sure which one he would pursue.

I ground my teeth together, and set my chin to the road. I was at my limit. I – *we* – wouldn't tolerate this, and I would need every one of these people's help.

Yes, it would take some convincing on my part, and strong arguments would need to be made to not only Cardona, but also to Monzon and his entire rag-tag crew spread across these three tanks, bound for nowhere. There would have to be a great reckoning of our great peril.

Most of all, there needed to be no "good, fine American warriors here," as Captain Benson so proudly and eerily called them back at Base One on the Cumberland. They needed to be filled with human souls, without prejudice, understanding that life – *all* life, even those of your supposed human enemies – is sacred, and that revenge only ever leads to dead-ends, as Rosie had said.

Justice leads to receiving.

I watched as the front view faded, and the tank's headlights began to replace the waning sun, shining brightly onto the highway ahead like two beacons, but the road was foggy, and they bounced off of white wisp as we rumbled forward: four tanks, alone, and on the frontier of all-out war.

Our time had come to fight back. Not just against the gorgons, but against a deranged lunatic who desperately wanted to cling to power, but was in fact a narcissistic, delusional psychopath who was long past deserving her role.

In truth, she never deserved it.

I would take her down.

I did the sign of the cross, as Rutty would have, in preparation for what was to come.

Be with me, Rutty. Be with me, Ally. Be with me, Joe. I need you now more than ever, for whatever's to come.

The only way out was through. It was stuffy in this tank, and moreover, in life.

I'd had enough.

THE END

The war for humanity continues.
Visit dissonancetheseries.com for news and updates.

Read all the books in the series, in chronological order:

Dissonance Volume Zero: Revelation
Dissonance Volume Up: Rising
Dissonance Volume I: Reality
Dissonance Volume II: Reckoning
Dissonance Volume III: Renegade
Dissonance Volume IV: Relentless

I AFTERWORD

I had no idea that my first volume in this series would be such a solid work nor such a raging success.

My endless gratitude to those of you who have taken to Cameron's adventure (and plight) and wanted more information on gorgons and the war against them. Thank you for taking in what I heartfully sculpted.

Of course, any author's dream is for his book and characters to captivate his readers, and for those readers to plead for more content on said books and characters.

My dream was fulfilled, and I thank you. I want to thank all the agents and publishers I've talked to, specifically Stu at Nef House Publishing, for their invaluable feedback.

Thanks also to my cousin Josh Barnwell as well as Andrew Howe of Oak Ridge Tennessee who provided some essential help and feedback on Mammoth Cave as I sought to take our characters through it much like the Fellowship had to thread their way through Moria in *The Lord of the Rings*. The fear that that section conjures up in me, of being trapped in the dark with aliens about, is primal. I hope the same was true for you as you read through it.

I knew going into the first volume that I wanted to pen a trilogy. Any good story deserves a sequel unless, of course, there is an inescapable element of finality to that first story where a sequel would be simply beating a dead horse. No one wants a dead horse, much less a beaten one. But the underpinnings of Cameron's adventures and the subtext present in his odyssey abroad were not readily apparent to me until I was well into the first few chapters of the first book. I knew characters had to die, that much was certain, but *why* they had to die was another story.

As my fingers pounded the keys, I found myself becoming acutely and ravenously hungry to peel back the onion and reveal what was brimming below the surface: the subtle undercurrent, the nefarious subplot that dogs our protagonist during his noble pursuits.

Several arteries of possibility lay before me in the sculpting of the overarching story, but none of them were really cemented until that first DTF, when Cameron (and I) became painfully aware and suspicious – concretely so – that something larger and more sinister was developing behind the scenes.

There had to be an illuminati of sorts.

In reflecting on the first novel in my series, I also had to do some heavy introspection related to the gorgons. The 1981 movie *Clash of the Titans* remains a cult classic for many reasons, not the least of which is the Claymation version of Medusa the Gorgon, the portrayal of someone so cursed, so mystical, so deadly, it was – shy of the jerky and stuttery cinematography – one of the seminal fears of my childhood.

Those eyes terrified me. The fact that one would be so handicapped were one to fall under her gaze was a danger so visceral and real. And the sound effect they gave her when she did that? *Yeeshk.* I remember play-acting it with other children my age.

In many ways, short of the glowing green eyes, I see Medusa in the gorgons of *Dissonance*. They are cursed, they are mystical, and they are deadly. But they are also misunderstood, some of them, and so I trust in this second novel of the series, you were as interested as I was to learn more about them, their evolution, and their purpose here.

I also wanted to expound more on the character development. I appreciate learning more about the characters as the story progresses, letting the action and developments lead to character revelation as opposed to setting up a narrative from the start.

I don't feel you should "know whom you're dealing with" right away; I feel there is more mystique to learning more and more bits and pieces about characters as their story arc progresses. I've tried to do that here.

As for Cameron, where will he go now? Read on and find out. You are as much discovering this journey in the reading as I was discovering it in the writing, being led down organic primrose paths of epiphany as I went, and discovering along the way that this was going to be one heckuva compelling journey.

Thank you once more for journeying with Cameron and me through the *Dissonance* series.

With love,

Aaron Ryan

I ABOUT THE AUTHOR

Aaron Ryan lives in Washington with his wife and two sons, along with Macy the dog, Winston the cat, and Merry & Pippin, the finches.

He is the author of the bestselling "Dissonance" sci-fi alien invasion quadrilogy, the sci-fi thriller "Forecast", the business reference books "How to Successfully Self-Publish & Promote Your Self-Published Book" and "The Superhero Anomaly", several business books on voiceovers penned under his former stage name (Joshua Alexander), as well as a previous fictional novel, "The Omega Room."

When he was in second grade, he was tasked with writing a creative assignment: a fictional book. And thus, "The Electric Boy" was born: a simple novella full of intrigue, fantasy, and 7-year-old wits that electrified Aaron's desire to write. From that point forward, Aaron evolved into a creative soul that desired to create.

He enjoys the arts, media, music, performing, poetry, and being a daddy. In his lifetime he has been an author, voiceover artist, wedding videographer, stage performer, musician, producer, rock/pop artist, executive assistant, service manager, paperboy, CSR, poet, tech support, worship leader, and more. The diversity of his life experiences gives him a unique approach to business, life, ministry, faith, and entertainment.

Aaron's favorite author by far is J.R.R. Tolkien, but he also enjoys Suzanne Collins, James S.A. Corey, Marie Lu, Madeleine L'Engle, C.S. Lewis, and Stephen King.

Aaron has always had a passion for storytelling. Visit www.dissonancetheseries.com for information on the release of the final chapter in Cameron's odyssey for truth and accountability.

If you liked Aaron's book, please visit the Amazon and Goodreads pages for this book and leave a positive review. Once it shows up, please email the screenshot of it to me@authoraaronryan.com for a discount on your next book purchase from him! Thank you so much! Reviews really do help a ton!

Visit his author website and enlist at the blog:

Subscribe to Author Aaron Ryan

Follow Aaron and connect on Social Media:

Made in the USA
Columbia, SC
25 September 2024

42393103R00198